JANET'S SWAP-
2410 W AVE.
SAN ANGELO, TX. 76904

P9-EKD-532

MOUNTAIN PASSAGE

Jason Manning

Pixie Dreams Bookstore
2222 Main St.
Woodward, OK 73801
580-254-2770

A SIGNET BOOK

SIGNET
Published by the Penguin Group
Penguin Putnam Inc., 375 Hudson Street,
New York, New York 10014, U.S.A.
Penguin Books Ltd, 27 Wrights Lane,
London W8 5TZ, England
Penguin Books Australia Ltd, Ringwood,
Victoria, Australia
Penguin Books Canada Ltd, 10 Alcorn Avenue,
Toronto, Ontario, Canada M4V 3B2
Penguin Books (N.Z.) Ltd, 182–190 Wairau Road,
Auckland 10, New Zealand

Penguin Books Ltd, Registered Offices:
Harmondsworth, Middlesex, England

First published by Signet, an imprint of Dutton NAL,
a member of Penguin Putnam Inc.

First Printing, November, 1998
10 9 8 7 6 5 4 3 2 1

Copyright © Jason Manning, 1998

All rights reserved

 REGISTERED TRADEMARK—MARCA REGISTRADA

Printed in the United States of America

Without limiting the rights under copyright reserved above, no part of this
publication may be reproduced, stored in or introduced into a retrieval system, or
transmitted, in any form, or by any means (electronic, mechanical, photocopying,
recording, or otherwise), without the prior written permission of both the copyright
owner and the above publisher of this book.

BOOKS ARE AVAILABLE AT QUANTITY DISCOUNTS WHEN USED TO PROMOTE PRODUCTS OR
SERVICES. FOR INFORMATION PLEASE WRITE TO PREMIUM MARKETING DIVISION, PENGUIN
PUTNAM INC., 375 HUDSON STREET, NEW YORK, NEW YORK 10014.

If you purchased this book without a cover you should be aware that this book is
stolen property. It was reported as "unsold and destroyed" to the publisher and
neither the author nor the publisher has received any payment for this "stripped
book."

Chapter 1

I.

Though he was only sixteen years old and had never been in a boat larger than a river skiff—and on that occasion always within a few yards of dry land—Gordon Hawkes was not afraid of the sea. In fact, when his father announced that they were going to make the long sea voyage to America, Gordon was thrilled at the prospect.

The same could not be said for his mother, but then nothing brought joy to Mary Hawkes anymore. Since Gordon's birth, which had not been accomplished without difficulties, Mary had suffered two miscarriages and a stillbirth. These tragedies had taken their toll on her both physically and emotionally. Mary Hawkes was no longer the robust and rosy-cheeked Scottish lass Thomas Hawkes had married twenty years ago. She was constantly ailing. Only laudanum appeared to easy her physical suffering, though by now Tom Hawkes was convinced that his wife's dependence on the opium-based elixir caused her to magnify and sometimes even manufacture her aches and pains. Only the Bible seemed to ease Mary's tortured soul. Mary feared she wasn't strong enough to make the long voyage to the United States. But her husband hoped a new beginning would restore to him the lively, smiling, fun-loving girl he had wed.

Of course, Tom Hawkes had other reasons for deciding to emigrate to America in the year 1832. His father had been one of the Scots lured to Ireland by British promises of abundant land forty years ago— part of England's attempt to undermine the hold over Ireland exercised by the Catholic Church. As a good Protestant, Tom Hawkes was at least spared the persecution suffered by Irish Catholics since as far back as 1690. Catholics could no longer vote or hold office. They could not enlist in the army, carry a weapon, or even own a horse. Catholic schools and churches had been shut down. The Penal Laws banned all public practice of the Roman Catholic religion, and priests were occasionally hunted down like dogs. Catholics could not purchase land, and other repressive laws made it exceedingly difficult for those who already owned land to keep it. These days, less than one fifth of the land in Ireland remained in the possession of Catholics.

But that didn't mean the land rested in the work-callused hands of plain Protestant farmers like Tom Hawkes. Noblemen had acquired title to vast tracts, creating estates worked by tenants. They appropriated the best land, and there wasn't a lot of that to go around. Much of Ireland was marsh or mountain or peat bog. Like so many other plain sowers of the field,

Tom Hawkes could successfully raise little more than a crop of potatoes and a bit of barley.

Land in America, though—now that was a different story altogether. Fertile land was to be had there, good land for the asking, where a man could grow everything he needed for himself and his family. Americans seemed to be well on their way to realizing Thomas Jefferson's dream of a nation of independent farmers, equal one to the other and beholden to nobody but themselves and their Maker. It was that, Tom told Mary, or in a few years he would lose the farm from an inability to pay the taxes. Then he would be forced to live out his years as a tenant farmer, dependent on some high-and-mighty absentee English landlord for his livelihood. Worse, their son would be doomed to the same fate.

Gordon's future was Mary's only concern. She cared nothing for her own tomorrows, and not enough for her husband's to risk an arduous sea passage to a dangerous new land. And even if they survived the crossing, then what? A precarious existence on the American frontier, set aflame year in and year out by savage Indians encouraged in their depredations by the Spanish in the south and the British in the north? But Tom was right—there was no future for her only son in Ireland. And so, eventually, Mary grudgingly gave her assent to the move.

Gordon's concern for his mother's health and state of mind could not dampen his enthusiasm for the journey that lay ahead. It all sounded like such a great adventure for a boy who had seldom strayed from the farm where he'd been born. Why, they might set eyes on a giant whale, or be menaced by pirates flying the skull-and-crossbones! And as if that were not enough to fill a lad's daydreams, a wilderness populated by fierce aborigines wearing war paint and feathers awaited him across the ocean! Ireland seemed a dull place indeed when compared to a land so full of exciting possibilities.

II.

They would sail from Dublin, Ireland's major port. The River Liffey and Dublin Bay played host on any given day to hundreds of vessels—a prime anchorage called home by nearly a hundred and fifty square-riggers that sailed the seven seas. So it was that on a blustery March day, with an armada of clouds driven by the sea breezes scudding across the sky, Gordon Hawkes found himself standing on the cobblestones of Custom House Quay, nearly overcome by the sights and sounds that encompassed him. Burly work gangs unloaded cargoes onto carts that would trundle loudly down the narrow streets branching off from the docks, or onto barges that plied the canals leading to the old city. The aroma of sugar, rum, and molasses were carried by the breeze as it wafted up from the holds of ships just arrived from such exotic places as the West Indies.

Vendors, beggars, and thieves lurked along the quay as well, and Gordon's father had charged him with defending their belongings, which lay piled beneath a canvas on their mule-drawn cart, while he'd gone in search of the captain whose ship would carry them to America. Gordon was big and brawny for his age, and he was proud that his father put such trust in him. He sat atop a pile of trunks and carpetbags and tried to keep a wary eye peeled for suspicious-looking characters who might be lurking too near for comfort. But in spite of best intentions, his eyes were drawn to the forest of masts and spars that rose into the sky all along the quay.

All manner of craft filled the river and bay: mail cutters, river colliers, sloops carrying livestock, produce, and passengers to England, the big three-masted brigs and barques built for the high seas trade, even a pair of mighty frigates bristling with guns. The Custom House—considered by many the most magnificent structure in a city filled with grand Georgian mansions—towered above everything. Built by the renown London architect, James Gandon, the gray-stone structure was embellished with statues representing Navigation, Industry, Commerce and Wealth.

Gordon wondered which of the vessels arrayed before him was the one destined to carry him and his parents to America. Reaching under his linsey-woolsey shirt, he took out the folded broadside that his father had brought home many months ago—the one Tom Hawkes had been so engrossed in for what seemed like weeks, on those cold winter evenings when they sat around the hearth and Mary read aloud from the Bible. Gordon carefully unfolded the brittle paper and for the thousandth time read its contents.

BOUND FOR NEW YORK
The Barque PENELOPE
of Dublin
800 tons berthen
J. Warren, Commander

This sturdy barque is coppered and copper-fastened, made
of choice
Canadian timber and commanded by a veteran of
numerous Atlantic crossings.
She will sail from the above port on
Friday, 12th March.
She will proceed to sea on the appointed day.
The Owner will have her comfortably Berthed,
and attention will be paid to the comfort of her passengers.
No Fever or Sickness on board.
Plenty of good Water and Breadstuffs will be put on board.
A few Cabin passengers will be taken.
For Freight and Rate of Passage, apply at once to
JOSEPH SOMERVILLE
53, Merchants Quay

"Your father is coming back now, Gordon," said
Mary. She sat on the cart's bench, Bible open on her
knees, a shawl over her head as protection against the
salty breeze, and she spoke without enthusiasm, without even lifting her head.

Tom Hawkes arrived in the company of a short,
bowlegged man wearing a blue tunic with brass but-
tons over a white waistcoat, white knee breeches, and
stockings, and a blue tricorner hat adorned with gold
braid. For all this, his cuffs and collars were threadbare, but Gordon was too impressed by the man's
quasi-military garb to notice.

"This is Captain Warren, the *Penelope*'s skipper,"
said Tom Hawkes. "Captain, my wife Mary and son
Gordon."

Warren removed his hat and bowed with as much
flourish as his potbelly would permit. A smile creased
his craggy, red Irish features, displaying crooked, yel-
lowing teeth. "A pleasure to make your acquaintance,

Mrs. Hawkes. And this is young Gordon? A fine, strapping lad you've got there, Mr. Hawkes."

"The captain wants to take a look at our belongings, Mary," Tom explained.

"Aye, we'll have better than two hundred passengers, and a cargo of linens and shoes besides, so space is at a premium."

"Gordon, set aside the tarpaulin."

Gordon did as his father commanded. With one glance at the trunks and valises in the cart, Captain Warren clucked his tongue with a rueful shake of his head.

"Alas, much as it pains me to say so, you folks must travel more lightly than this, good sir. One trunk and one valise is all you'll be able to take aboard, I'm afraid."

"Then we shall just have to take passage on another ship," said Mary.

"Beggin' your pardon, ma'am, but you'll have no better luck with another ship. Look about you. The quay is crawling with scavengers, as you can see. Every person bound for America ends up leaving most of their belongings behind, and many's the bloke who makes a fair living absconding with what's left behind."

"We must sail on the *Penelope*." Tom sighed. "I've already paid for our passage. Five pounds sterling for you and me, Mary, and another three pounds for Gordon."

"But you can't very well expect me to make a new start in some wild and heathen country without at least a few of my things," protested Mary. Noting the edge to her voice, Gordon looked at his mother and was shocked to see her on the verge of tears.

Tom Hawkes was visibly shaken by the depth of his wife's consternation. He felt guilty, besides. He had dragged Mary from her home, forcing her to leave behind nearly everything they owned. That hadn't been much, but Mary was attached to all of their things. Of course he had tried to assure her that in America he would prosper as he had never been able to do in Ireland, and with prosperity would come more and better things. But the tactic failed miserably. Mary wasn't one for dreams; in her opinion planning for the future was a waste of time. She'd suffered too much tragedy to put stock in tomorrow.

Discomfited by Mary's emotions, Captain Warren cleared his throat and laid a hand on Gordon's shoulder. "Come along, then, lad, and I'll show you where to find the *Penelope* while your folks tend to the baggage. With your permission, Mr. Hawkes."

Tom Hawkes nodded and Warren started off along the quay with Gordon, who looked back once to see his mother covering her face with her hands and shaking her head as his father spoke to her in a supplicating manner.

"My mother hasn't been feeling well, sir," he told Warren, compelled to take up for her in the event the captain thought less of her as a consequence of the emotional outburst.

"No need to explain, son. Going off to a new land can be a fearful experience, especially for the weaker sex."

"She's afraid she won't survive the passage."

"One looks forward to the sea but does not expect to

find a grave there," said Warren. "An old Irish proverb. I'll get you and yours safely to America, lad, never fear."

"How long will the voyage take, sir?"

Warren shrugged. "Six weeks if we have luck. It depends on the weather."

"Will we chance upon any pirates, do you think?"

Warren chuckled. "None, boy. No pirates so far to the north. The southern route is too long, and with two hundred passengers, not to mention a crew of thirty, we couldn't carry sufficient provisions. Nae, we'll keep to the northern latitudes. The wind and sea is a bit more precocious, but at least we'll not have to worry about pirates. Now, we will need to keep a weather eye out for icebergs."

"Icebergs!"

"Aye. Now, I've heard of only two ships that wrecked on a reef of ice, and that in all my years of sailing the Atlantic. Ah, here's the *Penelope*. She's a true ship, lad, rely on it."

Gordon gaped at the vessel, with her sleek gray hull and towering white masts. Warren left him standing there to join his first mate, who was stationed at the gangplank to make sure that those who boarded the barque had paper to show they'd paid for their passage. Not the least interested in his fellow passengers, Gordon spotted men scrambling like monkeys up the *Penelope*'s rigging and along her yardarms. Mesmerized by their daredevil agility, Gordon moved sideways to get a better view, failed to watch where he was going, and collided with someone moving briskly along the quay. The impact sent Gordon to his hands and knees.

"Here now!" he yelled crossly, bounding to his feet and spinning around with a stormy expression on his face. "Look where you're going, why don't you?"

The man who stood before him with amusement dancing in his dark eyes was tall, swarthy, wide-shouldered, with black hair, a rakish mustache, and a prominent, hooked nose. In fact, he was nearly a spitting image of what Gordon had imagined a pirate would look like. This man had the look of someone who had seen the world. Capable, self-reliant, and a bit jaded, too. And he looked dangerous. Gordon's anger fled, and with it his ill-advised belligerence, and he tried without success to swallow the lump that had suddenly lodged itself in his throat. Besides, it was obvious by the man's garb—scarlet swallowtail coat, waistcoat, snowy white shirt of French linen, doeskin breeches tucked into shiny black blucher boots—that he was a gentleman. And the homespun-clad son of a dirt farmer did not speak to a gentleman in the way Gordon had just spoken.

"My apologies," said the man, smiling wryly. "Somehow I did not notice you standing there."

Witness to the collision, Captain Warren rushed over. "Captain Stewart!" he gasped. "I'm terribly sorry! He's a clumsy farmboy, this one."

With effort, Gordon held his tongue. The dangerous-looking man saw that he was fuming, and chuckled.

"Quite all right, Captain. No harm done. Perhaps you would introduce me to the young gentleman."

Clearly Warren didn't think it at all appropriate to introduce the likes of Gordon Hawkes to an officer and a gentleman, but he couldn't decline.

"Captain William Drummond Stewart—Gordon

Hawkes." Scowling at Gordon, Warren added, "Captain Stewart is the brother of Sir John Archibald Stewart, eighteenth duke of Grandtully. He is a hero of the battle of Waterloo, serving with the King's Hussars."

"Hardly a hero," said Stewart. "Many men conducted themselves in a far more gallant fashion than I on that day. Are you bound, then, for America, young man?"

"I am," said Gordon. "With my father and mother. We're going to find a new place to live on the frontier."

"I, too, am bound for the wilderness. I've been placed on half pay. My battalion was mustered out, now that the Corsican ogre is safely tucked away. I have it in mind to do a bit of hunting. Bag a buffalo or two. Have a look at those savage Indians I've been hearing so much about."

Gordon's eyes gleamed. "That sounds very exciting, sir!" he said enviously.

Stewart smiled. "I fervently hope that it will be. Frankly, I'm going mad from boredom. Well, it's too bad you can't come along with me. You appear to have an adventuresome spirit." He turned to Warren. "The tide will be going out in a couple of hours, if I'm not mistaken, Captain. I trust it is your intention to sail with it."

"Indeed it is, Captain Stewart. Indeed it is. You will find all your luggage stowed away in your cabin. I have seen to it personally."

Stewart glanced over his shoulder, scanning the bustling quay with what Gordon thought was a fugitive's intensity. Yet it hardly seemed likely that a man of Stewart's caliber—a man who had with unflinching

courage faced Napoleon Bonaparte and his vaunted
Grande Armee—would be running from anything.

"Splendid," said Stewart. He gave Gordon a friendly
nod, spared another for Warren, and made for the gangplank with long strides.

"Go fetch your parents, boy," said Warren, "and be
quick about it. The *Penelope* sails in two hour's time."

III.

The voyage of the *Penelope* began as a great adventure
for Gordon, but it quickly became a terrible ordeal. Two
hundred emigrants had been crammed into an unventi-
lated space 'tween decks. With no lights and no port-
holes, the only fresh air passed through the hatchway,
and the hatch was often closed during rough seas and
bad weather. Double tiers of bunks less than three feet
deep and five feet wide lined the hold, and only one
bunk was made available to each family.

Water was strictly rationed almost from the first day,
and what little food was provided proved very poor fare
indeed—a meal usually consisted of moldy sea biscuits
and half-cooked porridge. The filthy, oppressive atmos-
phere in the hold was one Gordon sought to escape at
every opportunity. The problem there lay in the attitude
of the captain and crew toward the *Penelope*'s human
cargo. Now that he had their passage fare in his pocket,
Captain Warren ceased to pretend to be the least bit so-
licitous about the welfare of his emigrant passengers.
And the crew treated the emigrants with indifference at
best—and all too often with open contempt. Once a day
the passengers were briefly allowed above deck to
stretch their cramped limbs and breathe fresh air. They

were brought up in groups of twenty-five at a time; any more than that would interfere with the operation of the ship, said Warren. Tom Hawkes had no illusions about their captain. It was his opinion that Warren allowed them this privilege only because he didn't want his entire cargo to sicken and die. It would be bad for business if the *Penelope* became known as a "coffin ship." Of course, the privilege was withheld when the sea was rough, and that seemed to be quite often.

A half hour's respite from the claustrophobic squalor of the hold was not sufficient for Gordon, and he sometimes managed to slip up on deck at other times. Since he did his best to stay out of the way, many of the crew members tolerated his presence. Until Mick Maguire ruined everything.

Mick Maguire was an emigrant boy, a year older than Gordon, and a bully. He was quick to establish a 'tween-decks gang of young rowdies who took to pilfering the baggage stowed away in steerage. Tom Hawkes tried to curtail their activities, but his efforts fetched up hard against the opposition of Maguire's father, and the fathers of the boys who ran with Mick. Tom tried to organize the rest of the passengers, not only for the purpose of keeping order in the hold but also to petition the *Penelope*'s captain for better treatment. It was no use. "We've already come to the point where it's everyone for himself," a grave Tom Hawkes told his son. "They are concerned only with their own survival. I suppose you can't blame them."

Inevitably, Mick Maguire went too far. He and his rowdies began to carry out "raids" above deck, antagonizing the crew and worsening relations between the men of the *Penelope* and the emigrants. The climax came when a crewman's knife turned up missing. It was found on Mick Maguire's person. Captain Warren made an arrangement with Mick's father—Mick would serve as cabin boy for the duration of the voyage. "I will teach him discipline, sir," said Warren. "Discipline, and respect for his elders. The experience will stand him in good stead." Mick's father had no choice but to acquiesce. And so Mick was isolated from the rest of the emigrants, and without his leadership the gang disintegrated. But Gordon was banned from loitering on deck. Though never a participant in Mick Maguire's activities, he suffered guilt by association. He was an emigrant youth and that made him suspect.

From the start it was apparent that the passage would be a difficult one. Following only two days of fair sailing, the sea began to rise, and the crew warily eyed the rapid approach of a line of dark and angry storm clouds. The barque began to roll heavily, pitching the unprepared in the emigrants' hold to and fro like so many rag dolls, and those who had not yet been afflicted by seasickness began to groan and writhe in discomfort. Some heaved the contents of their stomachs onto the deck to mingle with the effluvium escaping from overturned buckets that had been provided for human wastes. Even Gordon, who had prided himself on being endowed with a set of sea legs, felt a trifle queasy. Rain began to hammer the deck overhead. The first mate cried out, "All hands aloft! Take in sail!" A torrent of water cascaded through the hatchway until someone up above remembered those huddled below and battened down the hatch. Some of the emigrants began to pray. A woman cried out that all was lost. Gordon was struck by just how small and flimsy the *Penelope* was as she was tossed about by the violent seas.

Close-hauled before the wind, the *Penelope* lay sharply over, and the gale screamed like a banshee in the riggings while the sea hammered against the bow. One of the topsails slipped her halyards and the canvas slapped against the mainmast, booming like cannon. The crew scrambled aloft and reefed the topsail and some laid out on the yards and there rode out the fury of the storm's leading edge. Down below, in the stench and the pitch dark, Gordon saw none of this. He huddled on the bunk next to his mother and father and listened to the mumbled prayers for deliverance and doubted whether he would live to see the wonders of the American wilderness.

The storm raged for the better part of the day, only to give way to a week of light squalls and unpredictable winds. This was followed by a period of dead calm. Abandoned by the wind, the *Penelope* wallowed on a glassy sea. The men kept the sails wetted, but to no avail. The sun blazed without mercy in a cloudless sky and the heat became oppressive, particularly below deck. Eavesdropping on the crew, Gordon learned that they had been blown off course and that Captain Warren's prediction of five or six weeks' sailing time to New York would prove recklessly optimistic.

From the first he worried about his mother's health, doubting her ability to adapt to this new situation, much less endure it. Mary took drops of laudanum in her porridge every day. She kept to herself and said very little and spent most of her waking moments reading her Bible, when there was light enough to read. But when the fever struck it wasn't Mary who fell prey to it. Tom

Hawkes was one of the first of the emigrants to be afflicted.

The fever struck suddenly, about four weeks out of Dublin. No one knew for certain what caused it, though Gordon heard someone say it was transmitted through the water, while someone else believed it was carried by the shipbound rats that shared the hold with them, and yet another was of the opinion that the disease was caused by the fetid, 'tween-decks air. Whatever its source, the fever came on with frightening swiftness. Within twenty-four hours Tom Hawkes was delirious, and in forty-eight hours more he lay in a coma. There was no doctor among the passengers, and no medicine to be had. Fearful of the disease, the captain and crew prevented anyone from leaving the hold. Within a week one-third of the emigrants were sick. Day and night the hold was filled with the moans and cries of the ill, the awful sound of retching, the sobs and helpless queries of men and women who could only sit by and watch their loved ones die by inches, powerless to relieve their suffering.

One night, Mary Hawkes turned to Gordon and said, "Your father must have quinine or he will surely die. I must go to the captain."

"I'll go," said Gordon. "They post a watch on the hatch day and night, but I think I know of a way. Forward, in steerage, there's a small hatch covered with an iron grate. But the grate isn't bolted down. I think I can just squeeze through."

"Go, and take care."

In steerage, Gordon stacked several trunks, climbed on top of the stack, and strained to move the grate aside. He squirmed through the hatch, which was barely large enough to accommodate his broad shoulders. Crouched behind the anchor's windlass at the bow, he spotted a sailor sitting in the gunwales abreast of the main hatch—a brawny man wearing duck trousers and a checkered shirt and smoking a pipe as he gazed at the constellations shining like brilliant clusters of diamonds in the clear night sky. It was the orange glow from the pipe that gave his position away, because the *Penelope*'s heeling deck was a kaleidoscope of moving shadows. There was no moon, but the masts and the sails and the shrouds all united to cast a chiaroscuro of moving shadows in the silver starlight.

Gordon peered aft. The helmsman stood at the wheel on the quarterdeck, and a third man stood near the taff rail—it was the first mate, using a sextant to determine latitude and longitude by the altitude of specific stars. Gordon could see him fairly clearly thanks to the throw of light from a storm lantern on the quarterdeck. The captain's quarters could be accessed by means of the amidships hatch, but Gordon knew that would take him through the crew's quarters. The other means was the companionway below the quarterdeck. Somehow Gordon had to make his way from bow to stern under the very noses of three crew members. His heart sank. It appeared impossible. But the image of his father's pale, sweat-drenched face allayed his doubts and fears. Captain Warren was bound to have some medical stores aboard. Clearly he was not disposed to "waste" them on his emigrant passengers; nonetheless, Gordon was determined to get something that would help his father, and Captain Warren's opinions in the matter be damned.

Crawling on his belly, Gordon used the coaming of

the forward hatch to conceal himself from the crewman on guard. Beyond that, however, he had no cover and could only trust to luck. The crewman was still gazing at the stars. Gordon wondered if he was armed. In the darkness it was impossible to tell. How would he react to Gordon's presence on deck? No doubt violently, since the crew had no desire to expose themselves to the contagion raging in the hold below. He would kill me, like as not, thought Gordon, possibly by throwing me over the side. Such worrisome ruminations weren't making the task at hand any easier, so Gordon forced them from his mind, steeled himself, and crept onward, sliding on his belly in the shadows that gathered in the starboard scuppers. The crewman on guard was on the port side, a scant sixty feet away, but Gordon kept to deep shadow and made no sudden movement.

Abreast the foremast, Gordon began to entertain a slight hope of reaching the companionway unobserved; abreast of the main mast he turned his attention to the helmsman, confident that the crewman stationed in the bow no longer posed a threat. Beneath him the deck pitched and rolled. Overhead, sail canvas shivered and flapped, making a sound like the report of a cannon as it struck the masts.

"Winds shifted to larboard, Mr. Wolford," said the helmsman, addressing the first mate, and Gordon was close enough to hear every word clearly.

"Very well. Call the watch."

Gordon froze. For weeks he had been an intent observer of the ship's operations, and he knew what was about to happen. The helmsman would call up the watch to man the braces, and if Mr. Wolford's intention was to put the barque's stern to the wind the crewmen would haul in the starboard braces and let out those on the larboard side, and then the helmsman would turn the wheel upon the first mate's cry of "Helm a lee!"

But, as interesting as all that had been to Gordon on previous occasions, it was at this moment the worst thing that could have happened, because as soon as the helmsman called up the watch at least a dozen sailors would swarm the deck and Gordon would most assuredly be discovered. There would be no place for him to hide.

In a panic, Gordon gathered himself up and made a dash for the companionway.

The helmsman had filled his lungs to bellow for the watch, but seeing Gordon appear seemingly out of nowhere startled him so that he froze, speechless, giving Gordon a few precious seconds, so that by the time the helmsman had recovered, Gordon was at the top of the companionway directly below the quarterdeck.

"Passenger on deck!" roared the helmsman. "God help us, thars a bloody emigrant lad on deck!"

Gordon paused and shot a quick glance forward. The crewman stationed to watch the forecastle hatch was running aft. More sailors were clambering up out of the hatch amidships.

"Hey you! Stop right there!"

Gordon looked up. The helmsman and the first mate were peering over the quarterdeck rail, scowling fiercely down at him. Wolford, though, was momentarily distracted by the unattended helm. "Back to your station!" he rasped at the helmsman, and then leaped over the rail. Gordon gasped, for it seemed as though Wolford would land right on top of him. But if such had been the first mate's intent, he misjudged in his haste, and hit the deck a few feet away from Gordon. With no one minding her wheel, the *Penelope* heeled over sharply, and the deck's rising angle betrayed Wolford. The first mate was an agile man who had spent his whole life at sea; notwithstanding that, he lost his balance and went sprawling.

Gordon hurled himself down the dark companionway. Also endowed with considerable agility, he might have negotiated the steep narrow stairs but for the fact that the ship was turned now into a wave. The *Penelope*'s bow lurched skyward. The ship teetered for an instant on the crest of the wave and then plunged sharply down into the trough. The steps seemed to fall out from under Gordon's feet and he pitched forward just as they came back up, and a yelp of pain escaped him as he landed on his shoulder and toppled head over heels to the bottom of the companionway.

Stunned, Gordon lay there, certain that he must have broken at least half of the bones in his body. He couldn't move—it hurt too much to move. He tried to drag some air into his lungs but his lungs didn't want to work. Then he saw the shape of a man at the top of the companionway, and a raspy voice growled an incoherent curse and Gordon knew it was the first mate. Wolford started down the companionway, but the ship's bow tilted skyward again and the first mate caught himself lest he pitch headfirst down the steps as Gordon had done.

"Damn your eyes to everlastin' hell, Lynch!" he roared, and Gordon assumed he was addressing the helmsman. "Put the helm a lee or I'll skin you alive."

With that he started down the companionway, and Gordon turned to run—straight into Captain Warren, who had thrown open the door to his cabin. Gordon expected the captain to grab him and hold him until Wolford had descended the steps—and then God only knew what horrible fate would befall him. Instead, Warren recognized him and cringed, so great was his fear of the contagion that raged in the emigrant hold, and Gordon managed to slip past him and into the cabin. It was the only place left to run. He saw a dirk on a table. The blade weighed down one end of an old nautical chart. He grabbed the weapon, whirled to face the door, and it was then that he saw Mick Maguire. He almost didn't recognize the rowdy. Mick stood with his back pressed against a bulkhead. He was pale and gaunt in the cheeks and his eyes were sunk deep in their sockets. He looked very old and haggard for a boy of sixteen—no longer the brawny, ruddy-faced lad Gordon remembered from a fortnight ago, when he and his gang had been terrorizing the rest of the passengers.

Gordon was shocked by Mick's appearance—but he could spare Maguire only a brief glance, because now Wolford's bulk filled the cabin's doorway, and behind the first mate stood Captain Warren, scowling darkly.

"Get that filthy rascal out of my cabin, Mr. Wolford."

The blade in Gordon's hand gave Wolford pause. He grinned like a wolf.

"Take care with that now, boy. You might hurt yourself."

"I'll hurt you if you take another step."

"At once, Mr. Wolford," rasped Warren.

"Put the dirk aside, lad," Wolford said with a sneer, "or I'll use it to cut you up into little pieces and feed you to the sharks."

Suddenly Captain Warren and Wolford pitched violently forward into the cabin. Gordon jumped back as they fell in a cursing tangle of arms and legs. Into the doorway stepped William Drummond Stewart.

"You'll do no such thing, Mr. Wolford," he said cordially, but steel laced every quietly spoken word.

Wolford pounced to his feet, but the tension went out of his body at once when he saw that Stewart's hand rested lightly but meaningfully on the butt of a belted pistol. He didn't take his eyes off Stewart as he helped Captain Warren to his feet.

"This matter doesn't concern you, Captain Stewart," said Warren.

"I respectfully disagree. I was pleasantly employed reading a fellow officer's reminiscences of his visit to America when all this commotion interrupted me."

"It's nothing, sir, I assure you," said Warren, adopting a more conciliatory tone as he recovered his reasoning processes. "Just one of those Irish rowdies. We mean only to teach him his manners."

Stewart glanced at Mick Maguire. "I see you've done a bit of work on this lad, Captain," he remarked dryly. Then he turned his attention to Gordon, and recognition illuminated his features. "I remember you. Hawkes, isn't it?"

"Yes sir."

"What's the meaning of all this, boy?"

"It's my father, sir. He's dying. He must have some medicine or he doesn't stand a chance. Captain Warren, I beg you to help us . . ."

"What's this?" Stewart looked sternly at the *Penelope*'s skipper. "You told me, sir, that you were doing everything in your power to help those poor people. I took you at your word and, as you suggested, concerned myself no further with the matter. I thought you were an honorable man, Captain. Apparently I was wrong."

"I have limited medical supplies on board, Captain Stewart. I—I have my crew to consider. All would be lost if they fall prey to the fever."

"So you kept your medicine for the crew. My God, Warren, you're a gold-plated fool, aren't you?"

"You have no right to speak to me in that manner," said Warren resentfully.

"If you had done all you could to treat the first cases, the fever might have been contained, perhaps even conquered. The fact is, you wouldn't give a farthing for all those emigrants you carry 'tween decks, would you? Why, I've seen slavers treat their human cargo better."

"Slaves are worth more alive than dead," said Wolford.

"Shut your trap," snarled Warren.

"I see," said Stewart with a deep sigh. "You've got their fare, so whether they live or die is of little consequence to you now, is that it, Captain?"

"No one has died."

"Not yet. I insist you honor this lad's request and provide his father with medicine."

"But no one knows for certain how to effectively treat ship fever," protested Warren.

"Damn your hide," snapped Stewart, anger blazing in his eyes. "Assume the worst. Assume it is typhus."

"And who are you to be giving orders aboard this ship?" asked a truculent Wolford.

"Belay that," Warren told him.

"Sound advice," said Stewart, fastening his cold smile on the first mate. "Your captain is no fool after all. I personally have little influence. The same cannot be said for my brother, however, who could make life perfectly miserable for a ship's captain."

"Break out the medical stores, Mr. Wolford," Warren said with a sigh.

"I'm not going down into the hold," said Wolford.

"You'll do as you are told or suffer the consequences."

Wolford frowned at Warren then at Stewart—and stormed out of the cabin with a muttered. "Aye, aye, sir." Warren gave Gordon a dark look and followed.

"What is your father's condition, boy?" asked Stewart.

"He went into a coma several days ago and hasn't regained consciousness, sir. His heart seems scarcely to be beating. At times he appears to have difficulty breathing. His condition scares me."

"You've done a brave thing tonight. This is a desperate crew and an unprincipled captain."

"I had to do something. I couldn't stand idle and watch my father die by inches."

"Don't place too much faith in medicines, Gordon. It may be that your father is past the point of helping. Prepare yourself for the worst."

Gordon shook his head. He refused to consider the possibility that his father would die. Without his father, what would become of him and his mother? What would they do if they reached America? The enormity of the responsibility that would befall him in that event was too great for Gordon to contemplate. The grand adventure had become a grim nightmare.

Stewart turned to Mick Maguire, who through it all

had remained motionless, backed up into a corner of the captain's cabin.

"He's treated you damned harshly, hasn't he, son?" asked Stewart. "Seems our good captain is a little too fond of the cat-o'-nines. I've heard you cry out a time or two. But by the looks of it I'd say it's been much worse than I imagined."

"No," rasped Mick. "I don't cry out. That wasn't me. Stay back. Don't come any closer."

"I'll have a look at your back," said Stewart, and put a hand on Maguire's shoulder.

"No!" sobbed Mick, and flinched at Stewart's touch. Eluding the Scotsman's grasp, he bolted from the cabin, screaming, "Keep away from me! Everybody just keep away!"

"Poor boy," said Stewart. "The devil's aboard this accursed ship." He glanced at Gordon. "Go to your mother. She needs you. Stay clear of the captain, and be brave. Life doesn't play fair. But no matter what happens, it's still worth living."

IV.

Tom Hawkes died three days later.

He was one of the first to be claimed by the fever. Within the week two dozen emigrants perished. Captain Warren's medical stores proved to be too little, too late.

Gordon wept when his father's shrouded body was commended to the gray melancholy of the sea. His mother, on the other hand, didn't even seem to be aware of what was going on. The trauma was too much for her. That night she sat up until dawn, hugging her knees to her body and rocking back and forth, back and forth, humming a spiritual melody and staring into space. The next morning she smiled sadly at Gordon and patted his cheek. "Poor boy," she crooned. "All alone in a strange new land."

"But I'm not alone, Mother. We have each other."

"Poor boy. All alone. What will become of you?"

In black despair Gordon sought refuge in steerage. Crouched among the baggage of the *Penelope*'s emigrant cargo, swamped by his own sorrow and surrounded by the manifestations of grief demonstrated by other passengers, he feared he would go mad. His world had lost all its meaning, its hope, its sanity, and for days he simply hid away, wanting only to be left alone. Wanting to escape, too. But there was no place to run. He seldom slept, and when he did drift off to sleep he awoke exhausted and shivering, for his sleep was haunted by nightmares populated with images of being sewn up in a canvas shroud while still alive, and being tossed over the ship's side, and sinking into the cold black depths of the ocean, and fighting to get out of the shroud, and hearing his father's mournful voice, his father calling to him as though from a great distance, and then, unable to hold his breath any longer, he let the ocean into himself and in that brief, writhing agony he would awaken, sobbing and drenched with sweat.

At some point—Gordon lost track of time—his mother came looking for him. Her appearance alarmed him. She was gaunt and colorless. There was no life in her eyes. He was afraid the fever had found another victim, but she assured him that all she needed to put herself to rights was a dose of laudanum. You must go to the captain, she told him, and if there is laudanum to be

had you must get it for me. The supply—two bottles—
that she had brought with her, was all gone now. Gordon's father had been meticulous in measuring out
small doses to mix with her porridge, and there would
have been enough to last the voyage had she adhered to
this strict rationing after her husband's death. Instead,
she had consumed all that remained in a matter of days.

Gordon refused to go to Captain Warren. The laudanum was slowly but surely killing his mother, suck-
ing the life out of her by degrees, and he would
not—could not—act as an accomplice in her self-
destruction. Managing Mary's addiction had been his
father's responsibility—a responsibility too great for a
confused and frightened and grief-stricken lad of sixteen years to take upon himself. Besides, Gordon had
no wish to tangle again with the captain or crew—especially Wolford, the first mate.

Angry at her son for his lack of cooperation, Mary
Hawkes arranged to see the captain herself.

Later she came again to steerage and Gordon could
tell by her placid, somewhat dazed attitude that she had
found more of the elixir her body so desperately
craved.

"I've had a good long talk with the captain," she told
him, "and have made certain arrangements with your
best interests at heart. The captain is in need of a new
cabin boy."

"What about Mick Maguire?"

"Oh, you don't know, do you? That troubled lad cast
himself into the sea two nights ago. There was no hope
of finding him in the darkness. And to be truthful I
doubt that they tried. Poor Captain Warren. He exhausted himself trying to straighten that boy out. But

Mick Maguire was a bad seed, Gordon. There was no hope for him."

Gordon was horrified. Though Mick had brought him nothing but trouble, he was saddened by the rowdy's death, and he was fairly certain that Captain Warren's sadistic habits had driven Mick to take his own life. Gordon couldn't get the image of Mick Maguire—frozen like a gaunt statue in the corner of the captain's cabin, staring with wild and haunted eyes—out of his mind. Now his mother had unwittingly condemned him to the same hell that had forced Mick to the last resort of suicide, the only escape from Warren's brutal attentions.

"How could you?" he gasped. "You don't know the captain, Mother. He is an evil man. Just ask Captain Stewart. He knows the truth. He'll tell you what Warren is really like."

"Captain Stewart? What in the world does he have to do with this?"

"Please, Mother. You don't realize what you've done."

"I know very well what I have done, young man. It is for the best. We cannot stay in America now. Captain Warren has been good enough to guarantee us passage back to Dublin. Of course, it will be a long journey, for first the *Penelope* must sail to the West Indies for a cargo of sugar and tobacco."

"But why can't we stay in America?"

"That should be obvious. Your father is dead. We can't venture out to the frontier alone."

"Why not? I'm strong. I work hard. I can take care of everything. I'll take care of you. We won't be any better off back in Ireland. We couldn't afford to buy a new farm, and even if we could the available land would be so poor that we couldn't survive."

Mary Hawkes shook her head. "I have no intention of living on a farm, in either Ireland or America. No, I shall find some kind of work in Dublin. And perhaps your experience as a cabin boy on this ship will inspire you to make your livelihood on the sea. You will have to make your own way from now on. I won't be able to support us both."

"I hate the sea," said Gordon resentfully. "And I can't believe you've done this to me. You don't care about your own son. All you care about is your next bottle of laudanum."

Mary was no less taken aback than if he had struck her with his fists. Then anger knitted her brows.

"I think you are in need of some stern discipline, young man. One of your father's faults was that he went too easy with you."

"I won't do it. I won't!"

"Yes, you will. The arrangements have been made. You belong to Captain Warren until we arrive back in Dublin."

"And how much did that arrangement cost him?" asked Gordon bitterly. "How much laudanum did it take to buy me?"

She slapped him, and the tears welled up in her eyes, and with a quivering lip she turned quickly away as though unable to bear the sight of him, and in spite of everything Gordon regretted his harsh words. His poor mother hadn't realized what she was getting him into, and her mind was so befuddled by the opiate that she just couldn't think straight. Yes, that had to be it. Had she been of sound mind she never would have done this.

"Very well," he said. "I'll do as you say, Mother."

Mary Hawkes turned back and embraced him. "You're a loving son, aren't you, Gordon?" she whispered gratefully. "You know I won't let anything happen to you. You know that, don't you?"

"Of course," he said flatly.

"Good. Now run along and see the captain. He is expecting you."

"Yes, ma'am."

He was stopped at the hatchway by the sailor on watch, and told the crewman that the captain wanted to see him, and when he said it he thought he glimpsed a glimmer of pity in the seaman's eyes. The man let him pass and he went aft to the companionway and Mr. Wolford was on the quarterdeck glowering down at him—this was not a man who forgot a grudge. Then and there Gordon made up his mind because it was quite clear to him that he would not survive the voyage back to Dublin. If Warren didn't do him in, the *Penelope*'s first mate would see to it, with relish.

On his way to the captain's cabin he paused at Stewart's quarters and rapped lightly on the door. Stewart swung the door open, took one look at the expression on Gordon's face and said, "Good Lord, what's happened to you?"

"It's what's about to happen, sir."

"Come in and tell me what it is that's troubling you, lad."

Once inside Gordon told the Scotsman everything, and tried his best to remain calm and collected in the telling. In conclusion he said, "I've decided to jump ship as soon as we get to New York. Even though it means leaving my mother . . ." His voice broke, and he choked on strong emotion.

"Your mother can take care of herself," said Stewart. "It's time you struck out on your own. But I fear Captain Warren will take precautions when we reach port—precautions that might make it impossible for you to get off this ship."

"I've got to get away. Will you—will you help me, sir?"

"Yes," said Stewart, without a moment's hesitation. "You can rely on me, Gordon. But until then . . ."

"Yes, I know." Gordon felt safe in Stewart's presence; he wanted to stay right here in the Scotsman's cabin until the *Penelope* reached New York—it was his only haven on the ship. But he knew he couldn't.

"Listen, lad. Do everything Warren tells you. Don't give him the least cause to indulge his taste for the whip. We're but a few days from our destination. Make do as best you can until then—and leave the rest to me."

"Thank you, sir. I don't know how I'll ever repay you . . ."

Stewart shook his head. "It's high time I did something. I've stood back and let Warren mistreat that Maguire boy. I didn't do a thing to help your father and the other sick. I'm thinking you would want to come along with me on my excursion into the American wilderness."

"Do you mean it, sir?"

"I always mean what I say. How about it, then? Do we have ourselves a bargain?" Stewart stuck out his hand.

Gordon took it with alacrity. "Yes sir!"

Stewart nodded. He hoped that would give Gordon something to look forward to in the dark days that lay ahead.

A moment later, heart hammering against his rib cage, Gordon mustered up all his courage and knocked on the door to the captain's cabin.

"Who is it?"

"Gordon Hawkes, sir."

The door opened and Warren looked him up and down and nodded. "So your mother has told you all about our little agreement, I take it. You might say you've been indentured into my service for a time, though no document exists to record that fact. Your duties will not be severe. You will clean my clothes, keep my shoes polished, maintain the cabin in order, serve me my food, and run any errand I might need of you. You would do well to be prompt and respectful at all times. Failure will bring swift retribution. Is that clear, Hawkes?"

"Quite clear," said Gordon, and began counting the minutes to New York and freedom.

V.

A week later the *Penelope* ended her journey across the Atlantic, moored to an East River dock. Thirty-four of the emigrants had perished during the crossing. City officials boarded the barque and promptly ruled that she had to be quarantined, and Captain Warren's heated protests availed him nothing. Gordon fell deeper into despair. Leaving the ship was twice as impossible now. Warren was watching him like a hawk, and he had in-

formed the *Penelope*'s first mate of his suspicions that
the cabin boy might be plotting something, so now
Gordon was not even permitted above deck. And even
if he could get over the side somehow, constables were
on watch dockside, around the clock, to prevent anyone
from disembarking.

Several days passed, and with hours spent waiting
for the quarantine to be lifted Captain Warren's mood
worsened. He took his frustrations out on Gordon, finding fault with everything his cabin boy did, and twice
in three days Gordon felt the sting of the cat-o'-nine
tails. Though he had tried to follow Stewart's advice,
he'd been whipped a dozen times, and his back was a
mass of raw, bleeding welts that were never allowed to
heal. It was all Gordon could do to refrain from turning
on his tormentor and trying to kill him.

Physicians boarded the *Penelope* daily to treat the
sick, and it was hoped that in a fortnight the quarantine
could be removed and the emigrants allowed to go
ashore. The Irish Emigrant Relief Society brought fresh
food, and some of the female members of the benevo-
lent association volunteered to stay on board and serve
as nurses. Conditions in the emigrants' quarters gradually improved. But they didn't improve for Gordon.
The only thing that kept him going was the idea of accompanying Captain Stewart on his excursion into the
American frontier. *Life doesn't play fair,* Stewart had
said. *But no matter what happens, it's still worth living.*
Those words were Gordon's lifeline; he clung to them
even as his hope faded.

But then, eight days after the *Penelope*'s arrival in
New York harbor, Captain Stewart and a city official
came to Warren's cabin.

"I am satisfied that this gentleman is not afflicted with typhus," announced the official, "and therefore I have provided him with a pass permitting him to go ashore at his convenience. I am confident you will have no objections, Captain."

"Certainly not."

The official nodded, gave a stiff bow in Stewart's direction. "If I may be of further service to you, sir."

"Thank you."

Warren studiously avoided looking at Stewart until the official was gone—and then he leered at the Scotsman.

"You must have paid a pretty penny for this privilege, sir."

"Not really. I've found that if you demonstrate the proper respect for a man's position he quite often lets you off with just a modest token."

Warren chuckled, but he was unable to conceal his resentment. "I suppose you must be accustomed to such favoritism, being a gentleman and a hero."

Stewart refused to rise to the bait. "Still, it is always a pleasant experience. Now, I shall be ready to leave your fair ship in an hour's time. But first I must make myself presentable. My boots need a good polishing." He glanced for the first time at Gordon, who out of habit had made himself as inconspicuous as possible in a corner of the room. "Send your boy to my cabin, if you please, Captain."

Lips pursed, Warren thought it over. He didn't want to accommodate Stewart but he didn't have just cause to refuse the request. During the passage he had come to dislike Stewart with a resentment born of envy. Stewart was everything that he was not—articulate, dashing, courageous, a gentleman and hero of the realm.

"Oh, very well," said Warren. "Go with the captain, Hawkes, and be quick about it."

Once they were in his cabin Stewart grabbed Gordon by the shoulder and led him to an empty, open trunk.

"Get in."

"What?"

"Get in the bloody trunk, lad."

"But I . . ."

"You want off this ship, don't you?"

"Well, yes, of course, but . . ."

"Then do what I tell you. Get in the trunk and make no sound or movement."

Gordon reluctantly climbed into the trunk and sat down. He didn't care for the idea of being confined in such a small space for no telling how long. But the thought of Warren—and the captain's fondness for his cat-o'-nine tails—prompted him to obey Stewart. At the Scotsman's bidding he leaned well forward with his head between his knees. Stewart brought the lid down. It wouldn't quite close; Gordon was larger than the Scotsman had calculated. Muttering a curse, Stewart pushed down on the lid. Inside the trunk Gordon winced at the pressure on his shoulders and spine, and fought a moment of panic as he heard the latches click shut.

Stewart went up on deck and informed Mr. Wolford that he was ready to leave the ship. The first mate already knew about the Scotsman's arrangement with the city official, and he was no more pleased about it than Captain Warren. It wasn't right that Stewart was free to leave the *Penelope* while all the rest of them were imprisoned on board. Wolford knew the seamier side of New York quite well, and he had been looking forward to visiting a few bar rooms and a bordello or two. Grimacing, he barked at a pair of crewmen lounging about on the main deck to lend the *gentleman*—he sneered the word—a hand with his luggage.

The two men were carrying the trunk containing Gordon out of Stewart's cabin when Captain Warren emerged from his quarters.

"Cor blimey," muttered one of the crewmen. "This flamin' thing is heavy. What have you got in here, sir? A cargo of cannonballs? Or bars of gold bullion?"

"You've found me out," joked Stewart. "It's the Crown Jewels."

The crewmen laughed and moved toward the companionway steps with their burden.

"Hold on there," said Warren. He peered past Stewart into the Scotsman's quarters. "Where is the Hawkes boy?"

"I changed my mind about the boots," said Stewart, "and told him to go about his business."

"Damn!" Warren rushed for the steps, jostling the crewmen, and one lost his grip on the trunk, which hit the deck with a jarring thud that made Stewart wince.

Reaching the main deck, Warren bellowed for his first mate. "Have you seen Hawkes?"

"He hasn't been up here, Captain."

Warren turned to descend the companionway, but had to wait for Stewart and the two crewmen with the trunk. Stewart touched the brim of his hat in passing.

"Farewell, Captain Warren, and good sailing."

Warren muttered a reply and disappeared down the companionway.

Once the trunk was safely ashore, Stewart sent the crewmen back for the rest of his baggage, and sat on the trunk to wait for them to carry out the task. When all was done he gave them each a half crown. He gave another half crown to the cartman who loaded the trunk and valises into the back of his cart, all the while assuring Stewart that he knew of clean, safe accommodations suitable for a "furrin gennelman."

Stewart chuckled. "I don't care if it's safe, old fellow, so long as I can get a hot bath and a decent meal. Oh— I almost forgot."

He popped the trunk's latches and lifted the lid.

"Mother of Jesus!" cried the cartman as Gordon came out of the trunk like a drowning man who breaks the sea's surface for one last gasp of life.

"There's another crown in it for you if you forget you saw this young man," said Stewart.

"What young fellow was that?" asked the cartman, the sight of the gold coins in Stewart's palm helping him recover from his shock.

"Fine. Let's be off, then," said Stewart, with a backward glance at the *Penelope*. He noticed the way Gordon was gazing at the barque, and read his thoughts. "You will have plenty of adventures to relate to your mother when you see her again, Gordon."

"Yes, of course," said Gordon—even though somehow he knew that he would never see his mother again.

CHAPTER 2

I.

Gordon didn't think he would ever get tired of New Orleans when he first arrived at the fabled Crescent City, but after a few weeks of the hustle and bustle and exotic sights and sounds of the Vieux Carré's narrow streets he started to long for some peace and quiet, some wide open spaces where he could get a breath of fresh air that wasn't redolent with humanity.

The Vieux Carré—French for "old square"—had been established over a hundred years earlier by the explorer Jean Baptiste Lemoyne, Sieur de Bienville. Envisioned as a capital city for New France, positioned to guard the mouth of the Mississippi River against possible encroachment by British and Spanish rivals, La Nouvelle Orleans had begun as crude huts lining cramped streets populated by adventurers, scoundrels, black sheep aristocrats, and undesirables culled from Paris jails. "Casket girls"—young women from poor families who were willing to risk the perils of the New World to better their lot—also came, along with Ursuline nuns and Acadian trappers who lived in the swamps that encircled the settlement.

In 1762 the French king Louis XV gave Louisiana to his cousin Charles III of Spain. Children born from the intermarriage of French and Spanish families became known as Creoles. Though devastated by two fires, floods, hurricanes, and epidemics of yellow fever, New Orleans prospered. And then, with the Louisiana Purchase of 1803, in which the United States acquired New Orleans, the Americans began pouring in. New Orleanians did not choose to make the rough and rowdy Americans welcome, and with Creole society closed to them, the "Yankee barbarians" created their own community nearby. The Vieux Carré retained, therefore, its uniquely exotic flavor.

Captain Stewart had rented rooms in a boardinghouse on Chartres Street, in the heart of the old quarter, and for the first few days Gordon enjoyed touring the city with the Scotsman. From dawn to well after dusk the narrow streets were always alive with a delightful variety of people. Street vendors peddled wares of every description, from pralines and hot rice fritters to palmetto fronds and Spanish moss, the former used for cleaning chimneys and the latter for mattress stuffing. There were wagons and carts carrying produce in from outlying farms, as well as goods unloaded from sailing ships and bound for local emporiums. Each day Gordon and Stewart would pause at a coffee shop located on Bourbon Street, sitting at a sidewalk table in the shade of a striped awning, and as Stewart read a newspaper Gordon would watch the people passing by—Creole aristocrats and French sword masters mingling with slaves and Indians and sailors and swamp-rats.

But after a while the sightseeing began to bore Gordon. He longed to proceed upriver, for it was his understanding that Stewart intended to embark on his excursion into the wild frontier from a town called St. Louis, which lay many days' travel to the north. He wondered why Stewart was lingering in New Orleans, but he didn't broach the subject. He owed the Scotsman a great debt, for without Stewart's help Gordon knew he would not have escaped the sadistic Captain Warren. What right had he to express dissatisfaction with his lot? They had spent a fortnight in New York, and Stewart had bought him a new set of clothes and introduced him to the opera and the lyceum and even taken him along to a grand soiree in an opulent mansion on Washington Square, and it had been quite an experience for an Irish farm boy whose only experience with cities had been a few visits to Dublin. And Dublin was not nearly so full of wonders as New York—or New Orleans, for that matter.

Stewart had met a young woman at the soiree and Gordon had feared the captain's dalliance with the beauty would delay their departure, but they were soon taking passage on a coastal steamer, stopping briefly at Charleston and Savannah and Mobile before arriving at last, in early summer, in New Orleans. Though there had been no shipboard fever and no brutal captain to endure aboard the steamer, the voyage had been an unpleasant one for Gordon. He was sick to death of the sea. Where were the uncharted plains? The savage Indians? The herds of buffalo that Stewart talked so much about— millions of shaggy brown beasts moving in herds so vast that travelers had been stopped for days to await their passing?

These wondrous things were all that Gordon had left to look forward to. They were all that remained of the grand adventure he had dreamed of back in Ireland from the moment his father had spoken of a new beginning in America. Beyond these things Gordon entertained no expectations, no prospects. He had no idea what he would do with his life. Separated by circumstances from his mother, his father dead, Gordon Hawkes had nothing left to cling to besides the alluring images of the frontier dwelling in his imagination.

Then, as they sat one day at their usual table in front of the coffee house, Stewart suddenly put down his newspaper and fastened a speculative eye on his brooding companion.

"I suspect you must be wondering why we linger here. I can tell by the look on your face that the wild country is calling you."

"It's just that if we don't get to St. Louis soon and start west we'll be snowed in before we can get anywhere."

"I see. Yes, you're quite right."

Gordon shrugged. "I realize it's not my place . . ."

"Rubbish. You're entitled to your opinion, and never hesitate to make your feelings known to me, my friend. It will take us two weeks to reach St. Louis, and that is assuming our steamboat makes the journey without mishap—and I am given to understand that mishaps are commonplace on the Mississippi River. Then we must outfit ourselves, and find suitable traveling companions, for I am also told that white men should trek west in large parties if they want to keep their scalps. But I have a confession to make. I don't have the funds for a proper outfitting. That's why we linger here. I'm waiting to hear from my banker. Remember, lad, I'm a soldier on half pay. I am also the youngest of two brothers. In jolly old England that means my brother controls the purse strings. A silly thing called primogeniture is responsible for this damned sorry state of affairs. Now John is a generous soul, and he forwarded funds to a New York bank for me. I was assured that those funds would be transferred promptly to a bank here in New Orleans. But they haven't been. I'm trying to find out why."

Stewart sipped his chicory blend coffee and ruefully shook his head. "With the benefit of hindsight I can say that it would have been wiser to withdraw all the funds in New York and carry them with me. But, in my own defense, I wasn't aware until recently how deplorable the American banking system really was."

"Deplorable? How so?"

"Well, you know there is a fellow by the name of Andy Jackson in the White House. A military man—he has that much going for him. But apparently high finance and economics are not subjects in which he is too well versed. When he was elected in '28, the Bank of the United States was for all intents and purposes in full control of the country's finances. You see, the B.U.S., as it is called, had a charter from the federal government and enjoyed the exclusive right to hold the government's funds. Its banknotes circulated throughout the country as a dependable medium of exchange. It kept the state and local banks from issuing more paper money than they could redeem with the gold and silver reserves in their vaults. The president of the B.U.S., a chap by the name of Nicholas Biddle, could set interest rates, establish branch banks, and decide who would get credit and who wouldn't. In short, Mr. Biddle and his bank controlled the national economy. Following me so far?"

Gordon nodded, though he had no idea what all this had to do with the fact that they were wasting the summer away in New Orleans.

"Jackson and his associates are 'hard money' men," continued Stewart. "They think paper money is dangerous, and to an extent they're right—a bank is allowed to print all the paper currency it wants to, even if it doesn't have the specie to cover that paper's redemption, and so it is quite possible that you may be conducting your business with notes that will be practically worthless tomorrow if the bank falls on hard times. Jackson called Biddle's B.U.S. 'The Monster,' and he set about destroying it. Some say it's because Biddle used Bank funds to finance the political campaigns of the general's opponents. Others say Jackson doesn't want to share power with Biddle. The end result is that for whatever reason Old Hickory set himself to destroying the Bank of the United States. He defeated the Bank's recharter and is in the process of withdrawing the federal government's deposits, placing them in state and local banks."

"Is that good?" asked Gordon hesitantly. "Or bad?"

"It's politics, lad. New 'wildcat' banks are popping up like weeds and printing paper and making loans without the reserves to cover their issue. And the B.U.S. is no longer powerful enough to control them. I left my funds in just such an institution as that." Stewart shrugged, and added, "So that is why we sit here and wait." A passing belle, all lace and silk and the faint fragrance of jasmine, caught the Scotsman's attention. He smiled, and the Creole beauty gave him a coquette's sidelong glance around the rim of her parasol. "But you must admit," said Stewart, "we could be stuck in a much less congenial place than this."

As it happened, their wait was almost over. Two days later, Stewart returned from his daily visit to a New Orleans bank to inform Gordon that bad news had finally arrived from New York. The bank that had held his funds had closed its doors and the bank president was suspected of having made off with most of the institution's operating capital.

"I am afraid we are stone broke," announced Stewart.

Gordon was stunned. "You mean . . . you mean we can't go on?" He felt sick to his stomach.

Stewart laughed. "We can't even pay for our board. But don't worry, lad. I've been in tighter spots. You'll see your wild Indians and fire-breathing shaggies, I promise you."

"But how? You said yourself we had to outfit ourselves, and that takes money." Gordon frowned. He didn't like the way his complaint sounded. Stewart wasn't responsible for paying his way in the first place. "You'd do well to leave me behind, sir."

"We're in this together to the bitter end. If you'll forgive the presumption, I've come to think of you as a younger brother. I suppose it's because you remind me so much of myself when I was your age."

Gordon was moved. "Then I'll find some work. Make some money so we can go on."

"That's the spirit. Even though life doesn't play fair, you have to stay in the game. I see you've learned that lesson. But no, I've thought of another way to recoup our losses. It is a risky business, and if it fails then we will both have to roll up our sleeves and resort to manual labor. But if it succeeds, we will be on our way to St. Louis within the week."

"What is it that you have in mind?"

"There will be a fight in Slave Town tomorrow night. A big buck named Gabriel is the reigning champion in bare knuckle brawling. A sugar planter by the name of Remairie is bringing in one of his slaves to take this Gabriel on. No one gives Remairie's boy much of a chance. The odds are twenty to one in favor of Gabriel. I'll put everything I have left on the challenger. I've already pawned my saber and pistol, and I have a hundred American dollars to place on the fight."

"But what if you lose?"

"If I lose then we'll both have to work our way to St. Louis. God knows I hope we don't have to do that." Stewart laughed again. "I guess it's the blue blood in my veins, but I am damned averse to hard labor!"

II.

The bout was scheduled to take place at sundown in the courtyard of what had once been a large stucco house at the end of Royal Street. The building had been largely destroyed in the great fire of 1794; though most of the exterior walls of brick and stucco were still standing, most of the interior of the house had been gutted. This end of Royal was part of what was now called Slave Town. It was a rough and tumble area, known for its saloons and bordellos, its pickpockets and cutthroats. But that didn't prevent dozens of affluent locals from attending the event. Gleaming carriages and thoroughbred saddle horses lined the cobblestone streets. Gentlemen in broadcloth suits and beaver hats, sometimes alone, sometimes accompanied by wife or mistress, mingled with slaves and dockworkers, sailors and professional gamblers. Gordon figured there were at least two hundred people on hand.

Stewart placed his bet, one hundred dollars on Joe Lightning, Remairie's slave, giving the money to a man who placed it in a strongbox guarded by a pair of pistol-toting men who both stood about six feet six and weighed in at about three hundred pounds, all of it brawn. They were identical twins.

"Who are those two?" asked Gordon, as he and Stewart turned away from the bet maker.

"Those are the Vargot brothers," said Stewart, pocketing his chit. "They have a very bad reputation in these parts, I'm told. There must be a lot of money in that strongbox, but it is as safe as if it were in a bank's vault." Stewart smiled ruefully. "Safer, I should say. Come on, lad. We'll have a good view of the fight from up there."

Gordon looked warily at the wrought-iron balcony at which Stewart was pointing. It was attached to the wall of the burnt-out hulk of the house, and Gordon wondered how secure it could be. A dozen people had already braved it, but how much more weight would the balcony take before it collapsed? Stewart didn't seem to give the danger a second thought. He bounded up the narrow iron steps to the balcony, and Gordon followed much more cautiously.

Stewart was right—they had a fine view of the crowded courthouse below. The brawl was about to begin. Gabriel and Joe Lightning had been put up on crates for the spectators to compare. Both fighters were big—nearly as big as the Vargot brothers, but Gabriel was older and looked much the meaner of the two, in

Gordon's opinion. Joe Lightning seemed to enjoy immensely being the center of attention. He posed for the audience, flexing his muscles and flashing a big grin. Gabriel, on the other hand, just stood there and watched his adversary's antics with the stoicism of a statue, and even from up on the balcony a hundred feet away, in a quickly gathering darkness, Gordon thought he could detect a quiet menace in Gabriel's scarred countenance. He feared that Stewart had bet on the wrong man.

By the light of numerous lanterns and torches, the arena was roped off, and the fighters were introduced to lusty cheers and boos from the spectators.

"Here we go, lad," said Stewart, caught up in the excitement. "Within an hour's time we should know what our future holds in store for us."

As Joe Lightning was introduced, so was his owner, and the Creole planter named Remairie acknowledged the crowd from a balcony directly across the courtyard from where Gordon stood. He was a tall, rail-thin man with iron-gray hair swept back from a long, gaunt face, and he was clad in the finest broadcloth, linen, and silk. He greeted the crowd as a monarch might acknowledge the adulation of the masses.

But Gordon spared M'sieu Remairie scarcely a glance, because standing beside the planter was the most beautiful young woman he had ever seen. She wore a pale yellow organdy dress adorned with white lace, in sharp contrast to the raven black hair that fell in ringlets to her bare shoulders.

"Who is the girl standing next to Mr. Remairie?" he asked Stewart.

"I'm glad you have a discerning eye where the ladies are concerned," replied the Scotsman. "Her name is

Lorine, I believe. She was with him when I made his acquaintance a few days ago, and I understand she is his current mistress. He is married, of course, but Madame Remairie rarely leaves the plantation. It isn't unusual for a man of Remairie's stature to keep a mistress. Truth be known, it would be unusual if he did not."

"But he's so old, and she looks very young."

"I daresay she is your age, Gordon, or younger. By the way, she is a quadroon."

Gordon had heard about the legendary quadroons of New Orleans. They were brought up to become the mistresses of white gentlemen, and the gentlemen prized them highly. Well educated and accomplished in all the social graces, they were presented to society at quadroon balls, to which the gentlemen flocked to select a lover. The man was responsible for setting his mistress up in high style—there were rows of houses on the Ramparts occupied by quadroon beauties—for one did not keep a mistress unless one could afford to lavish every extravagance upon her. To do less would be dishonorable. When the man eventually married a woman of his own race and class he might give up his mistress, but he would not turn her out onto the street; she would be allowed to keep all her gowns and jewels and furniture and house, and quite often she would receive a generous monetary gift—a kind of severance pay. Sometimes, though, the gentleman would keep his mistress even after his marriage to another.

Oddly enough, southern society justified the keeping of mistresses—and sexual relations between slaveholders and female slaves—with the argument that the custom relieved white women of the distasteful duty of serving their husbands' lust. Thus did white men release their passion harmlessly on women of a lower class, and thus was the virtue of white women protected.

This justification notwithstanding, Gordon decided then and there that he didn't at all care for the institution of mistress-keeping. Especially in Remairie's case; the old man had no business corrupting a girl like Lorine. No doubt this arrangement was not to her liking.

A roar went up from the crowd—the fight had started, and Gordon dragged his gaze from the quadroon beauty to see Joe Lightning attack Gabriel with a flurry of blows. Gabriel threw up his arms to protect his head and took a dozen blows to the midsection that didn't seem to faze him in the least. Joe stepped back, breathless, momentarily spent, and Gabriel faked with a left and then hit Joe with a right hook that sent Joe reeling. Before he could regain his balance, Gabriel was on him, connecting with several blows to the head. Joe went down, blood dripping from his mouth to mingle with the sweat glistening on his heaving chest. But he didn't stay down. He drove a fist into Gabriel's groin. Gabriel doubled over and Joe seized the opportunity. Bouncing to his feet, he drove a knee into Gabriel's face. Gabriel sprawled flat on his back and Joe delivered a kick to the ribs. He made the mistake of attempting another kick; Gabriel grabbed him by the leg and twisted. Joe went down again and Gabriel pounced on him, pinned him down, and methodically delivered four or five punches to his opponent's face. Gordon could see the spray of blood every time Gabriel connected. The spectators roared with delight. It seemed as though the fight was over—but Joe Lightning wasn't finished yet. He managed to get through Gabriel's defenses and claw at his eyes. Gabriel let out a shout of pain and rolled away. Joe staggered after him, coming in from behind and hooking an arm around Gabriel's neck. Laying a knee against Gabriel's spine, he did his best to break his adversary's back. Gabriel was too strong for that. He reached up and got a handful of Joe's hair and flipped Joe over his shoulder. Then a bell rang out. The fighter's keepers entered the ring to separate the pair and guide them to their respective corners. Both men were covered with blood.

"Well, Gordon, what do you think?" asked Stewart, caught up in the excitement of the moment. "No holds barred, isn't it? The Marquess of Queensbury wouldn't approve, but it makes for great sport."

"Frankly, I don't see much sport in it. They're trying to kill each other."

"Just remember, we stand to win two thousand dollars if our man prevails. I think Joe has a splendid chance. He's the younger of the two. If he can outlast his opponent . . ."

But Gordon wasn't listening. He noticed that Lorine was leaving Remairie's side, descending the balcony steps, and he watched her until she turned toward the courtyard gate. Beyond lay the street, where the carriages were parked. Gordon couldn't help himself. He had to have a closer look.

"I'll be back," he told Stewart, but the second round of the fight had begun and the Scotsman's attention was riveted to the action in the courtyard below.

Gordon left the balcony and worked his way through the crowd, making for the gate through which Lorine had passed. As he reached the gate, the crescendo of the crowd noise soared, and he paused, ears ringing with the shouts of the spectators. He couldn't see the fighters and he couldn't tell what had happened, but he sensed that the fight was over, or nearly so, which meant he didn't have much time if he wanted a closer look at Remairie's quadroon mistress.

The street beyond the gate was packed with carriages of every description. To one side of the gate stood several drivers, all clad in livery, engaged in conversation that dwindled as they caught sight of Gordon. Thanks to Stewart, Gordon was dressed well enough to pass for a gentleman, and he considered asking the men if they had noticed in which direction Lorine had gone, but then he saw her, about fifty yards down the street, talking to a driver who sat atop a gleaming black carriage sporting red-rimmed wheels, tasseled curtains on the windows, and a coat of arms emblazoned on the doors.

People were beginning to emerge from the courtyard, and Gordon realized that time was running out. Heart pounding, throat dry, Gordon started toward Lorine, wishing he had the nerve to speak to her, perhaps something as innocuous as a comment on the pleasantness of the evening—but he knew he couldn't. He would simply walk past her and hope for at least a glance from her.

He was twenty paces away when she first noticed him, and he thought she gave him a longer look than one might expect—but then it was probably just his imagination. To his horror she turned and started walking toward him. Gordon almost panicked. There was nothing for him to do but proceed. She kept her eyes demurely downcast until they had closed the distance between them, and by that time Gordon had come to the conclusion that she was going to walk right on by—no doubt returning to the courtyard to find Remairie. In passing he touched the brim of his hat, deciding at the last instant not to trust his voice in a pleasantry, but she responded to his acknowledgment with a smile that took Gordon's breath away. A flutter of white caught his attention, and he looked down to see a lacy handkerchief on the ground. Lorine took another step, stopped, turned, looked at the handkerchief, and then at Gordon, and Gordon felt like an utter fool because he was just standing there like an idiot.

"Oh," she said, "I seem to have dropped something."

"My apologies," gushed Gordon, picked up the handkerchief, and held it out to her, and she smiled sweetly as she took it, and her gloved fingers brushed against his and he felt a jolt of electricity shoot up his arm and straight through his heart and then down to the soles of his feet.

"Thank you, sir," she said.

Bewitched, he gaped at her, having not a clue what to do or say next, and she stood her ground, obviously waiting for something more from him. But what? Then he remembered how Stewart had presented himself to the ladies at the New York ball.

"Gordon Hawkes, at your service, Miss . . . ?"

"Lorine. I don't believe we've met, have we? Do you live here in New Orleans?"

"No. I'm . . . I'm on my way to St. Louis."

She glanced over her shoulder at the people who, having quit the courtyard, were coming up the sidewalk, and she put her arm through Gordon's and led him into a doorway—or what used to be a doorway in the derelict mansion. They stood in the shadows, and beyond lay piles of rubble, and Gordon could have looked up and seen the crumbling walls rising like a canyon of charred brick and timber into the star-studded sky—only he couldn't take his eyes off Lorine. He was lost in her dark, liquid eyes, mesmerized by her rose petal lips.

She waited until two gentlemen had passed the doorway; she kept her back turned lest they glance her way, and Gordon took her cue and pulled the brim of his hat low to conceal his face. When the men had gone she clutched Gordon's arm and whispered, "Do you know Anton Remairie?"

"We've never met. I know of him, though. My friend just bet a hundred dollars on Mr. Remairie's slave, Joe Lightning."

"Your friend was ill-advised to do that. You see, Remairie struck a bargain with Gabriel's owner. It was agreed that Joe Lightning would lose the fight. Do you understand what I'm saying?"

"You mean—you mean the fight was fixed?"

Lorine nodded.

"But why are you telling me? Aren't you . . ." Gordon stopped short; it hardly seemed gallant to comment on Lorine's concubinage.

She knew exactly what he meant, though, and if she was offended it didn't show. "I am his mistress," she affirmed quietly. "He has purchased my company, but not my love or my loyalty. He is a mean-spirited and avaricious man. I despise him."

"Then why don't you leave him if you feel that way?"

She smiled sadly. "You do not understand the way of these things."

"You're not a slave. You are free to come and go as you please."

"I am bought and paid for, just like the slaves on the auction block. Remairie has provided for my mother and younger sisters. I live well, but that is not important. What *is* important is that my family wants for nothing."

"I'm sure your family wouldn't want you to . . ."

She put a finger to her lips. "Hush. This has nothing to do with what my family wants for me, but rather what I want for them. I will not leave Remairie unless I can find some other way to provide for the people I love."

"I see."

"By now he is looking for me. I must go."

"Wait, please . . ."

"I must go." She smiled that melancholy smile of hers once more, and then she was gone.

Gordon lingered in the shadows of the doorway. Lorine's beguiling scent lingered, too, in the sultry night air. He tried to convince himself that he was a fool for feeling this way about a girl he had first seen less than an hour ago. Nevertheless he was indescribably saddened. Then he remembered Stewart, and St. Louis, and the frontier, and the fact that they had been cheated out of the funds they needed to leave New Orleans. And now, more than ever, Gordon wanted to put this city behind him. Maybe if he put a thousand miles between himself and Lorine he would be able to get her off his mind. Maybe.

Heading back for the gate, he met Stewart emerging from the courtyard. The Scotsman was clearly disappointed, but he shrugged and smiled gamely when he saw Gordon.

"Well, lad, Dame Fortune has turned her back on us tonight. Gabriel won in the second round. Experience prevailed over youth. Where did you disappear to?"

Gordon pulled him aside and took a quick look

around to make certain no one was within earshot. "The fight wasn't fair and square."

"Oh, I don't know. There at the start I thought Joe Lightning had a good chance."

"No, I mean it was rigged. The fight was rigged. Remairie and Gabriel's owner were in on it together."

Brows furrowed, Stewart stared at him, slow to comprehend. "You mean the whole bloody thing was a confidence trick? How have you come by this information?"

"Lorine told me."

"Lorine?" It took Stewart a second or two to make the connection. "Remairie's mistress? How do you know her?"

"I never met her before tonight. But I—well, I followed her when she left the courtyard."

The light dawned for Stewart then. "Oh, I see. Yes, well, some women have the same effect on me. It has proven to be one of my most conspicuous weaknesses."

"She told me about Remairie. It must be true. She'd have no reason to lie about something like that."

"But why, lad? Why did she tell you?"

"She hates Remairie. Wants to strike back at him, I guess. I don't know for sure, but what does it matter? We've been robbed."

"Indeed, it seems we have been," agreed Stewart, anger welling up inside him. "I don't mind losing on the square. But I cannot abide cheats and swindlers."

"What are we going to do now?"

"M'sieu Remairie owes us some money," replied Stewart grimly. "We shall collect it this very night. This could be dangerous, Gordon. Are you with me?"

"I am."

"Good. Let's be off."

III.

It was necessary to sneak out of the boardinghouse, as Stewart did not have the money for the bill. That made Gordon feel bad—the lady who ran the house had been very kind to him, showering him with little attentions; Stewart said it was because she was a widow who'd never had children healthy enough to survive the trauma of birth. The Scotsman assured him that they would be able to send the woman the money they owed, assuming they succeeded in getting what Remairie owed them. "But we won't be welcome back here once we're finished with Remairie," he warned. "We will head straight north for St. Louis."

They would have to travel light, and for that reason Stewart left his trunk and many of his belongings behind, taking only what he could pack into a single valise. For his part, Gordon owned nothing but the clothes on his back—he could travel very light indeed.

Successful in slipping away from the boardinghouse undetected, they confronted their next problem. Remairie's plantation was several miles away from New Orleans, north along the well-traveled river road, but it was late in the evening, and the chances of their hitching a ride on someone's wagon was so slight as to border on the nonexistent. They could not hire saddle horses or a buggy for lack of funds, and Gordon was afraid Stewart's next step might be the theft of some sort of conveyance. The Scotsman was accustomed to taking great risks, and his conscience seemed to be of the flexible variety. Gordon had visions of rotting in some dark cell for the remainder of his youth. To his immense relief, Stewart informed him that they would walk to Remairie's plantation. It would take several hours, but that suited Stewart just fine. "We'll fare better if everyone at Remairie's place is fast asleep when we arrive," he said.

"You're not intending to kill him, are you?"

"I'm not a murderer, Gordon. All I want is the money that is due us. Of course, I shouldn't be surprised if Remairie makes trouble. He is a proud man, even though he is bereft of honor."

They walked for what seemed an eternity just to put New Orleans behind them, and then the road took them through forest and swamp and an occasional cultivated field. At times moss-draped trees arched their massive limbs over the road, blocking out the moonlight. Occasionally they passed a gateway marking an entrance to one of the plantation homes that lined the river. Once they heard someone coming up the road behind them. Stewart seized Gordon and led him into the shadows of the forest, where they hid until the carriage had passed.

"No doubt a gentleman on his way home from a pleasant evening of debauchery in the city," remarked Stewart.

"But maybe he could have taken us to Remairie's plantation."

"It is just as likely that he would have wondered why we were paying a call on M'sieu Remairie at such a late hour. No, we're better off remaining unobserved. Come on, it can't be much further."

Gordon was tired, but he didn't complain, consoling himself with the thought that at least they were finally on their way to St. Louis. His only concern was that they would not make it any farther than Remairie's. This was a dangerous business, and a lot of things could go wrong.

By Stewart's timepiece it was after one o'clock in the morning when they finally reached their destination. Remairie's home was a spacious whitewashed house perched on brick pillars and encircled by a broad gallery, set at the end of an oak-lined lane. The slave quarters, located some distance from the main house, were dark and silent. A dog barked, and Stewart froze in his tracks, only to realize that the canine was deep in the woods behind the house. He proceeded, motioning for Gordon to follow. To their left and right lay vast fields of cotton, so their only cover were the oaks, and they walked on up the lane, crouching behind the last tree and giving the house a careful scrutiny. Lamplight gleamed through French windows standing open.

"No horse or carriage in sight," whispered Stewart. "I hope it's safe to assume that Remairie has no company."

Gordon hardly heard him. He was thinking about Lorine, whom he surmised was in New Orleans, and he wondered what she was doing at this very moment. Sleeping, no doubt, in the well-appointed quarters Remairie had provided for her. It saddened him to think that he would never see her again.

"Gordon, pay attention, lad."

Gordon mumbled an apology that Stewart impatiently waved aside.

"Listen well. In less than a half hour the moon will set. We will wait until then. Now, once we're inside, your job will be to watch my back. I'm certain Remairie has house servants, and they may well be quartered in the big house." He handed Gordon a knife.

Gordon stared at the weapon, with its gleaming

double-edged blade, curled brass guard, and ribbed handle.

"I served under Wellington in Portugal," said Stewart. "Took that one and its mate off a Basque assassin hired by the French. Finest Toledo steel. Very sharp. Do be careful and don't cut yourself." Stewart grinned, waving an identical dirk admonishingly at Gordon. "I'm afraid this is all we have, since my saber and pistol now reside in a Bourbon Street pawnbroker's shop. I thought we might need weapons of some sort, so I didn't part with these."

Gordon weighed the dirk in his hand. It was perfectly balanced. Excellent for throwing, or close-in work—a weapon designed for a killer of men. He wondered how many lives had been taken with this blade. Wondered, too, how he would react should it become necessary for him to use it once more for that purpose tonight. He had never killed a man, and had no aspirations in that regard.

"Don't worry, Gordon," said Stewart, reading his young friend's expression and accurately assessing the tumult of mixed emotions Gordon was suffering. "This will go smoothly enough. In the end Remairie will have to see reason."

Gordon didn't say anything. If Stewart was trying to reassure him it hadn't worked. As far as he was concerned, Remairie and the money he had cheated them out of could go hang. Far better to find honest work on a boat bound upriver and forget this entire affair. But he knew there was no point in trying to make Stewart see things his way. The Scotsman was as proud as Remairie; he had been robbed and he would not rest until he had settled the score.

They waited in silence and shadow until the moon

had slipped below the tree line. The light still gleamed inside the big house. Stewart motioned for Gordon to follow and started for the house in a running crouch, leaving his valise at the base of the oak tree. Gordon had no choice but to follow, even though a premonition of disaster made very fiber of his being ache to turn and run the other way. He owed Stewart a steep debt; he had to do what the Scotsman asked.

Reaching the gallery, Stewart slowed to a walk and cautiously tested the planks beneath his feet, lest a loose or warped board betray him. Gordon stayed close behind, shooting a worried glance over his shoulder every few seconds. At the open French windows, Stewart pressed his back to the wall and took a quick peek in. Then he took a longer look and, nodding at Gordon, turned into the doorway, walking boldly into Remairie's house like he owned the place. Saying a silent prayer, Gordon followed him in.

The room they entered was a handsomely appointed study with rich burgundy carpet on the floor, gleaming glass-fronted bookcases, brocaded damask on the walls, and mahogany furniture with mohair or velvet upholstery. It was as elegant a room as any Gordon had seen in New York. Remairie sat in a high-backed wing chair with his back to the open French windows, reading by the light of a lamp perched on a marble-inlaid taboret. Gordon could see only the top of the Creole planter's head, crowned by that distinctive mane of white hair.

"Remairie," said Stewart softly.

The planter shot to his feet—the book that had been resting in his lap fell to the floor with a thud muffled by the carpet.

"Do you remember me?" asked Stewart cordially. "We met a few days ago in New Orleans."

"I meet many people," replied Remairie, quickly regaining his composure. "Do refresh my memory."

"You approached me, sir, and said I had the look of a gentleman not averse to a friendly wager. You informed me of the fight between your boy Joe and the man called Gabriel. You told me I would do well to put a wager on your boy, as the odds were twenty to one against him, and you shared with me your confidence that Joe would prevail against the champion." Stewart moved closer, and his tone lost much of its congeniality. "But you failed to inform me of one important fact. That the fight had been fixed. Joe was guaranteed to lose because you had made an arrangement with the man who owns Gabriel."

"That is a lie," said Remairie, but his expression betrayed him. He tried to muster up some outrage. "What is your name, sir?"

"The least you could do would be to remember the name of the man you have swindled."

Remairie threw a quick glance at the door which led to the rest of the house, and Gordon moved swiftly to block his path. The Creole aristocrat stared at the Spanish dirk in Gordon's hand—Stewart had concealed his own blade behind his back.

"Why have you come here?" asked Remairie, fear pitching his voice higher than normal. "What is your intent?"

"You owe me two thousand dollars, sir," said Stewart. "I have come to collect."

"Nonsense. Gabriel won that fight fair and square. You have no proof to the contrary . . ."

"I don't need proof. This is no court of law. Gentlemen don't require a court to settle their differences."

"If it is a duel you're after, m'sieu, I will be more than happy to oblige."

"Alas, I am leaving Louisiana tonight. I'll take the money due me and postpone our final reckoning for another day."

"You are common thieves, both of you!" shouted Remairie contemptuously.

"Keep your voice down," rasped Stewart. "My friend will kill the first person who comes through that door."

Remairie nodded disdainfully. "Yes, he has the look of a cold-blooded killer about him. Well, I shall have to disappoint you, m'sieu. I do not keep that kind of cash laying about. My funds are safely locked away in the vault of the Bank of New Orleans."

Stewart sighed and brought the dirk hidden behind his back into Remairie's view.

"My patience is running out. You fooled me once. Don't try a second time."

Remairie was silent a moment, gauging Stewart's sincerity and measuring the Scotsman's willingness to use the weapon in his hand. Finally the Creole nodded, and Gordon breathed a sigh of relief. He hadn't been sure what Stewart would do had the planter persisted in his obstinance, despite Stewart's assurances that he wouldn't kill anyone. Because there was something tangibly dangerous about William Drummond Stewart. Remairie had detected it, and concluded that a paltry two thousand dollars wasn't worth losing his life over.

"Very well," he said, still contemptuous. He turned to a bookcase, opened the glass door, removed several thick leatherbound tomes from a shelf, and reached into the recesses of the case. Stewart quickly stepped up behind him and placed the tip of the dirk's blade against Remairie's spine.

"No tricks, sir," warned Stewart, "if you care anything about seeing tomorrow's sunrise."

"I will see it, but you will not. By sunrise the both of you will be hanging by your necks."

"Defiant to the bitter end. Get on with it."

Remairie removed a small iron box from the bookcase, placed it on a table, and brought a skeleton key from a waistcoat pocket, with which he unlocked the box. As he lifted the lid, Stewart pushed him roughly to one side and opened the box himself. It was stuffed with cash and coin. And beneath the cash lay a small pocket pistol, loaded and primed. Stewart appropriated the pistol, turning it on Remairie.

"I had no intention of using that," said Remairie stiffly.

"Make no mistake. I will use it. Now, count out two thousand dollars in cash, if you please."

"Take it all. You might as well. You'll hang just as high for two thousand as for twenty."

"I'll take only what is due me, thanks all the same."

Remairie counted out the money and handed it to Stewart.

"I am curious," he said as Stewart counted the bills. "How did you find out?"

Stewart glanced at Gordon, and Gordon shook his head, afraid that the Scotsman would commit an indiscretion that might place Lorine in grave jeopardy.

"I am sorry," said Stewart. "But I can't help you."

"Only four people knew," said Remairie. "Joe and Gabriel, of course. Gabriel's owner, and myself. No, wait just a moment. There was one other." He looked at Gordon, and it was as though Gordon's expression somehow revealed the whole truth to him. "It was she! The whore. She told you."

"Watch your tongue or I'll cut it out of your head," snapped Gordon.

Remairie laughed. It was a harsh and ugly sound grating on Gordon's nerves. Gordon wasn't sure why, but the more Remairie laughed the more irate he became.

"The ungrateful wench," Remairie said with a sneer, his amusement overtaken by resentment. "After everything I've done for her and her family. Why do you suppose she told you? Out of the goodness of her heart, perhaps? But she has no heart, that one. She accepted everything I offered her, but she was never satisfied, and she repaid me with infidelity. She has a fondness for younger men, you know."

"Infidelity?" echoed Stewart. "Talking about your mistress that way, sir, you must admit is highly ironic."

Remairie ignored the Scotsman's comment. "She told you because she hoped you would come here and kill me. That would free her to take up openly with a younger man. In particular, a rakehell by the name of Simon Terrebonne. Lorine thinks I don't know what she has been doing behind my back. But I know. I have had her watched."

"If you knew you would have done something about it," said Gordon. "These are lies. All lies."

"No. I am telling you the truth. I did nothing because . . . because I am beguiled by her. Just as, obviously, you are, young man. Beware of her embrace. She is like the black widow spider."

"This is all well and good," said Stewart impatiently,

"but we really must be going. I regret, M'sieu Remairie, that we will have to bind and gag you."

"And if I give you my word that I will not raise the alarm until, let us say, the sun rises?"

Stewart shook his head. Remairie shrugged his indifference.

"It doesn't matter," he said. "I will have you both hunted down. No matter how far you run, my men will find you. I will spend ten times the money you have taken from me to see you dead."

Stewart ripped the sashes from the window's draperies and escorted Remairie outside. They walked down the lane to the oak tree where the Scotsman had left his valise. While Stewart held the pistol on the Creole planter, Gordon bound the man to the tree with one of the sashes and gagged him with the other.

"I am sure you'll be found in the morning," Stewart told Remairie. "Until then, sweet dreams."

Putting the money and dirk in his valise, Stewart belted the pistol and, with Gordon tagging along behind, headed down the lane toward the river road. They turned north on the road, and neither spoke for the distance of more than a mile, until at last Gordon said, "Do you think he was telling the truth?"

Stewart glanced at Gordon and decided he had better choose his words with care; it was obvious that his young companion was disturbed by Remairie's revelations concerning his quadroon mistress.

"It may be that he was," replied the Scotsman. "We shall never know for certain, I suppose. But don't let it bother you too much, Gordon. You have had too little experience with the opposite sex. You haven't as yet learned their ways."

"Their ways?"

Stewart nodded. "A woman will quite often say one thing while meaning just the opposite. All too often they measure love by what they can gain from it. And they are not averse to using their feminine wiles to get exactly what they want. Don't take this the wrong way, lad. I don't hold any of that against a woman. I enjoy her company as much as the next man. But I don't trust them. And when they tell me something I always tend to look for the hidden motive."

Gordon shook his head. "I don't believe what he said about Lorine," he said adamantly. "She isn't that way."

"Ah, well." Stewart shrugged. "Think what you will. Where's the harm in it? We will never see her or Remairie again."

"I'm thinking we should go back to New Orleans and warn her that Remairie knows she betrayed him."

That stopped Stewart in his tracks. "Are you daft? You heard what Remairie says. If we don't clear out of Louisiana we'll end up decorating a tree with our corpses. Remairie wasn't making idle threats. We humiliated him and he'll not soon forget it."

"But she might be in danger."

"From Remairie?" Stewart laughed. "Not a chance. Gordon, the man is bewitched by that girl, just as you are. No matter what she did to him, he would never harm so much as a hair on her head. There lies the power of woman, lad. That is precisely what makes her the most dangerous creature on earth. Trust me, your Lorine will come to no harm. But we most certainly would were we foolish enough to go back to New Orleans."

Gordon trudged along in moody silence, mulling over Stewart's words. He simply refused to believe it was even remotely possible that Lorine had ulterior motives in telling him about Remairie's deceitful scheme.

They walked the rest of the night, and as the first threads of daylight became woven into the darkened sky they arrived at a remote landing on the Mississippi River, a collection of huts around a wharf where, much to their relief, they saw a sternwheeler docked. The ship was taking on firewood and a load of tobacco bound for northern markets. A Chickasaw who went by the name of Long Tom ran a tavern and trading post here, and it was in his establishment that they found the sternwheeler's skipper. Stewart learned that the vessel was bound for St. Louis and then Cincinnati by way of the Ohio and that, yes, they were welcome to take passage aboard her so long as they didn't mind doing without a cabin. A blanket and bed of tobacco leaves was the best the riverman had to offer. Stewart said that would suit them fine, and as he and the skipper decided on a reasonable fare, Gordon studied Long Tom with keen interest. This was the first Indian he had ever laid eyes on—and he came away from the experience thoroughly disappointed. Clad in white man's clothes, his black hair shorn, Long Tom didn't look at all like the noble savage Gordon had imagined.

An hour later, the sternwheeler left the landing and churned upriver. There was a handful of other passengers, Kentucky and Tennessee farmers who had floated their produce down the Mississippi to New Orleans on flatboats and were now returning home with their pockets full of money. Many of their kind went north by way of the Natchez Trace, but that route had become so infested with thieves and cutthroats that, at least for Gordon's fellow passengers, avoiding such perils was worth a riverboat's fare.

Though she struggled valiantly against the Mississippi's mighty current, the riverboat could scarcely make five or six knots, with the result that it took two full days for her to reach Natchez. Gordon spent the time watching the murky greenish brown water being churned into white foam by the boat's stern wheel, or gazing at the wooded shoreline slowly sliding by. The river was bustling with other craft—riverboats, flatboats, broadhorns, piroques, and rafts. Gordon had a sense that he ought to be appreciating the panorama that lay before him. After all, he was at last well and truly on his way to the wild frontier. But he was tortured into a state of perfect misery by thoughts of Lorine. The frontier's allure had faded. It was overshadowed by the taunting memory of the quadroon as she stood so close to him in the darkened doorway of that derelict building in Slave Town. Why, why couldn't he put her from his mind? Why was it that he had this nearly overpowering urge to return to New Orleans, in spite of the danger? He had the foolishly romantic notion that he might appear just in time to rescue her from a wrathful Remairie. Of course that was absolute rubbish. If he showed his face in New Orleans again Remairie would have him hanged. Yet the chance to see Lorine once more was almost worth the risk.

The sternwheeler docked the second night out at Natchez, and Stewart tried to get Gordon to come along with him and sample the charms of the town's notorious red-light district, called Under the Hill. Gordon wanted no part of that. In the early morning hours Stewart returned to the ship and shook Gordon out of a troubled sleep.

"I've got a bit of bad news, lad," said the grim Scotsman. "The word has come upriver ahead of us. It's the kind of news that spreads like wildfire."

"What kind of news? What's happened?"

"They found our friend Remairie tied to that tree where we left him. But his throat had been cut."

Gordon cast his blanket aside and jumped to his feet, his blood run cold. "It can't be true! There must be some mistake!"

"It's no mistake. At first they thought it must have been one of his own slaves that did the deed. They found that money box of his, empty. But all the slaves were present and accounted for, and the authorities soon came to realize by the tracks they found that three men had been there that night. Mind you I said three men. Blood-hounds were brought in, and the trail of two of those men led to the landing. They got descriptions of us from that Indian tavern keeper, I'm thinking. Fortunately, they aren't very good descriptions."

"What are we going to do?" asked Gordon, with rising panic.

"Nothing. We sit tight and keep our nerve. With luck we will make it through to St. Louis."

"But I wonder who killed him? It doesn't make any sense."

"She did it," replied Stewart. "Or rather someone did it for her."

"You don't mean Lorine . . ."

"That's precisely who I mean."

"You're dead wrong. She couldn't have."

"Listen, boy. Remairie was telling us the truth about her. That's obvious now. She was hoping we would kill him. But she wasn't going to leave anything to chance. So she comes along behind us, and we'll never know who she had with her, but there were tracks of three men, remember, and only two leaving the plantation afoot, and those belonged to us. So it seems fairly certain that Lorine and her accomplice arrived by carriage after we had gone, and when they found Remairie tied to the tree the accomplice got out of the carriage and cut his throat. Lorine probably knew about the money box, and she had it emptied to make it look like robbery. Then her accomplice got back in the carriage and they rode away, neat as you please."

Gordon shook his head. "I don't believe you. It can't be. There must be some other explanation. You have no proof that she was involved. You're just guessing."

Stewart relented. "Women," he said wryly. "They do have the power, don't they? A single brief encounter, and now look at the state you're in. Oh well, it doesn't really matter whether you believe me or not. The fact remains that Remairie has been murdered and we are the prime suspects. If we're fortunate enough to make it to St. Louis, we shall have to split up, until such time as we head west. And, needless to say, we'll not be able to come back this way ever again. Sorry, lad. If and when the times comes for us to leave America we will have to do it from some Pacific port."

"That doesn't matter," muttered Gordon. He had no intention of ever returning to New Orleans now, or to any place east of the Mississippi, for that matter. Deep in his heart he knew Stewart was probably right about Lorine. She had used him. Worse, she had framed him for murder. He was sick to death of being used and lied to, and vowed to himself that he would never be so gullible again. Now his only refuge was the frontier, and if he ever got there he would never leave.

CHAPTER 3

I.

St. Louis could boast of a population exceeding seven thousand in the year that Gordon Hawkes and Captain Stewart arrived. Like New Orleans, this city possessed a strong French flavor; the Chouteaus, the Bertholds, the Prattes had all settled here a hundred years earlier and made their fortune by establishing a trade with the western Indian tribes. St. Louis was the gateway to the American frontier. It was here that all the trappers and traders began their westering enterprise. But St. Louis also looked east. A thriving river town, her mile-long wharves were always packed with riverboats and broadhorns. Above the wharves stood the long rows of warehouses. Some were filled with the plews that came down the Missouri and other western rivers, bound for New York and London and Paris and Athens and St. Petersburg, the harvest of fur that by its nature was opening up the West. Other warehouses contained the bountiful harvests of midwestern ploughsmen, produce bound for New Orleans. St. Louis was destined to succeed because of her location, on the Mississippi near where the Missouri came in from the west and the Ohio came in from the east. Naturally, then, the city's inhabitants were an exotic blend of French voyageurs, buckskin-clad trappers, burly and profane river men, hardy farmers from Illinois and Ohio and Kentucky, factors and merchants and gamblers in their broad-cloth.

And there were Indians, too. Real, honest-to-God Indians, and Gordon was amazed at how different they were from the Chickasaw tavern keeper he had met in Louisiana. These were Mandans and Arikaras and Nez Percé who had made the long journey across the plains from their distant villages to learn more about the white man's powerful "medicine." The trappers and traders had demonstrated the extent of the white man's power, for the whites made guns and gunpowder, alcohol and tobacco, mirrors and musical instruments, pots and pans, scissors and needles, beads and woolen blankets—all those things that made Indian life easier, and yet at the same time made it more complicated, too. The Indians needed to understand the source of this astonishing power, and they sent representatives to St. Louis to mingle with the white man on his own turf. Sometimes, though this quest for knowledge bore a steep price, as the Indian envoy fell victim to the diseases the white man also brought with him, and against which the Indian had no defenses.

Despite the fact that he was a man on the run, Gordon was keenly excited by what he saw and heard in the cobbled streets of bustling St. Louis, and he refused to remain cooped up in some hotel room. The town was cloaked with the aura of the frontier, and he had to breathe it and taste it and hear it. At last Gordon stood on the verge of making the dream that had sustained him all these long months into a glorious, adventuresome reality. Best of all, he could rest assured that Stewart would not tarry long in St. Louis, not with a noose ready and waiting for him in Louisiana. News of Remairie's gruesome end had swept upriver to St. Louis and beyond, receiving considerable attention in the local newspapers. The sooner they lost themselves in the Great American Desert, the better.

Since the authorities were looking for two men traveling together, Stewart put himself up at the Union Hotel and Gordon at another hostelry some blocks away. The Scotsman gave him more than enough money to buy clothing better suited to the trail than the broadcloth Gordon had been wearing since New York. Stewart also told him to purchase a good plains rifle, and encouraged him to call on the Hawken brothers, the famous St. Louis gunsmiths. As for the horses and the provisions they would need, Stewart said he would take care of all that. This suited Gordon just fine, because he had no idea what a properly outfitted plainsman actually required, and neither did he know a thing about horses. They would meet, Stewart said, in three or four days; the Scotsman would get word to him at his hotel as to exactly when and where the reunion would take place.

Gordon had no doubt that Stewart would prove as good as his word. He didn't worry that the Scotsman might run out on him, even though it would be safer for them to split up for good. He knew he could count on Stewart as he could have counted on an older brother.

The first order of business was to change his appearance—Gordon bought some sturdy mule-ear boots, stroud trousers, one linsey-woolsey shirt, and another of muslin, a long woolen coat and a broad-brimmed hat. He tied the broadcloth suit up into a bundle and discarded it in an alley. Such clothing would be of no use where he was going, and besides, he couldn't be sure just how complete the descriptions that Long Tom—and possibly others—had given the authorities might be. Looking over his shoulder quickly became a habit. He was a hunted man and he didn't like the feeling one bit. His only consolation was the fact that St. Louis was a fairly large and crowded city, and the chances of his being picked out in this motley crowd were relatively small. So he hoped.

Next he visited the gunsmiths Stewart had recommended. Jake and Sam Hawken had learned their trade from their father, whose Pennsylvania rifles had been highly prized on the Ohio and Kentucky borderlands a half century ago. In 1807, Jake had departed Maryland and set up shop in St. Louis, figuring that the trappers and traders who were venturing West would need the services of a man who knew how to make a reliable long gun. He was absolutely right. In 1821 the Missouri Fur Company commissioned him to produce a large number of percussion rifles. The following year, Jake's brother came to join him. Sam was fleeing from bad memories—his beloved wife had passed away—and he soon decided to make St. Louis his home. Together, Jake and Sam prospered. In a few short years the Hawken Plains rifle became legend. Many a mountain man swore by that particular brand of long gun as far and away the most dependable weapon to be had.

So it was a Hawken rifle that Gordon was determined to acquire.

Over the years the gunshop of the Hawken brothers had become a meeting place for trappers and traders, their favorite St. Louis haunt, and when Gordon walked into the establishment he was confronted by three buckskin-clad mountain men sharing a stick of tobacco, a jug of corn liquor, and a passel of tall tales. The only guns he saw in the place were the ones that obviously belonged to the trio of buckskinners. Beyond a counter in the rear of the room was a curtained doorway leading to another room. The walls were adorned with several maps of the frontier region, some Indian paraphernalia, and a couple of grizzly bear pelts.

When Gordon came in, the mountain men fell silent and gave him long once-overs.

"I'm looking for Mr. Hawken," he said, self-conscious beneath their impassive scrutiny.

"What you be wantin' him fer, younker?" asked one of the men.

"I'm going west and I want to buy one of his Plains rifles."

The man who had spoken glanced at his comrades. "He's headed west, boys. Take a gander at that top-knot. Reckon we'll see it on some Injun's scalp pole before the winter is out." He broke into laughter and his two companions joined in.

Gordon's cheeks burned. "If and when I lose my scalp is my concern and none of your own!" he shot back.

All three men abruptly stopped laughing and Gordon, thinking he had offended him with his tone of voice, dwelled for one unhappy moment on the prospect that these men might kill him right where he stood. Then one of them smiled slowly beneath his sandy red beard and said, "We were all greenhorns once, I reckon."

"Not that green."

"Leastways he's got some bark on him." The sandy-haired one nodded amiably at Gordon. "The name is Ben Talley, boy. What handle do you go by?"

"My handle?"

"Your name."

"I'm Gordon Hawkes, sir."

"From Ireland, if I'm not mistaken. That would explain your gift for talkin' first and thinkin' second. Well, this feller here, the one that's so godawful ugly that grizzly bears have been known to keel over dead after one look at him, is called Johnny Ornsdorff. And this one here is Bill Batterson, but most call him Three Fingers, or sometimes something worse."

Batterson held up one hand and Gordon saw that the thumb and forefinger were missing. "Got in a ruckus with an Arapaho squaw one night and she bit 'em both clean off. She war meaner than a treed cougar, that one."

"So you be headed for the Shining Mountains, then," said Talley. "Aimin' to hunt for brown gold?"

"I don't know what I aim to do," admitted Gordon. "Worry about that when the times comes."

"My sentiments exactly. Ussens, we trap for the Rocky Mountain Fur Company. Ever heard of it?"

Gordon had to admit that he had not.

"Well, you got the Rocky Mountain Fur Company—that's us—and then there's the American Fur Company. We're both after the same thing. I'm talking about brown gold. Beaver plews. Only we go about gettin' them plews in different ways."

"Yeah," growled Batterson. "We trap the varmints ourselves, but Astor's boys—the American Fur Company—why they ain't nothin' but Injun traders. Thievin' no-accounts who get the redskins to do all the hard work of trappin' the beaver. Then they trade likker and guns and powder and such in exchange for the plews the Injuns bring in. So the Injuns turn around and use them guns on us, the opposition. Pretty damned clever, you must admit." Batterson spat a stream of yellow-brown tobacco juice into a bucket placed on the floor nearby for just that purpose, a colorful way of expressing his profound contempt for the American Fur Company and its methods.

Gordon didn't know how to respond. He knew nothing about the fur trade, or the competition between American and Rocky Mountain Fur companies.

"Boils down to this," drawled Talley. "Iffen you aim to join up with Astor's crew, why then we'll probably just kill you here and now and save ourselves the trouble of havin' to do it later on."

Gordon felt a chill shoot through his body, and he gaped at Talley, who couldn't keep a straight face for long. He broke out laughing and was joined by the other two.

"Just pullin' your leg, younker. Don't go and have a heart attack on us. My conscience would bother me—for at least an hour."

"What you aim to do out yonder in the big country?"

queried Ornsdorff. "Iffen you ain't goin' to trap beaver, how come you headed for the Shinin' Mountains in the first place?"

"I don't plan to do anything in particular," said Gordon defensively. "Except I'm going to hunt buffalo. That's why I need a good rifle. And they say the Hawken brothers make the best there is. So here I am."

Talley nodded. "If it's a good rifle you're wantin' you've come to the right place."

"You ever shoot a rifle before, boy?" asked Ornsdorff.

"Sure I have." Occasionally Gordon had been allowed to go hunting with his father's fowling piece, a temperamental gun in the best of times, missing fire on a regular basis. And yet, in spite of that, he had become a pretty decent shot, he thought, able to bring down a pheasant on the wing at a fair distance. Of course, that didn't mean he could hold a candle to men like these in terms of marksmanship. He'd heard stories, mostly from Stewart, about how these men could shoot the eyes out of a squirrel at a hundred yards.

Ornsdorff grunted his skepticism. "I dunno, you look like a plowpusher to me, and I ain't never known a plowpusher what could hit the broad side of a barn."

"Well, now, Johnny, I was a farmer once, remember," said Talley.

"Proves my point. You're the worst shot in the country, bar none."

Talley snorted. "I could outshoot you any day of the week and twice on Sundays." He turned his attention back to Gordon. "Yes sir, I was the son of a farmer, just like you, I reckon. But I was born to be a mountain man. Never know, mebbe you were, too."

"He won't live to see the mountains, I tell you," opined Batterson.

A man emerged from the shop's back room—a stocky, balding man with a round and pleasant face. An unlit pipe jutted from his mouth. He wore a canvas apron over his clothes. "What's going on out here?"

"I've come to buy a rifle, sir," said Gordon. "Are you Mr. Hawken?"

"I'm Jake Hawken." Sizing Gordon up, he added, "I've got a couple of old Pennsylvania flintlocks I'll sell cheap."

"No, sir. I want one of your Plains rifles. I've got the money to pay for it." He took the wad of notes from his pocket to show Hawken.

Ornsdorff whistled. "Where did a sodbustin' kid like you get that kind of money, boy?"

Gordon realized he had made a mistake. What if Hawken or one of these mountain men had heard about Remairie's murder? It was assumed that whoever had killed the Creole planter had also made off with the contents of the strongbox found in his study. And most of the notes in Gordon's hands had been issued by Louisiana banks. He was going to have to talk his way out of this, and fast.

"I—I sold everything after my father and mother died," he said, hoping his expression would not give him away.

They believed him. "Sorry for your loss, younker," muttered Talley.

"Sure," said Hawken. "I can make the rifle you want. But it will take at least two weeks. I've got more work than my brother and I and four apprentices can keep up with."

"Two weeks! But I can't wait that long. I'm leaving in just a day or two."

Hawken shrugged. "I'm sorry, but that's the best I can do."

Reading the disappointment on Gordon's face, Talley said, "You can give him mine, Jake."

"What?" exclaimed Batterson. "Are you touched? We've been hangin' around here for days waitin' on your new Hawken. And now you just give it away? We can't sit here for another fortnight, Ben, and you know it. We got to get back before the snows come."

"I know," said Talley.

"You won't make it to green-up with that ol' trade musket you've been carryin' ever since you tangled with them Blackfeet."

Talley nodded. "I run foul of a Blackfoot huntin' party," he explained to Gordon. "They took my plews and my rifle and they would've got around to takin' my scalp only I got away from them dirty, thievin' scoundrels."

"You sure you want to do this, Ben?" asked Hawken.

"I didn't say it just to hear myself talk, Jake."

"Okay. If that's what you want. Young man, you come back tomorrow morning and I'll have your rifle ready."

"Mr. Talley, I . . ." Gordon didn't know what to say.

"Save it. One day you might get to return the favor."

"Thanks," said Gordon, humbled, and left the gun shop.

"He won't last long," muttered Batterson. "And then some heathen redskin'll have your rifle, Ben."

"Don't be so sure," said Talley.

II.

The Hawken Plains rifle that Gordon purchased the next morning was a sight to behold. Weighing about twelve pounds, it had a thirty-four inch octagonal barrel, metal rib, crescent-shaped butt plate, half stock, set trigger, and a percussion lock with a steel basket called a "snail." A .53 caliber, the rifle fired a half-ounce ball in a paper cartridge containing two hundred grains of powder and could drop a charging buffalo. Gordon paid eighty dollars for the rifle and a shot pouch containing fifty cartridges and as many caps.

"She's a thing of beauty," gushed Gordon.

"You can buy a fancier looking gun," Jake Hawken told him. "But, if I say so myself, none are more dependable. She won't fail you, I'll stake my reputation on that."

"I wish Mr. Talley were here so I could thank him."

"You thanked him already, and once was enough. I've known Talley for eight, ten years. He's a good man, and a fine judge of character. I figure he saw something worthwhile in you, Mr. Hawkes, else he would not have parted with this rifle."

"Seen what, I wonder?"

Hawken shrugged. "I guess he expects you'll make your mark in the high country. I don't know. You can ask him when you see him next. It's a big land out yonder, but it's funny how mountain men don't seem to have any trouble finding each other out there, when they're of a mind to share a jug and a chew and a little talk. And then there's always the annual rendezvous. If Talley doesn't show up for one of those sprees it means he's eating dirt. Every year Sublette brings a load of trade goods out to some likely spot that's been picked during the previous year's rendezvous, and comes back with his mules loaded up with plews. I'd say that's just about the only time you'll get nearly all the Rocky Mountain Fur Company boys together in one place. Talley and Ornsdorff and Three Fingers came back with Sublette this summer."

"Is the American Fur Company as bad as they say, Mr. Hawken?"

"What you've got is a feud, sure enough. I try not to get in the middle of it. Fact is, the competition for beaver is fierce. I fear the end of the fur trade is near, because the demand for beaver fur is on the decline, and so are the beaver themselves. In some parts they've been hunted out completely. If you're of a mind to seek your fortune in brown gold, son, you had better be quick about it."

Gordon thanked him and took his leave.

Walking down the crowded St. Louis streets, Gordon felt ten feet tall with the Hawken rifle racked on his shoulder and the shot pouch bouncing against his hip. At last he stood on the verge of the grand adventure that had occupied his thoughts for nearly a year. All the trials and tribulations that had afflicted him since his departure from Ireland no longer mattered. He could put them behind him and look to the future.

And yet—what Jake Hawken had said about the fur trade gave him pause. What *would* he do with himself, especially when Captain Stewart decided to go home to England? The prospect of returning to Ireland held no allure for Gordon. And once he left St. Louis he would never be able to return. The East was no place for a fugitive wanted on a charge of murder. It seemed the only recourse left to him was to remain on the High Plains or in the Shining Mountains for the rest of his days. At least he wouldn't have to worry about sadistic sea captains and deceitful beauties and arrogant aristocrats in the wilderness. He would learn to fend for himself in the wild country. He would live alone, and in that solitude he would find security. Never again would others hurt or betray him. As he walked back to his hotel he gazed at the sights of the city with the eyes of one who knew he would never return to civilization. There were no regrets. Civilization was highly overrated.

As he neared his hotel, Gordon was startled out of his reverie by Stewart sticking his head around the corner of the building and calling out his name. The Scotsman made a curt come-hither gesture and then fired a wary glance up and down the street. With a sinking feeling in the pit of his stomach, Gordon entered the trash-strewn alley, sensing that something had gone very wrong.

Stewart, too, had changed his appearance. He wore buckskins and a plainsman's hat, looking not at all like the dashing officer and gentleman in his scarlet hussar's uniform or impeccable clawhammer coat that Gordon had become accustomed to.

"Well, lad, I see you've done right by yourself," said Stewart, admiring the rifle in Gordon's hands. "That's a Hawken if I'm not mistaken. Milton Sublette was carrying one just like it when I made his acquaintance yesterday."

Gordon had momentarily lost interest in his new possession because even though Stewart was trying to maintain his devil-may-care facade, it was obvious that he was deeply troubled.

"Something's wrong," said Gordon. "What is it?"

"A bit of bad news, I confess. We've a price on our heads." Stewart reached under his hunting shirt and produced a broadside which he unfolded and showed to Gordon. "Seems Madame Remairie has offered ten thousand dollars to the person or persons who bring her husband's murderers to justice. As you can see, they've got some fairly decent descriptions of us here."

"Ten thousand dollars!"

Stewart nodded. "These came upriver yesterday. They are plastered all over town today."

"We've got to get out of here." Gordon could feel the noose tightening around his neck.

"I've made arrangements . . ."

Gordon winced. Arrangements. He didn't like that word. His mother's arrangement with Captain Warren of the *Penelope* had put him through weeks of pure hell. And then there was Lorine's arrangement with Remairie, and Remairie's arrangements with Gabriel's owner—two more sources of grief for him.

"I've had a long talk with Sublette. He and Jedediah Smith and Dave Jackson bought out Colonel William Ashley, who formed the Rocky Mountain Fur Company. Sublette and his partners own the company now. Jackson is in charge of the trapping operation, while Sublette handles the business end. As for Smith, he was by all accounts an inveterate wanderer, forever off exploring, and it got him killed. They say the Comanches caught him alone down on the Cimarron.

"The Rocky Mountain boys have decided to establish a trading post on the Missouri River not far from the mouth of the Yellowstone, where their rival, the American Fur Company, has already built a post. Sublette is taking supplies up the Missouri by keelboat for the new post, while a fellow named Robert Campbell is leading a wagon caravan overland along the Platte, bound for the same destination. We'll be going with Campbell."

"We ought not to travel together. It's too dangerous."

"We'll be safe enough once we get out of St. Louis."

"But what if Sublette or one of the others sees this broadside?"

Stewart shook his head. "You worry too much, Gordon. It doesn't matter to those men what you've done in the past. All they care about is whether you can be counted on today if the need arises."

Gordon wished he could be as sure of that as Stewart seemed to be. In his opinion the wisest course was to slip out of St. Louis now. Tomorrow might be too late. But he didn't argue. It wouldn't do any good, not with Stewart. The Scotsman enjoyed flirting with danger. Gordon realized it would be safer for them to part company. Yet the debt he owed Stewart prevented him from doing the sensible thing.

"Tomorrow morning," said Stewart, "go to the livery at the other end of Market Street. There will be a horse there for you. If I don't show by noon, ride north out of town to Cleve's Landing. That's where you'll find Campbell. Got it?"

Gordon nodded, though it was obvious that he could muster no enthusiasm for the plan.

"Believe me, lad, I've been in worse spots. Just keep

your nerve and we'll come through with flying colors."

Gordon spent the rest of the day in his hotel room. He passed a restless night. Dawn found him pacing his room like a caged animal. It was all he could do to wait several hours before starting out for the livery.

True to his word, Stewart had paid for two saddle horses at the livery on Market Street. The proprietor was expecting Gordon, and showed him a tall buckskin and a blaze-faced sorrel with three white stockings. "Your friend took a liking to the buckskin, I believe," said the proprietor, "but I suppose you can take either one. Makes no difference to me."

"This one suits me fine," said Gordon, indicating the sorrel.

The man brought him a saddle, and stood back with arms folded to watch as Gordon tried to strap the hull on the sorrel's back.

"None of my business, of course," said the man, "but you'd best give that cinch a couple of hard tugs and loop the end of the strap through the ring there."

"I don't know what I'm doing," confessed Gordon. "I guess it shows."

The man shrugged. "No matter. You'll learn quick enough. Fresh off the farm, I reckon."

"Is it that obvious?"

"No shame in that."

Gordon was put at ease. "We didn't have any horses when I grew up. Just a mule or two for the wagon and the plow."

"This nag won't give you much trouble. She's strong and quick and has a lot of bottom, but she's good-natured as horses go." The man checked the tightened cinch and nodded his satisfaction. "That'll do. You're all set to go."

"If you don't mind I'll wait around for my friend. He should be here soon."

"Make yourself at home."

The livery man went about his business. Gordon sat on an overturned feed bucket just inside the livery's doors and watched the activity in the street beyond. A one-eyed yellow dog wandered up, tail wagging, to keep him company. Gordon didn't have to worry about keeping track of time. The steeple bells of a nearby church rang out the hours.

By the time those church bells chimed the eleventh hour, Gordon was getting worried. He had a hunch something was wrong, but tried to convince himself that he was mistaken. What was keeping Stewart? The next hour crawled by. When the bells rang twelve times he was on his feet and turning toward the sorrel tethered nearby. He couldn't wait a minute longer to get out of St. Louis. It just wasn't safe. Stewart had told him not to wait, so he was going. The Scotsman would catch up at Cleve's Landing. The fool took too many chances. Sometimes it seemed as though he lived to take unnecessary risks, to push his luck to the limit. *Well, not me,* thought Gordon. *I've got a good horse and a good rifle and the frontier is waiting just the other side of the town limits.*

And yet he felt bad about leaving. What if Stewart really was in some kind of trouble? After everything the Scotsman had done for him, Gordon couldn't just run out on him. *Even if it costs you your life?* Disgusted and afraid, Gordon knew the answer had to be—*Yes, even then.*

There was one other option—he could wait another hour or so. Maybe Stewart was just running late. But Gordon couldn't sit still a moment longer. He had to do something. So he climbed aboard the sorrel, rode out of the livery, and turned the horse down Market Street toward the Mississippi River. He was no horseman, but the sorrel seemed to have a smooth gait and a good disposition, and Gordon's mind was much too filled with bigger apprehensions to address the relatively inconsequential problem of learning the proper way to sit in a saddle and use the reins.

As he neared the hotel where Stewart was staying, Gordon decided to approach the building by the back way, and steered the responsive sorrel down a side street and then up an alley. Tethering the horse behind the hotel, he tried a side door which led to a narrow hallway. This in turn took him to the lobby. Peering cautiously around a corner, he saw nothing to alarm him in the lobby—a man was sitting in a chair reading a newspaper and the clerk stood behind his counter filing letters and telegrams into room mail slots. Gordon made straight for the counter and cleared his throat. The startled desk clerk turned.

"I didn't see you come in, sir," said the clerk. "How may I help you?"

Since he wasn't sure if Stewart had registered under an assumed name, Gordon relied on a description of his friend. The clerk immediately knew who he was talking about.

"Oh yes, you mean Captain Stewart. Room twelve. Up the stairs and to the left."

Gordon nodded—he should have known that Stewart would disdain the simple precaution of registering under a different name.

As he turned toward the staircase, the clerk added, "Are you with those two men who came here earlier, by any chance?"

A cold chill raced down Gordon's spine.

"I mean, they described him just the way you did," explained the clerk, puzzled by Gordon's expression. "They arrived about an hour ago, and they're still upstairs."

"Yes, thanks," said Gordon, and took the stairs two at a time. Pausing in the second floor hallway, he checked his Plains rifle to make certain all was in order. The two men with Stewart could be from the Rocky Mountain Fur Company—but Gordon doubted it. Somehow he just knew they were bounty hunters or lawmen who were here to take Stewart into custody on the charge of murdering Anton Remairie.

But then why had they been here for an hour? Why hadn't they just taken Stewart away? What were they waiting for?

He cat-footed down the hall to Stewart's room and, kneeling, tried to see through the keyhole. No luck. The key had been left in the lock on the inside. Hearing voices, he put an ear to the door.

"It's after twelve noon and he hasn't shown up." Gordon didn't recognize this voice.

"He's just running a bit late." This was Stewart. "He's got a bad habit of doing that. But he'll be here, I can assure you."

"I think he's lying," came a second voice that Gordon couldn't identify.

"Why would I lie to you gentlemen? It was Hawkes

who killed M'sieu Remairie. I didn't want there to be bloodshed."

"Yeah," said one of the men with a sneer. "You're as innocent as a virgin, ain't you?"

"I realize I am an accomplice to murder, and that in all likelihood I will hang. But I will not hang alone. Hawkes did the deed, and he will be here soon enough. Have a little patience, gentlemen."

"I don't trust this bastard," said the second man, who was apparently endowed with a much more suspicious nature than his associate.

"What have we got to lose?" asked the other. "Except half the reward if we don't bring them both back. Thing is, Stewart, we don't have to bring you back alive. I'd just as soon kill you now. Make the trip back a lot easier for us. And believe me, I *will* kill you if you're lying to us."

They were bounty hunters, then—and Gordon knew exactly what Stewart was trying to do. The Scotsman was buying him time, assuming that at noon Gordon Hawkes would follow instructions and head for Cleve's Landing. Gordon was glad he had decided to come looking for his friend. His debt to Stewart was greater than ever now.

Standing, Gordon backed away from the door. His first instinct was to bust into the room and settle the matter once and for all. But even with the element of surprise on his side, what chance would he have against a pair of bounty hunters no doubt much better-acquainted with violent confrontations than he? Gordon desperately cast about for a plan. He needed a distraction. But what?

He tried the door to the room adjacent to Stewart's.

It was unlocked, and the room unoccupied. Throwing the covers off the bed, he used the blade of Stewart's dirk to rip open the mattress. A lamp stood on a table near the bed. Removing the glass chimney, he turned the lamp upside down and soaked the torn mattress with oil.

Taking a sulfur match from the waterproof metal case he carried in his shot pouch, Gordon struck the match to life on one of the bed's posters, hesitated, and then tossed it onto the oil-soaked mattress. He jumped back from an explosion of flame. Leaving the door open, he stepped back out into the hall. Dense, acrid gray smoke followed him. In less than a minute the four-poster bed had become a blazing inferno. The hungry flames leaped to nearby window curtains. Dollops of fire dripped to the floor.

"Fire!" yelled Gordon. "Fire! Everybody out!" At the end of the hall opposite the staircase was a narrow window. He ran to it, smashed it out, frame, glass, and all, with the butt of his rifle. Down below was the porch roof, and below that the street. Smoke was filling the hallway. Taking a deep breath and holding it, Gordon turned and went back down the hall to Stewart's room. A half-dressed man lugging a hastily packed valise bolted out of another room, colliding blindly with Gordon, cursed profusely, and staggered for the staircase. Further down, several more guests boiled out of their rooms, but Gordon could scarcely make them out in the thick, choking, eye-burning smoke. As he reached Stewart's room the door opened. Gordon raised his rifle and slammed it into the face of the man who emerged, a split second after he had ascertained it wasn't Stewart. Blood spewing from nose and mouth, the man was thrown backward, careened off the door frame, then slumped forward, out cold.

Stepping over the unconscious man, Gordon entered the room. Stewart shouted a warning, and Gordon dimly made out the shape of the second stranger, whirling from a window, turning a pistol on him. But then Stewart lunged out of the chair where he had been sitting and hurled himself at the bounty hunter, knocking the gun down just as it discharged, and the bounty hunter proceeded to use the pistol like a club to drive Stewart to his knees, striking once, twice, a third time, and as he lifted the pistol to strike again, Gordon brought the Hawken to his shoulder and fired.

The impact of the bullet at such close range picked the bounty hunter up off his feet and hurled him through the window. Gordon watched in horror. *My God, I've killed a man.* He couldn't believe this was really happening. He hadn't even thought twice about pulling the trigger. The bounty hunter had been intent on breaking Stewart's skull open and Gordon had simply reacted.

Stewart got to his feet, fell to one knee, got up again, and stumbled toward Gordon. Blood streamed down one side of his face. "You bloody fool!" rasped the Scotsman. "I told you to get out of town at noon. What the bloody hell are you doing here?"

Gordon just stared at him. Stewart's words didn't even register.

"Come on, lad," said Stewart, his anger quickly ebbing. "We've got to get out of here." He grabbed Gordon by the arm and pulled him out of the room. Gordon stumbled over the form of the unconscious bounty hunter. The smoke was by now so thick in the hallway that he could barely see the fallen man. Wrenching free of Stewart's grasp, he knelt to take the man's wrist, feeling for a pulse, praying for one.

"He's alive," he said. "We can't just leave him here."

Stewart was halfway to the window at the end of the hall. He turned, incredulous. "Are you mad? That bloke was going to be the death of us."

"I'm not leaving him here to die."

Stewart hesitated but an instant. "Fair enough. Take his arms. I'll get his legs."

They carried the bounty hunter to the staircase. Gordon took one last look down the hall. Flame was darting like a serpent's tongue through the doorway of the room next to Stewart's. There would be no saving the hotel. He could only hope that everyone would get out unscathed.

By the time they got down the stairs and across the lobby and out into the street Gordon was gasping for air. His lungs were on fire from the smoke and heat. They put the man down on the street and Gordon dropped to one knee, coughing uncontrollably. He was vaguely aware that a crowd was gathering. A knot of people had collected around the corpse of the bounty hunter Gordon had killed. The sight of his handiwork made Gordon sick to his stomach. Bile rising in his throat, he retched. Stewart got him around the shoulders and helped him to his feet.

"Come on, Gordon. We'd better get moving before the authorities show up. I don't fancy answering a lot of questions."

"Horse," gasped Gordon. "Around back."

He was feeling better when they reached the sorrel.

Climbing into the saddle, he helped Stewart on behind him and returned to Market Street the way he had come. In minutes they were at the livery, and in a few minutes more Stewart's horse was saddled and they were putting St. Louis behind them.

"I apologize for shouting at you, Gordon," said the Scotsman. "You saved my life. Now I am in your debt."

Gordon just shook his head. Stewart had been willing to give his life to buy time—time for Gordon to make good his escape from the city. The debt he owed Stewart was, if anything, greater now then it had been before. He could only wish it weren't so.

As usual, Stewart seemed capable of reading his mind. "I've killed several men in my time," he said, "and it doesn't get any easier. I know well how you feel. Believe me I do."

Still Gordon made no reply. Stewart looked at him, then over his shoulder, and chuckled.

"I can see the smoke from here. I hope you haven't burned St. Louis to the ground."

Gordon didn't look back. He wanted to forget St. Louis—and New Orleans, and Lorine, and New York, and Captain Warren, and everything that had gone before. He wanted nothing more to do with that world, and set his sights on the far horizon, hoping that the new world he was about to enter would treat him better.

III.

Cleve's Landing was located north of St. Louis, near the confluence of the Missouri and Mississippi rivers, a collection of shanties in a clearing carved out of the forest. It was here that Gordon and Stewart were to meet Campbell and the Rocky Mountain Fur Company's westbound expedition of wagons carrying supplies to a new company post on the upper Missouri.

That afternoon, a bank of storm clouds rolled in from the northwest, bringing with it a cold and drizzling rain. As he rode down the single muddy street of Cleve's Landing, Gordon was wet and miserable. If nothing else, the weather served to remind him of the summer that had been wasted away. But when he and Stewart entered the tavern where Campbell was waiting for all the members of his expedition to show up, Gordon forgot about his discomfort. At last he could well and truly put the past behind him. Meeting Robert Campbell was the first step in realizing the dream that had sustained him since his departure from Dublin on the *Penelope*.

Campbell had been with the Rocky Mountain Fur Company almost from the beginning, signing on with Major William Ashley for the early expeditions as a tubercular youth who had come west for the sake of his health. No one knew the fur trade better than Campbell, who had served as a brigade leader, or "partisan," before partnering with William Sublette to act as the company's supplier. He and Sublette made their money carrying goods to each year's rendezvous and then bringing the beaver plews back to St. Louis. It was an enterprise fraught with peril. A host of things could go wrong during the long journey across the high plains and back again, and if a single caravan was lost the Rocky Mountain Fur Company would face ruination. A capricious Nature, unpredictable Indian tribes, a hostile American Fur Company—so far, Campbell had prevailed against them all.

Tall, lean, weathered, the sandy-haired Campbell cordially greeted Gordon and Stewart and introduced them to the rest of the company. His most trusted lieutenant was Louis Vasquez, a living legend among the mountain men, one of Ashley's original trappers. French-born Charles Larpenteur, a refined and well-educated young man who had been raised in Baltimore's most genteel surroundings, was here to make his first trip West. He and Gordon were not the only greenhorns, though; Benjamin Harrison, a doctor by trade and the son of the famous Indian fighter, William Henry Harrison, was also present and accounted for, having only just arrived from St. Louis himself. There was an Arapaho youth named Friday who had been rescued from starvation in the arid wasteland of the southwest by Tom Fitzpatrick; Friday had been sent East to a white man's school, but he'd had enough of that and was going back to the mountains to be reunited with his adopted father, Broken Hand, as old Fitzpatrick was called. The rest of the men, thirty in number, were all experienced in the sense that they had made at least one overland trek, or made one voyage up the Big Muddy on a keelboat or piroque, with Campbell or Sublette. Some were of French extraction, some were half-breeds, a few were of Mexican extraction. But whatever their heritage, they were all hardened plainsmen, tough as nails.

As Campbell explained it to Gordon, each man would be responsible for three pack mules. Each mule would carry about two hundred pounds of goods. In addition, they would bring a remuda of about forty horses, as well as twenty sheep to provide the expedition with fresh meat until they had found their first buffalo herd. Stewart was assigned to herding the horses; a hussar, he was, of course, an accomplished rider. And since he was the Scotsman's friend and traveling companion, Gordon was also given the responsibility of watching over the remuda, based on Campbell's mistaken assumption that he, too, possessed equestrian skills. Gordon didn't think it was a very good idea, but he said nothing. In his opinion he didn't match up to these frontiersmen in any way, shape, or form. They were resilient and resourceful men, wise in the ways of the wilderness, excellent shots, and superior horsemen. They would not tolerate weakness, or brook excuses. So he kept his mouth shut, knowing he had to prove himself worthy of their trust, and knowing also that he would probably fall far short of their expectations.

He was astonished by the variety of goods stored in the packs. Staples such as powder and shot, traps, tobacco and alcohol, coffee and sugar, hatchets and knives, flints and steel, shirts, coats, blankets, fish hooks, awls and sewing needles. For trade with the Indians there were beads, mirrors, bells, vermilion, flannel and calico cloth, stockings and garters, trade muskets, and kitchen utensils. Of course, tobacco and alcohol and powder and shot were also earmarked for the Indian trade. Gordon learned that the majority of the trade goods had been loaded aboard Sublette's keelboat, which had embarked on its journey up the Missouri two days earlier. Five hundred strings of assorted beads, seventy-five pairs of Mackinaw blankets, bolts of fabric amounting to about three thousand yards, a dozen scarlet "chieftain" coats, blankets, woolen caps, half a ton of rifle balls, more than one thousand flints, three hundred shirts, one hundred and fifty smoothbore "Northwest" guns, and one hundred and fifty scalpers—as the mountain men called the knives destined for Indian hands.

Gordon later learned of the remarkable profits that would be made from these cheap goods. For instance, the Mackinaw blankets that might cost from three to ten dollars a pair were sold by the half pair for up to twenty dollars. Rifle balls that cost six cents a pound in St. Louis fetched a dollar a pound in the wild country. The bolts of fabric would bring a thousand percent profit. Of course, Indians and trappers alike acquired such goods with plews in lieu of hard money, and a beaver plew that might buy ten dollars worth of goods would in turn bring more than twice that sum on the eastern market, so that the Company—and jobbers like Sublette and Campbell—stood to make quite a tidy profit. In their opinion, though, it was by no means an unwarranted profit, for the dangers they faced were legion. The keelboat alone carried more than four thousand dollars' worth of merchandise. Its loss would be a disastrous blow. The traders risked their lives, and deserved big rewards. None of the trappers begrudged them what they made.

Over supper that evening Campbell announced that they would leave at first light on the morrow. All the packs had been made and all the members of the party, save one whom Campbell had decided would not show no matter how much longer they waited, were present and accounted for. He laid out the route, naming rivers and bluffs and rocks and other landmarks which meant absolutely nothing to Gordon. They broke out some liquor and began to swap tall tales. Stewart held up his end, regaling the appreciative buckskinners with stirring accounts of epic Napoleonic battles and incredible feats of heroism. He spoke of officers braving certain death to lead doomed charges against the enemy lines, all for the sake of God and country. He told, as well, of a few ribald experiences while on campaign, one with a hot-blooded Spanish marquesa and another with the wanton camp-following daughter of a sergeant major in the King's Hussars. The Westerners hooted, hollered, and soaked up every word of it.

In past months Gordon had heard all of these stories and more; he was far more interested in the tales Campbell and the other frontiersmen told. These men were natural born storytellers, and by evening's end Gordon had concluded that they were not adverse to embellishing on the facts. They spoke of hunting and trapping, of wild Indians and savage beasts, and of course there was the most unpredictable Nature. Sometimes the hero of the story was one of the legends of their own kind—Jim "Old Gabe" Bridger or "Broken Hand" Fitzgerald or Jedediah Smith or John Colter. Gordon heard how Colter had escaped from the clutches of Blackfoot Indians; naked and unarmed, he eluded his pursuers by diving into the icy waters of a creek and hiding inside a beaver's nest. He heard, too, about another mountain man who had also been captured by hostiles, and who taunted his captors until his last breath, even as the Indians tortured him without respite—torture which was described in sickening detail. The man's tormentors, or so the story went, were so ashamed of their own cruelty and so impressed by their victim's courage that they abandoned their village and moved far away, convinced that the dead man's spirit would continue to haunt the place and that the Great Spirit would curse it forever. One man told of a great golden grizzly bear that prowled the Wind River Range, an animal who could not be slain. Another told of a friend who had been cornered by fifty Arapaho braves and held them off for three days, forted up behind the carcass of his dead horse.

Louis Vasquez claimed he had escaped a band of Indians by leaping off a precipice, plunging into a river hundreds of feet below; swept downstream by the rapids, he lost his rifle and pack and very nearly his life. Unconscious, he was pulled from the river by a beautiful golden-haired girl who took him to ancient cliff dwellings where none but beautiful women lived. There he was nursed back to health and remained for over a year, enjoying the favors of all the women, until one day, weary of the sweet nectar and strange fruit upon which the cliff dwellers subsisted, he fashioned a bow and some arrows from an Osage orange tree and went hunting for some meat, only to return and find that the dwellings, and the women, had vanished. Stewart remarked that the story bore a striking resemblance to one of the adventures of Odysseus, immortalized by Homer—another great storyteller. At which point Vasquez blithely announced that he hadn't met a feller by that name in the high country, but he'd sure like to, because it was entirely likely that Odysseus had met up with those same gals.

Campbell had his story, too. He had run afoul of not one but two grizzly bears that seemed to work in concert as they attempted to corner him. For a while he managed to keep them at bay, but they wouldn't give up, wore him down, boxed him in. He had shot one of them but the other got to him before he could reload and proceeded to tear him to pieces. He describe the attack down to the last gruesome detail, and he told the tale with such flair that Gordon's skin crawled. He could almost feel the grizzly's claws ripping through his own flesh, could almost hear the mad, deafening roars of the giant bear and taste the blood in his own mouth. "Finally that ol' bear took one big swipe at me and ripped my belly wide open," said Campbell solemnly. "I tried to hold my guts in but they just slipped right through my fingers. I knew I was a gone beaver then, and I looked up at that grizzly and I'll be damned if he wasn't grinnin' at me. Then he picked me up and slammed my body against a tree trunk and I heard my spine crack clean in two."

"My God," gasped Gordon, horrified. "What did you do? What happened then?"

Campbell just looked at him, deadpan, and said, "Well, I got kilt, of course. What do you think happened?"

The others broke into a gale of laughter and Gordon had to join in. He didn't find out until later that the fact that he could laugh at his own gullibility raised his stock in the eyes of the buckskinners.

They drank and talked and talked and drank late into the evening. When Gordon awoke it was still dark outside, but the others were up and moving about, muttering curses as they fought hangovers and stubborn mules. Gordon thought his head was going to explode, and as he rode out to gather the herd, accompanied by Stewart, he thought he was going to have to die just to feel better. For his part, Stewart appeared none the worse for wear. Gordon envied the Scotsman's ability to consume liberal quantities of hundred-proof pop skull with the best of them. Stewart could drink these Westerners under the table, and they admired him for it. Apparently, the harder you drank and the bigger you lied the better off you were with such men. So Gordon tried not to let out that he felt so godawful bad. But his wretched condition dampened his enthusiasm for this important day—the day he had been looking forward to for the better part of one year. Something else put a damper on the occasion. Thoughts of Lorine still haunted him. He could only hope that as he put more miles behind him those bedeviling thoughts would release him.

The sky was still overcast, and a cold drizzle persisted, so that by the time they had gathered up the remuda Gordon was soaked to the skin. More than one of the buckskinners had been troubled by a recalcitrant mule that would try to throw off its pack or shed its burden by falling on the ground and rolling completely over. But eventually order was achieved, and the company took its leave from Cleve's Landing, heading west for the high plains and the Shining Mountains beyond, and Gordon wondered what lay in store for him in that vast and uncharted wild country. Who could say? But, for better or worse, it would be his new home. Gordon Hawkes turned his back on civilization forever, and was heartily glad to do it.

CHAPTER 4

I.

The route they took was one that Robert Campbell knew quite well. He had made the trip on a number of occasions, carrying goods to the annual mountain man rendezvous. West into Kansas they moved, then turning northwest, across the Big Blue and Little Blue rivers, and onward into the valley of the Platte. At the fork of the Platte they followed the southern branch, and after a hundred miles on this course they put the prairie behind them and entered the High Plains proper.

Here the grass was shorter and more sparse. The rivers were muddier and more shallow. The flatlands gave way to rolling swells that in turn became a more rugged country of ridges and ravines and distinctive rock outcroppings, the sculptured remains of ancient heights worn down by wind and rain. The elements of Nature ruled here. This world was more raw and wild in every way from the prairie. The storms struck more quickly and with greater violence. The lightning seemed to strike the earth with greater fury, and the wind howled as it tore at your clothes and snatched the breath from your lungs. The sun seemed closer—closer and meaner and more relentless by far. The sheer power and grandeur of this strange new land appealed to Gordon even as it shook his self-confidence. It appealed to him because clearly a man had to be possessed of more courage and wile and tenacity than the average fellow had at his command if he expected to survive in this country. It appealed, too, because here the land and the sky and the wind and the rain and the sun were the masters. In his naiveté, Gordon felt sure that civilization would never conquer this land. Truly here he would be safe from the disappointments and cruelties of the civilized world. Assuming, that is, he survived.

Watching the country change, become wilder and rougher and more demanding, Gordon understood why Campbell had opted for pack mules over wagons. Mules more readily navigated the broad rivers that barred their way. Unfortunately, however, mules were balky creatures by nature. A clap of thunder or a man's sneeze might cause them to kick or bolt. Out of pure spitefulness they would bite you if given an opportunity. They scoffed at gentle words and cajolery. Prodding, whipping, and cursing just made them more obnoxious. The braying of a mule was the most horrible noise God had ever made, Gordon decided. It was strident, raucous, nasal, nerve-wracking insolence personified. Gordon counted his lucky stars that he had been assigned to the horse herd.

As the days wore on Gordon's excitement grew, as he wondered which he would see first: a buffalo or an

Indian. As it happened, he was destined to make his acquaintance with the Indian first, but not under the circumstances he had expected.

When night camp was made the mules were usually kept on picket lines, as such was the nature of that particular beast that it would wonder off just for the hell of it, without regard for whether it had ample graze or water at its disposal. A mule was an individualist who preferred to go his own way. The cavallard, on the other hand, had become accustomed to banding together; after a few weeks the horses began to act as a herd, with a tendency to stick together, and nary a one wandering off in an act of solo defiance. If a horse wandered it would be with the herd, and a couple of night guards were usually sufficient to keep the remuda in place. While Gordon and Stewart were charged with moving the herd during the day, the entire company took turns acting as night guards. It just so happened that Gordon was on duty the night a band of Indians decided to help themselves to the company's ponies.

Some Indian sign had been found in the past week, and debate raged as to what tribe was represented by the warriors who had left the evidence, with some of the party certain that they were Arapahoes from the west, while others were just as certain they were Pawnee. The sign caused no undue concern; as Gordon understood, hunting parties of all the plains tribes were prone to range far afield during this time of year, looking for buffalo, so that they could lay in a stock of robes and smoked meat for the coming winter. That was not to say, of course, that a hunting party wouldn't get a notion to steal some horses or even take a stab at collecting a few scalps if the opportunity presented itself. You just never could tell about Indians. Many young bucks eager to make a reputation were on the prowl, and the one thing you could count on where Indians were concerned was their unpredictable nature. So every man in the company kept his eyes peeled.

It was Gordon's sharp eye that saved the horse herd that cool autumn night as he rode his blaze-faced sorrel in a slow circle counterclockwise around the quiet cavallard. The other guard, a fellow by the name of Sanchez, was making a clockwise circuit, so that the two men met twice every time they made a complete circle, just in case one had anything to report to the other. The problem with that was the fact that Sanchez wasn't a very amiable or communicative sort. He was a lean, swarthy half-breed whose father, it was said, had been a Comanche warrior of the Penateka band who had kidnapped Sanchez's mother, the daughter of a Santa Fe trader, and who'd had his way with the lady before giving her up for the ransom. The trader had wanted to do away with the bastard child, but the mother had saved Sanchez's life by giving him to a poor sheepherder who had raised the boy as his own.

It wasn't that Sanchez had any particular reason to dislike Gordon—he just wasn't the sort to make idle conversation. He was a loner who didn't need or want friends. Gordon had learned there were two kinds of mountain men. There was the friendly, garrulous sort who would greet you like a long-lost brother even if they'd last seen you only ten minutes earlier, and who would talk until the cows came home given half a chance, and who would give you the shirt off their back or their last chew of tobacco if circumstances called for it. And then there was the Sanchez type, taciturn and solitary and unreachable, who only tolerated human contact because sometimes it was just unavoidable. There were several such men in Campbell's company, but they were capable men, experienced in the ways of the wilderness, the kind that the others knew they could rely upon, and for this reason their unfriendly ways were overlooked.

The company camped that night where a creek emptied into the South Fork of the Platte, and they built their fires and spread their blankets about a quarter mile from the river. The horse herd grazed both sides of the shallow creek between the river and the camp, hemmed in by a low curving rise marking the southern bank of the south fork, with a break where the creek made its juncture with the Platte. As these were the High Plains, there wasn't a tree in sight; the campfires had been made of buffalo chips—a herd had passed this way a week earlier on its slow southern migration. For this reason Gordon tried to keep particularly alert, aware that an Indian hunting party might be trailing the shaggies. But he was tired. When he pulled night guard duty after a long day in the saddle he was hard-pressed to keep awake; he'd already learned the bad habit of dozing off while riding.

The sense that something was wrong came upon him very gradually—a vague uneasiness at first, the source of which he could not define, try as he might. There certainly didn't appear to be anything amiss. The night was clear and quiet. The herd was placid and well behaved. It was one of those crisp, clear autumn nights on the High Plains when the sky was bedecked with an uncountable array of stars and constellations that looked so close that it seemed a person could reach up and grab a handful. The early moon, a mere thumbnail sliver, had come and gone, but the starlight was sufficient to cast a silver glow across the nightscape. By this light Gordon could make out the occasional bushes that sparsely dotted the plains, and it eventually occurred to him that there was something peculiar about those shrubs. They seemed to be moving.

Every time he reached the northern perimeter of the herd, just before he crossed the shallows of the creek, he could glance in the direction of the river and see five or six dark clumps of shrubbery. But some of them didn't seem to be in the same place as before. At first he put it down to his own inattention. Then he wondered if maybe he wasn't simply overtired and seeing things. But when his sorrel began to act nervous he concluded that maybe there really was something very wrong here. And so he was confronted with the dilemma of having to tell Sanchez about his suspicions—only Sanchez had passed that same spot just as often as he had, and the half-breed, far more experienced in such matters than he, did not appear unduly alarmed.

He had to be sure. So after crossing the creek he left the herd and circled round to the north, putting himself against the backdrop of the low ridge, stopped the sorrel, and settled down to wait and watch. He could see the bushes well enough now, the nearest one being about a hundred yards east of his position. The sorrel whickered anxiously and Gordon leaned forward in the saddle and murmured, "Easy now, girl," into the animal's ear. He trusted the sorrel's instincts, and the horse returned that trust by accepting its master's reassurance and quieting. Meanwhile, off to the right, Sanchez had realized his partner was no longer making the circuit, and the half-breed, too, had checked his horse, letting out a low whistle that sounded uncannily like the call of a meadow lark, only Gordon knew it was Sanchez, knew also that Sanchez expected a response. Gordon kept silent. He refused to give his position away, and kept his eyes glued on the bushes.

There! One of them had most definitely moved! Just a few feet, a bit closer to the herd, but there could be no question. . . . There went another! A chill ran down Gordon's spine. He drew his Plains rifle from its saddle ties—it rode snugly against the hull beneath his right leg. This was no tumbleweed; this was someone impersonating a bush, and in all likelihood that someone was an Indian. Gordon had been told how warriors sometimes used shrubbery or animal skins as camouflage.

What to do? Go tell Sanchez. Alert the camp. If he fired a shot the horse herd might stampede and then there would be hell to pay. The company might lose as much as a full day trying to round up the scattered ponies. And they could not afford to lose a day. They had to reach the Yellowstone before the first snow, and winter was just around the corner. His duty clear, Gordon reined the sorrel to the right, returning to the herd, searching the darkness for Sanchez.

In the next instant all hell broke loose. A bloodcurdling shriek shattered the stillness. A gun spoke, and Gordon saw the bright orange muzzle flash—straight ahead of him, and a little to the left, from just about the spot where he figured Sanchez was located. And then the horses were running, their hooves making a sound like thunder that never stopped, the ponies themselves a long black shadow sliding westward across the dark ground directly in front of Gordon. For a moment he was torn by indecision. Should he go to the aid of Sanchez or stick with the cavallard? He chose the latter course. Kicking the sorrel into a gallop, he angled for the head of the herd.

A figure suddenly loomed in front of him, seeming to rise up from the earth. An Indian! The warrior launched himself at the sorrel's head, groping for the bridle. The sorrel snorted and veered away. The Indian's body struck the horse's withers. Gordon felt a hand clawing at his leg. Gordon got his foot out of the stirrup and kicked as hard as he could. The Indian fell, spinning away into the darkness, and Gordon rode on with his heart hammering in his chest.

Nearing the head of the thundering herd, he saw another Indian—this one astride a company horse, riding bareback, his long hair streaming as he bent low. Urging the sorrel to maximum effort, Gordon closed in on the horse thief. As he drew nearer, the Indian glanced over his shoulder, saw him, and steered his horse away from the rest of the cavallard, making a break for it, and leaving Gordon with the choice of staying with the herd or chasing after him. Gordon wasn't willing to let a single horse be purloined. Not on his watch. Without a second thought he raised the Hawken and fired at the Indian galloping across his front. The Indian's mount shrieked and went down; its rider was sent hurtling through the air. In horror Gordon realized he had missed the Indian and shot the horse. Angry with himself, he pressed on after the herd. Reaching the stampede's leaders, he whooped and hollered and tried to turn them. They pounded up a low rise and down the other side and there lay the river before them, and as suddenly as it had begun the stampede was over, and the horses spread out in the moon-silvered shadows, some drinking, others just standing with legs aquiver and nostrils flared. Not knowing what else to do, Gordon stayed with them, fumbling with his shot pouch and reloading the Hawken even as he tried to keep a sharp lookout in every direction for Indians, and thinking that the others would never let him live down the fact that he had killed one of their own horses.

A few minutes later he heard riders coming—and he was so jumpy he nearly shot Stewart and Campbell and Vasquez as they came over the embankment. All the men slept with a horse saddled up and near at hand for just such an occasion as this, and these three had set out after the stampeding herd while the rest prepared to defend the camp from attack and protect their precious mules and trade goods. When Vasquez saw the horses standing placidly in the shallows or along the bank he let out a whoop that set Gordon's already jangled nerves on edge. The first to reach Gordon, he drew his horse alongside the sorrel and grinned like a drunkard. "You done good, Hawkes! Mighty good. I figgered these cayuses were on their way to Mexico." He spat a stream of tobacco juice—Vasquez always seemed to be chewing on a wad whether it was day or night—and then, without warning, he reached out and slapped Gordon on the back so hard that Gordon was nearly knocked out of the saddle. "Thissun's got all the makin's, boss," Vasquez told Campbell as the partisan rode up with Stewart. "He'll do in a tough spot."

Gordon decided it would be prudent to make his confession now before all this undue adulation got out of hand. "I accidentally shot one of the horses," he said, ashamed. "I was trying to hit the Indian who was stealing it. But I missed him and hit the horse instead."

"Don't matter," replied Campbell. "By God I'd as soon shot a horse myself before I let one of them heathens make off with it."

"Sanchez. What about Sanchez?"

Campbell shook his head. "Don't know about him as yet. Let's get these horses back nearer the camp."

That task accomplished, Gordon accompanied Campbell into camp while Stewart and Vasquez watched over the herd. As they arrived, Sanchez came in; the half-breed was leading his horse, and a dead Indian was draped over the saddle. Sanchez tipped the corpse over and it fell, arms and legs akimbo. The mountain men gathered round for a closer look.

"Arapaho dog soldier," muttered someone, and the others nodded or grunted their accord.

"How many, you reckon?" Campbell asked Sanchez.

The breed shrugged as though it was a matter of supreme indifference to him. "I saw two. Killed 'em both. Couldn't find the other body, though, too dark."

Campbell turned to Gordon, and Gordon said he had seen two others.

"Well," said Campbell, "this one ain't done up for war, that's plain. Hunting party. Probably six or eight, all told. Just happened up on us and decided to try for the cavallard. But we'd better go out and make sure the dead are dead and them that's left above snakes have well and truly made for the tall timber."

A search was immediately commenced, with four parties of three or four men each setting off in different directions, each lighting its way with burning brands taken from the campfires, and every man on the alert. Gordon led one group, Campbell among them, to the general area where he had seen his two Indians. No sign was found of the first Indian who had attacked him. Soon, though, they came upon the dead horse, and a few yards away, an Indian just as dead as the horse. The Indian's neck had been broken.

"Looks like you killed yourself an Injun after all, Hawkes," remarked Campbell.

Gordon realized the Indian was hardly more than a boy. He felt sick to his stomach. The Arapaho youth wore a plain buckskin tunic and leggins. There was no war paint on his face.

"Reckon his scalp belongs to you," said one of the other men in the search party.

"I don't want it," said Gordon.

Campbell was paying attention—he could tell Gordon was unhappy with the way things had turned out. "You did what you had to do, Hawkes. Don't fret over it."

"Yeah," said the other mountain man. "We didn't ask this thievin' rascal to come along and make off with our ponies."

"I'll bury him," said Gordon flatly. "I killed him, so I'll bury him."

"Don't bother," counseled Campbell. "Injuns don't bury their dead. To their way of thinking, a person's spirit escapes the body through the mouth. If you put him in the ground his spirit will be trapped beneath the earth. No, leave him lay where he fell. His friends will come back after we're long gone and fetch him home. They would be dishonored if they didn't make the effort. He died a warrior's death and he'll get a send-off befittin' a warrior."

"What about the horse?" asked the other man.

"You can cook it up if you've of a mind to," replied Campbell. "I don't personally cotton to horse meat myself."

"Me neither, but I'm sick and tired of mutton, I can tell you that much. What happened to the damned buffalo, anyhow? That's what I'd like to know. I'd give my left arm for a chunk of greasy hump meat right about now."

The next morning, as he rode out to get the horse herd on the move, Gordon veered off when he spotted the buzzards that had gathered around the body of the Indian he had slain. His approach scattered the scavengers, but he knew they would be back as soon as he rode away. In spite of what Campbell had told him about Indian custom, it still didn't seem right and proper to leave this boy to the wolves and turkey vultures. He forced himself to take a long hard look at the corpse—and was shocked to see that the boy's scalp had been lifted. Anger surged through him. In camp that night, twenty-five miles further along the south fork of the Platte River, he was still mad, and challenged the man who had taken the scalp to identify himself. Gordon wasn't sure what he was going to do when the culprit stepped forward, but in his outrage at the mutilation of the Arapaho boy's body he wasn't thinking things through. As it happened, though, no one admitted to the deed. It didn't occur to Gordon that his cold fury and willingness to stand up for what he thought was right impressed these buckskinners. And it cowed at least one of them—the taker of the scalp—because Gordon never did find out who the perpetrator was.

II.

A couple of days later they left the south fork and turned northwest until they'd reached the north fork, a wide and shallow and muddy river notorious for its treacherous quicksand. The next day, much to everyone's relief, they spotted a distant herd of buffalo. It seemed to Gordon like an ocean of brown. He could not see all the way to the other side of it; nor could he see the tail of the herd. Like a slow-moving glacier of horns, hooves and shaggy fur, it crept inexorably across the undulating plain, grazing as it migrated south toward its winter range. Gordon was astonished when Campbell announced that this was a fairly small herd compared to some he'd seen. "I seen a herd once, some years back," remarked Vasquez, "that took a whole week to cross my path," and others nodded as though they had had similar experiences. Gordon couldn't be sure if they were exaggerating, as he knew by now that such men were prone to do. Surely no herd of bison could be larger than this one. Why, there had to be five, maybe ten thousand of the beasts stretched out across the plain in front of them.

Stewart was as excited as the others at the prospect of a buffalo hunt, but for a different reason. He reminded Gordon that this moment was the one he'd been waiting for. The chance to bag an American shaggy, along with an opportunity to confront a genuine Indian, were the reasons he had visited this country in the first place. Knowing this, Campbell appointed Stewart outright as one of the hunters. The rest of the men drew lots. The partisan wanted two hunting parties of three men each; the rest would have to stay behind with the mules and horses. Everyone wanted to participate in the hunt. It was great sport—great because it was dangerous, and to these men danger was the spice of life. They couldn't live without it. So Campbell had to restrict the number of hunters.

When the straws were done Gordon picked a long one; he and Stewart and an experienced mountain man named Rusher made up one of the hunting parties. "Kill no more than ten," Campbell told them. "More meat than that will just go to waste. Two of you will do the killing. The third will act as the lookout."

"I'll do that," said Gordon. He discovered that he could not share Stewart's enthusiasm for killing one of the great beasts. "But what am I on the lookout for?"

"You'll watch our backs," said Rusher. "You never know about them shaggies. Sometimes they'll just stand there and let you knock 'em down one by one. Sometimes they run. And sometimes one of 'em will get it into his head to charge. They'll for sure turn on a hunter if he don't kill it with his first shot, and he's close enough. That happens, you bring the critter down, and don't miss."

Gordon nodded, regretting that he had volunteered to be a lookout. If the hunt turned deadly he was responsible for keeping his partners alive. It should have been obvious, he thought, that he wasn't the best of shots. After all, only a few days earlier he had shot at an Indian and killed instead the horse that Indian was trying to purloin. But Rusher and Stewart didn't appear to harbor any doubts in that regard. Perhaps they were just too excited about the hunt to give appropriate consideration to their lookout's shooting skills.

Having heard plenty of stories about buffalo hunting across a campfire in past weeks, Gordon dredged his memory for important details as he and the others started out. He recalled that you had to shoot a buffalo through the heart or spine to be certain of stopping it, and even then the beast might sometimes run for a while despite its mortal wound. Gordon hoped Rusher and Stewart made their shots count.

They held their horses to a walk, keeping downwind of the slow-moving herd, advancing on it from due east as it crept from north to south before them. It was the middle of the morning, the sky was clear, and the cool breeze in Gordon's face carried the musky smell of the herd. The bison's eyesight was notoriously poor—it relied on its sense of smell to alert it to danger—but Rusher, who had hunted shaggies many times before, knew better than to charge straight at the herd. "We get up close as we can before we go to shooting," he told Stewart, and the Scotsman nodded, content to bow to experience.

As they moved to within three hundred yards of the herd, Gordon marveled at the sheer size of the shaggies. The bulls stood up to six feet tall at the shoulder, and ten feet in length from muzzle to rump. He figured a full-grown bull had to weigh at least a ton, twice as heavy as the average saddle horse. They ranged in color from yellow to sandy red to dark brown, with the calves generally lighter in color and the older bison darker with blond forequarters.

At the moment one of the bulls turned toward the approaching riders and let out a bellow that seemed to act as a warning promptly heeded by the buffalo near him, for they began to move more quickly, and their urgency was transmitted through the herd, rippling through the sea of brown so that in no time at all the entire herd was on the run. Rusher let out a yell and kicked his horse into a gallop. Stewart and Gordon followed suit. The bull that had sounded the alarm turned and bolted. The chase was on.

The thunder of thousands of hooves filled Gordon's ears. A cloud of dust closed in over him, so thick that in short order he could scarcely draw breath, and could barely see Rusher and Stewart directly ahead of him. He was dimly aware of the fringe of the herd off to his right. Now they were galloping headlong, parallel with the densely packed shaggies. Rusher's rifle spouted flame—Gordon didn't hear the sound of the rifle but he witnessed the result as a bull stumbled and went down. The herd broke around the fallen beast like a river around an island. Rusher's horse slowed as its rider concentrated on reloading his rifle. Now in front of his companions, Stewart fired into the herd. Gordon's heart leapt into his throat as he saw a buffalo veer out of the herd as though to charge the Scotsman.

Locking his knees tighter against the saddle, Gordon let go of the reins and gave the sorrel its head, raising the Hawken Plains rifle to his shoulder, remembering that in the course of one campfire conversation he had heard someone mention that to hit a shaggy's heart you had to put the bullet right behind the shoulder. Shooting at an angle from atop a horse, you had to be at close range; the buffalo's thick hide and tangled mat of wool around the shoulders could actually deflect a bullet fired from a distance. In this case Gordon didn't have to worry about that. He was within thirty or forty feet of the beast and coming straight on. Directly ahead of him, Stewart's buckskin recognized the danger and veered away. Gordon heard Rusher shout— probably yelling at him to shoot. His heart pounding, his throat dry as cotton, his eyes watering from the sting of the dust, Gordon pulled the trigger. The buffalo's front legs buckled and it went down, purplish blood spouting from nose and mouth with every labored breath. The sorrel carried Gordon past the mortally wounded shaggy; he retrieved the reins, checked and turned the horse. Suddenly he felt sorry for the buffalo he had shot. He fumbled with his shot pouch, eager to reload and shoot again just to put the creature out of its misery. But Rusher was reloaded, and did the job. The buffalo rolled over and died, legs quivering for a moment and then going stiff.

Stewart and Rusher turned their horses away from the herd, and Gordon gladly followed. They stopped some distance away from the stampeding mass. Gordon reloaded the Hawken then, keeping a wary eye on the bison as they thundered past less than two hundred yards away. He was relieved when none ventured out to challenge them. For a while no one spoke; it wasn't the noise that deterred them—the excitement of the chase and the kill had drained all three of them.

And then, abruptly, the herd was gone, leaving only a diminishing drumroll of sound and the haze of choking dust that the wind would gradually shred apart and carry away. Gordon and his companions had accounted for two bulls. The other team had dropped three of the shaggies. Neither horse nor man had suffered injury. But in Stewart's case it had been a close call and he knew it. As they dismounted to loosen cinches and let their sweat-lathered horses blow, the Scotsman grinned at Gordon. "Thanks, lad. You saved my hide, as they say in these parts. But then I knew I could count on you. That's twice, by the way, that you've stood between me and my Maker."

Gordon didn't know what to say to that. Stewart's compliment gave him a warm glow inside. "It was a lucky shot," he said with a modest shrug.

"Aye. Lucky for me, you mean."

Some of the other men came out to assist in the butchering. It took a half dozen of them to prop the carcass up on its belly; the first cut was made the length of the spine and the skin was pulled down along the sides. Nearly all the meat was taken: the "fleece," which lay between the spine and the ribs, covered with a thick layer of fat; the "side ribs" and belly fat; the "boss," a small hump at the back of the neck; and the big hump, including the "hump ribs." The liver was taken, too, and some of the intestines, as well as a thigh bone which would be used to crack other bones known to contain the tastiest marrow. The tongue, considered a great delicacy, was cut from the head and offered to the hunter who had made the killing shot. All of these cuts—save for the liver, which was cut up and split among the crew to eat raw, perhaps seasoned with a sprinkle of gunpowder—was placed in the skin and bundled up for transport back to camp.

Then the cooking and feasting began. Hump meat and boss were boiled in kettles. Cracked marrow bones were laid in the fire till they sizzled. Most other cuts were roasted over the fire, impaled on ramrods. Kidney fat and belly fat was melted into a greasy liquid and consumed. The aroma of the seared meat made Gordon's mouth water. Buffalo meat was rich, juicy, and tender, and after the first bite Gordon understood why these men had talked so much about it—he was quite certain he had never tasted anything finer in his life. Like all the rest, he ate until he simply could not eat any more. He tried the hump, the side ribs, the boss, the tongue, the bone marrow, even some of the melted fat. The only thing on the menu he passed up were the intestines, or "boudins," which the mountain men ate after a slight searing, squeezing the contents out with their hands as they swallowed the greasy coil.

All that afternoon and late into the evening the men ate themselves into oblivion. After dark, the aroma of the meat carried off on the wind attracted coyotes and wolves by the dozen, who lurked just beyond the firelight. An extra guard was posted on the horse herd as a consequence, but the wolves and their smaller cousins weren't interested in the cavallard, and the mountain men kept them out of the camp by hurling cracked bones and remnants of meat into the darkness, laughing at the savage noises made by the scavengers as they quarreled over the scraps. Gordon figured that each man in the company consumed eight to ten pounds of meat that day. Their faces, lit by the dancing flames of the windswept cook fires, were covered with grease and blood. Those faces, and the sounds of the snarling wolves and the howling of the wind sweeping over the High Plains and the realization that he was out in the middle of the wild country hundreds of miles from the nearest outpost or town—all of this combined within Gordon to produce a strange and soaring elation. He was at long last satisfied with his lot and at peace with himself.

III.

In the weeks to come they would strike the Big Horn River and travel along it until they reached the Yellowstone, thence along this river past the Rosebud, the Tongue, the Powder, and finally to the spot where the Yellowstone and the Missouri met. Four miles up the Missouri stood Fort Union, the chief outpost of the rival American Fur Company. Here Kenneth McKenzie ruled as the King of the Missouri, so called because this cosmopolitan gentleman lived like a potentate.

Officially, McKenzie was in charge of a division of John Jacob Astor's company called the Upper Missouri Outfit. His task as defined by Astor himself was to put the Rocky Mountain Fur Company out of business. It was McKenzie who had planned and built a series of outposts, these to serve in lieu of the annual rendezvous held by the Rocky Mountain boys for the purpose of exchanging plews and goods and information. It was McKenzie who, incredibly, established trade with the belligerent Blackfeet. Before, the Blackfeet had consistently killed any American trapper they happened to come across, and had steadfastly refused to have anything whatsoever to do with the white man. McKenzie actually got them to agree to a treaty that cemented the alliance between the tribe and the American Fur Company for as long as the rivers flowed. This was very bad news for the Rocky Mountain Fur Company, because McKenzie did nothing to dissuade his fierce allies from preying on the brigades affiliated with the RMFC. Quite the contrary, in fact. Kenneth McKenzie was a man of culture and refinement, but he was also completely ruthless.

Gordon had heard all about McKenzie long before he first laid eyes on Fort Union, and so he wondered why Campbell didn't avoid the stronghold of the RMFC's most dangerous foe. But as it happened, McKenzie greeted them with warm cordiality. He was, after all, a gentleman, an honorable and hospitable man and he felt honor-bound to welcome Campbell and his men into his home. He had been just as generous to Milton Sublette, who had come and gone on his keelboats nearly a fortnight earlier, moving on up the river to establish the RMFC's first permanent post. Campbell was relieved to know that Sublette and his party had successfully negotiated the wild Missouri without serious mishap; this was the first word he had received on the keelboat and its crew since Cleve's Landing.

McKenzie was a tall, sandy-haired man, a bit stocky, with a neatly groomed beard, a weathered but handsome face, alert and intelligent eyes like chips of pale blue ice carved out of a glacier, and a royal courtier's graceful manners. He traditionally wore a scarlet coat, his trademark garb by which all the Plains Indians identified him. Just looking at the man, Gordon found it hard to believe, at first, that McKenzie was the ruthless and cold-blooded competitor the other Rocky Mountain boys portrayed him.

Fort Union didn't look like much, especially in comparison to places like New York or New Orleans or St. Louis, but it was as close to a town as one was going to find north of Santa Fe and west of the Mississippi until one reached California. The stockade, located on high ground overlooking the river, wasn't very large, but a small village of huts, most made of sod but a few with wood cannibalized from wagons, and most with canvas roofs, had sprung up around the stockade. Gordon was surprised to see about two dozen teepees in the vicinity. He noticed that his Rocky Mountain Fur Company companions eyed the Indians who lived in those skin lodges with grave suspicion, but he wouldn't find out why until later. For his part, he was simply glad to know they had neared the end of their long journey across the plains. The RMFC's post—their final destination—was less than a day's travel further up the river. They had made it in the nick of time; for two days a curtain of gray clouds had blocked out the sun. A bitter and incessant cold wind roared down from the north. And on the day they sighted Fort Union the snow began to fall, a very desultory snowfall, but herald of worse to come.

Most of the men were content to mingle with the outpost's denizens—a polyglot of American, French, half-breed, and Indian men, along with a few Indian women—while keeping a keen eye on their mules and their pack of goods. Campbell, Vasquez, Stewart, and Gordon accepted an invitation from McKenzie. The latter was particularly interested in meeting Stewart, a fellow Scotsman, and because Gordon was Stewart's friend, the invitation extended to him.

The meeting took place in McKenzie's quarters, a room warmed by a blazing fire in a stone hearth and furnished with furniture that would not have looked too much out of place in the parlor of some fine eastern town home. A threadbare Belgian carpet and a grizzly pelt shared the puncheon floor. A case full of books stood in one corner of the room. A framed map on one wall caught Gordon's eye. He managed to edge closer to it as McKenzie and Stewart engaged in an enthusiastic discussion of the homeland they shared and how much they missed it. The location of Fort Union was prominently marked on the map, near the apex of the great arch marking the course of the Missouri River, and Gordon was astonished to see just how far he was from St. Louis at this moment, not to mention New Orleans. He had indeed succeeded in putting many hundreds of miles between him and Lorine—and much to his amazement he realized then that several days had passed since he had given her a thought. What an extraordinary turn of events! He was no longer the spellbound captive of the quadroon beauty's spell. A twinge of regret remained, but nothing like the torment he had suffered previously.

It came time for Gordon to be introduced to the King of the Missouri, and Stewart identified him as a fellow Scotsman notwithstanding the fact that he'd had the grand misfortune of having been born and raised in Ireland. McKenzie laughed and said Gordon looked none the worse for such an awful experience.

McKenzie's young aide, James Archdale Hamilton, was there, and it was he who poured and served brandy to all present with the exception of Vasquez, who insisted on a dose of raw whiskey instead. Hamilton was a slender, polished, and very English fellow—he looked altogether out of place here on the wild frontier in his doeskin britches and swallowtail coat. But he was fiercely loyal to McKenzie, was possessed of a keen business acumen, and could be as ruthless as his boss if need be. It was rumored that he had changed his name and fled England one step ahead of the authorities, though no one knew what sort of misdeed might have prompted his hasty change of venue. Some speculated that he had embezzled large sums of money from the Bank of London. Others guessed he had engaged in an illicit dalliance with the wife of a powerful member of the House of Lords, had been caught in flagrante delicto, an indiscretion requiring his prompt departure. He seemed to Gordon like an altogether personable sort of fellow. As did McKenzie, for that matter, in spite of all the uncomplimentary things he had heard about the autocratic chief of the Upper Missouri Outfit from the RMFC men with whom he had crossed the plains.

The brandy burned like fire in Gordon's throat, but he didn't really mind. It tasted much better than the raw whiskey he had occasionally sampled in past weeks. Coupled with the warmth from the crackling fire, the brandy seemed to instill in him a sense of complacency. And though he found himself in the den of the lion, so to speak—Kenneth McKenzie was the most ardent and dangerous foe the Rocky Mountain Fur Company had ever faced, and that included the entire Blackfoot Nation—there was nothing in the conversation going on around him that gave Gordon cause for alarm. McKenzie treated them all like long-lost friends. He listened to Campbell speak of the company's experiences during the trek out from St. Louis, and relayed what he had been told by Milton Sublette about Sublette's adventures coming up the Missouri River. He commented that there had been no major Indian trouble during the summer and fall, and that he hoped Campbell and Sublette would be able to get their post established before the snows came, observing that they were cutting it a little fine, in his humble opinion.

"Of course," he added pleasantly, holding out his empty snifter for Hamilton to refill, "you realize that you are doomed to failure. I am afraid we've got the upper hand now. Mr. Astor's goal is to have the beaver trade all to himself, and like it or not that day is fast approaching. By my reckoning we marketed two, perhaps three times the plews you Rocky Mountain boys did last season. Wouldn't you agree, Jim?"

Hamilton nodded. "Probably closer to three times, sir."

Smug, McKenzie beamed at Campbell. "So you see, the smart thing to do would be to join up with us. The Upper Missouri Outfit has need of experienced men. And we pay quite well, if I do say so myself."

"I can't speak for the others," replied Campbell, "but Hell will freeze over before I join the American Fur Company, McKenzie. I prefer to be my own boss. I've never worked for someone else's wages my whole life and I'm not about to start now."

"You don't own the mountains," added Vasquez coldly, "and you never will. You can't stop us from trapping beaver."

"No, I can't. But my friends the Blackfeet could."

"Is that a threat?" asked Campbell, bristling.

"Certainly not." McKenzie was shocked, or at least pretended to be. "But now that we have a peace treaty with the Blackfeet, the only white men left for them to hunt are, regrettably, Rocky Mountain men."

"Tell your savage allies to leave us alone," said Campbell. "They'll listen to you."

McKenzie shook his head. "You overestimate my influence with them. We pay a steep price to get them to leave our own people be. They don't do so out of any respect for me. So, I will repeat my offer. Join us." He glanced at Stewart. "What do you say, Captain? The company could use a good man like you. A born leader."

Stewart smiled. "I'm afraid I can't accept, though I thank you for the kind invitation. But Mr. Campbell and his colleagues have shown me every kindness, and it would be boorish of me to avail myself of your hospitality any further."

McKenzie shrugged. "Your loyalty is misplaced, Captain, but it does you honor." He glanced at Gordon. "I suppose it goes without saying that you share Captain Stewart's sentiments, young man."

"Yes, it does," was Gordon's ready answer. "And I most certainly do."

"My friend has been an underdog from birth, you might say," added Stewart. "He is not inclined to change."

"Well, then, I wish all of you the best of luck. While the task assigned to me is to put the Rocky Mountain Fur Company out of business, please know that I do not wish any of you ill will."

That night they camped near Fort Union, intending to get an early start in the morning, secure in the knowledge that they would reach their final destination on the morrow. Stewart questioned the wisdom of remaining so near the enemy during the night, but Campbell assured him that McKenzie wouldn't try anything underhanded. "He's dangerous and cunning, but he considers himself a genuine gentleman, and holds honor dear. That's not to say some of his Indian friends might not try to steal a few horses, but if it happens it won't be on McKenzie's orders."

"I see," said Stewart. "As long as we are his guests we're safe."

"We are safer tonight, I reckon, then we will ever be again."

"McKenzie's got plenty of nerve," growled Vasquez, agitating a chew of tobacco in his mouth as he spoke. "Askin' us to join up with him! And he must take us for fools if he expects us to believe he means us no ill will. But I ain't afraid of him or his Blackfoot pals. They cain't stop us. Never have and never will."

"I wish I could be so sure," said Campbell, somber in tone and expression. "McKenzie's got us by the short hairs and he knows it. The American Fur Company is pushing us out of the fur trade slowly but surely. I just don't know how much longer we can hang on, frankly."

"Well, I'll never join 'em," vowed Vasquez, "and I doubt many of the other boys will either, no matter how bad it gets. We'll just go back to bein' free trappers."

That evening several Indians and some of McKenzie's men from the fort strolled into camp. They seemed friendly enough, but Gordon and the others could tell that they had ulterior motives. The Indians were gauging their chances of stealing something. Gordon was reminded that to an Indian theft was not a crime but rather a game devoid of moral consequences. It would be a great coup for a brave if he managed to make off with a knife or a rifle or an unattended horse. But Campbell and his veterans were not going to be caught napping. They gave their Indian visitors no opportunities to practice their light-fingered skills. As for McKenzie's men, they were here to get a closer look at the goods the company was carrying. It was McKenzie who wanted to know, they would report back to him.

No one got much sleep that night. Campbell posted extra guards on the cavallard, the mule picket lines, and the packs. When Gordon finally did roll up in his blankets the night proved so bitterly cold that he could get precious little rest. At daybreak they were on the move. The snow flurries continued all morning long. Early that afternoon they reached the spot Sublette had chosen for the site of the Rocky Mountain Fur Company's first permanent post. The sound of ringing axes carried on the brittle winter air. The site was on high ground on the south side of the river, near a grove of cottonwoods and elms in a hollow where a creek joined the river. Sublette's men were already hard at work felling the timber. Mule teams dragged the logs up the slope to the construction site, where another crew notched the logs destined for the walls of a dozen cabins. More men were busy erecting the outer stockade wall. The work came to a standstill for a brief and hearty reunion. But Campbell wasted no time putting his own men to work.

While Stewart and a handful of others were sent out to do some hunting, Gordon was handed an ax and dispatched to the grove. Though weary, he didn't really mind the labor. At least the activity kept him warm.

And he was inspired to greater exertion by the steadily plummeting temperature as well as the realization that the sooner the post was finished the sooner he would find shelter, a warm berth in a cabin where he could idle away the long winter months. After the eventful trek from St. Louis, the prospect of a lengthy hibernation was kind of appealing. Little did he know at the time that his first winter in the wild country would be anything but uneventful.

IV.

They had the stockade and four long cabin barracks up in no time at all, every man save those guarding the cavallard or out hunting laboring from dawn to dusk at the task. The hunting crews were charged with bringing in as much meat as possible. This was smoked over slow fires and placed in one of two stone-walled buildings inside the stockade. The other stone structure was used for storing powder, shot, and trade rifles, kept under lock and key. Gordon would later learn why. The rest of the trade goods were stacked in the four barracks.

Several days after Gordon's arrival, the skies cleared and the temperature rose a little, melting the blanket of snow that lay upon the land. As the clouds broke apart and drifted away, he got his first good look at the Shining Mountains he had heard so much about. Several days' journey away, they rose in the distance like jagged blue teeth capped with white. Even that far away Gordon was impressed by their magnificence. He had never seen mountains like this before, and he desperately wanted a closer look. So did Stewart. Together they went to Campbell and asked him if they could engage, as the Scotsman put it, in a "little excursion."

Campbell thought it over carefully. "I'm not one to tell a man what he can or can't do. But a word of warning. The weather seems fair enough today, but in this country it can take a turn for the worse before you know what's happening. I reckon neither one of you has seen a blue norther the likes of which we'll have before too many days are passed. I've known it to get so cold it'll freeze a horse stone cold dead in its tracks. You don't want to get caught out in the open in that kind of weather, I can tell you."

Campbell went on to say that at least they probably wouldn't run into Indian trouble this late in the season. By now the tribes would be in their winter quarters.

When they heard that Stewart and Gordon were taking a sightseeing tour into the mountains, most of the veterans in the company just shook their heads. They were quite content to settle in at the outpost and wait out the winter. But Larpenteur, the French-born scion of a wealthy Baltimore family, and Harrison, the son of the famous Indian-fighting governor of Indiana Territory, wanted to go along. At the last minute Campbell prevailed on Louis Vasquez to go, too. "That way," Campbell told Vasquez, "if something happens, at least there'll be one man in the bunch that knows what to do." Vasquez wasn't thrilled at the prospect of babysitting four greenhorns, but he did what Campbell asked of him.

The five of them set out at daybreak the next morning, with a pair of supply-laden mules trailing behind on long leads, and Vasquez told Campbell that if they weren't back in a fortnight they wouldn't be back at all, most likely. After riding all day Gordon took a long look at the still-distant mountains and decided they didn't look one bit closer than they had the day before. He was cold clean through. The sky had been clear all day, but the sun didn't seem to have any heat, and when the sun went down so did the temperature— sharply. They scoured a rocky ravine for deadwood, built fires in shallow holes, covered the glowing coals with dirt, and spread their blankets over the fireholes. A little heat came up through the layer of dirt to warm them as they slept. The next morning they found a nearby creek frozen from bank to bank. Melting ice over a fire, they made thick, strong coffee, dined on two-day-old biscuits and jerked buffalo meat. Harrison commented that he wasn't sure this excursion had been such a good idea after all. Vasquez said he would be glad to go back to the post if the others were so inclined. But Stewart shook his head. "Go back if you like, chaps. I'm going on." Gordon decided he wasn't ready to give up on the mountains just yet, either, though he allowed that one more night as cold as the last might well serve to change his mind on that score. Harrison and Larpenteur agreed to press on. Annoyed by their mule-headedness, Vasquez just grunted, spat tobacco juice into the fire, and said nothing.

When he had occasion to think back on that morning's campfire conversation, Gordon would wonder how different his life might have been had the decision been made to return to the outpost.

It was sharp-eyed Vasquez who saw the wagons first, about a mile north of them, mere black specks on the dun-colored plain. At that distance Gordon couldn't be sure what those specks were, but Vasquez was sure, and he was perplexed, too. What were wagons doing way out here? As they drew closer they saw movement around the wagons, and then a sharp but faint cracking noise could be heard, followed a second later by a loud buzzing sound, and then Harrison let out a yelp of pain and toppled out of his saddle. "Damn fool's shootin' at us!" yelled Vasquez, and vaulted off his horse to go to the fallen man's side. Harrison sat up, wincing, and reached under his buffalo coat to feel his side.

"I could've sworn I was hit," he said shakily.

Vasquez picked the misshapen ball out of the buffalo coat. "You were. Lucky for you it warn't a Plains rifle that fool's usin', and that he's nearer to half a mile away than a quarter."

"Why is he shooting at us?" asked Larpenteur.

"Probably thinks we're Injuns. Can't tell otherwise at this distance, with the sun behind us and all."

Stewart was the only one among them who hadn't bothered getting off his horse; noticing this, Vasquez told him to step down.

"I've been fired at by a regiment of Bonaparte's Old Guard at one hundred yards, without effect," said Stewart mildly. "It isn't worth the effort."

"You must be tired of livin'," opined Vasquez. "Else you put way too much stock in your relationship with Lady Luck."

Stewart just laughed. "Not tired of living. Just tired. Charles, loan me your handkerchief."

Larpenteur brandished one of his white linen handkerchiefs, which Stewart tied to the barrel of his rifle, creating a makeshift flag of truce. "Wait here," suggested the Scotsman.

"No, I'm coming with you," said Gordon, and jumped back into his saddle.

As they drew within a few hundred yards of the wagons Gordon noticed two things: one of the wagons had been partially burned, and there were no oxen or mules or horses anywhere to be seen. As they got closer he spotted a man with a rifle crouched behind the burned wagon; then the man came out into the open and threw his rifle down and started running toward them, shouting something.

"What's he saying?" Stewart asked Gordon.

"Sounds like 'hallelujah' to me."

"Look there."

Three other people emerged from behind the other wagon, two women and a man, the latter shouldering another rifle.

When the first man reached them he clung to the bridle on Stewart's buckskin, breathing heavily. The buckskin shied, but the man wouldn't let go. Gordon figured he was in his forties, maybe fifties—a full beard perhaps made him look older than he really was. He had small cold blue eyes and his face—what Gordon could see of it—was deeply etched. His shoulders were narrow, his legs long, and he had a potbelly; his head seemed to be too large for the rest of his body. It was as though God had put him together with disparate parts that could not be assembled in any sort of acceptable symmetry.

"Praise the Lord!" the man cried out. "He has delivered us. A Divine Hand guided you to us, His lost and forlorn children."

"You very nearly delivered our friend back there—to the Pearly Gates," said Gordon. "You ought not shoot at someone until you know who he is."

"I thought you were the savages, returning to finish us off."

"You've had Indian trouble, then," said Stewart.

"They attacked our camp yesterday morning. Ran off all the stock. We held them off all day, but they came back last night and burned one of the wagons."

"Well, you're safe now," said Stewart, and introduced himself. "And this is my friend, Gordon Hawkes. We are with a band of good fellows who call themselves the Rocky Mountain Fur Company. We've built a post two days east of here. We'll take you there."

The man shook Stewart's extended hand. "I am the Reverend Marcus Hancock, sir. Come, and I will introduce you to the others—my wife and daughter and my associate, Jonathan Miller."

"I take it you are a missionary," surmised Stewart.

"I am indeed. The Methodist Mission Board has charged me with the noble task of saving the souls of the heathen in Oregon. I have found myself called to be the instrument of their salvation."

"And Mr. Miller. Is he a missionary, as well?"

"He is a layman, but a good and decent soul. A God-fearing man, though he lacks ordainment."

"You were bound for Oregon, you say?" asked Gordon. "You won't get there any time soon. That's west of these mountains, and you'll have to wait for spring to make the crossing."

"If we must wait then it is God's will."

Reaching the wagons, Hancock introduced Gordon

and Stewart to his wife, Letitia, and daughter, Eliza. Letitia was a stern-faced, matronly woman with iron gray hair pulled severely back in a tight bun. Her black dress, covered with dust, was gray—in fact, even her complexion was ashen. Gordon's first impression of her was of a woman whose very personality was as colorless as her appearance. She was as undemonstrative as her husband had been effusive in greeting Gordon and Stewart. Sparing them but an ambivalent glance, she put down her rifle and proceeded to go through what remained of the contents of the burned-out wagon.

Hancock's daughter was a willowy girl of about fifteen years, pale in complexion and shy by nature. She peered at the strangers with big blue eyes half hidden behind a veil of blond hair so pale it looked almost white. Gunpowder smudges on her cheeks made them appear even more hollow than they really were. She wore a drab gingham dress that hung like a sack on her slender frame.

Jonathan Miller, Hancock's associate, was a square-built, square-jawed man in his late twenties. His shirt-sleeve was bloodstained; a crude dressing had been secured around the upper portion of his arm. He explained that he had taken an arrow but that the wound wasn't serious.

Vasquez came up with Larpenteur and Harrison, the latter still visibly shaken by his brush with death. Taking a look at the arrows that jutted from the wagons and the ground all about, Vasquez concluded that the Indians who had attacked the missionaries had been Blackfeet. Hancock and Miller agreed that there had been about a dozen of them. Miller was certain they had killed at least one of the attackers, and wounded several more. Vasquez rode a wide circuit around the wagons, and came back to announce that in his judgment the Blackfeet had been on their way home, heading north, ending an excursion into the nearby mountains looking for a Crow village to hit—one more raid before winter set in.

"What I cain't figure," he said, speaking to Hancock, "is how you folks got this far without a guide. I wouldn't give a squirrel's tail for your chances of findin' your way to Oregon through the high country without somebody who knew the way."

"We had a guide," explained Hancock. "He was a half-breed Flathead Indian, a young fellow Dr. Jason Lee brought back East after his visit to this country. Dr. Lee vouched for him. However, a few weeks ago he simply abandoned us without warning. We decided to trust in the Almighty God and push on."

Vasquez grunted, and Gordon thought he knew exactly what the gnarled mountain man was thinking— that God looked out for fools and little children.

Gordon, Stewart, and the others agreed that they would have to cut short their trip to the mountains and return the Hancocks and Jonathan Miller to the outpost. Marcus and Letitia refused to leave their belongings—those that had not been destroyed in the burning wagon—so a makeshift sled was made of slats from the wagon sides. Trunks and valises were strapped to the sled using lengths of harness, and more harness was used to secure the sled to Harrison's horse. Everyone but Harrison would ride double, and Vasquez assigned Eliza Hancock to Gordon. Lifting her onto the sorrel behind him, Gordon noticed that she was light as a feather. Just skin and bones, really. When he told her to put her arms around him and hold on tight she shyly complied. Gordon glanced up and saw the disapproving way Letitia Hancock was looking at him. He felt like laughing. Eliza's mother didn't have a thing to worry about where he was concerned; he wasn't in the least attracted to the skinny waif who rode with him as they turned eastward, heading home to the company's Missouri River outpost.

CHAPTER 5

I.

By the time they got back to the outpost two mornings later, Gordon had learned a lot about Marcus Hancock and his wife—in fact, he knew more about them and their goals than he really wanted to know. Hancock was, after all, a very gregarious man; he talked at great length over the campfire that night, and Harrison and Stewart were too polite not to appear interested in what he had to say, while Larpenteur—the Lord only knew why—seemed genuinely curious to know all there was to know about the Hancocks and the mission that had brought them out West. Gordon noticed that Larpenteur was also keenly interested in Eliza. He smiled at her every chance he got, and Gordon caught him gazing raptly at the girl on a number of occasions. So did Letitia Hancock, for that matter, and she kept an eagle eye on the young Baltimore blade. Larpenteur had been a real lady's man back home and he had made no secret of the fact that he missed the company of the young ladies. On the first night of their trek back to the post, he asked Gordon to take Miller, who was riding with him, on the second day of travel, so that he might play host to Eliza. Gordon didn't really care, but he decided to string Larpenteur along just to see him squirm a little, and declined to make the switch. It was all in good fun—he had no animosity toward Larpenteur—but Larpenteur wasn't the least bit amused. He immediately assumed that Gordon was a potential rival for the attentions of Eliza Hancock. Of course, nothing could have been further from the truth; nonetheless, Larpenteur's childish behavior annoyed Gordon and he refused to tell Larpenteur so.

Hancock had been born in New York, the son of a minister, and had been ordained at an early age, for he had never wanted to do aught but spend his life in the service of the Lord. Such was his calling, and his passion for the task of saving souls had not waned, even after ten years in the saddle as a traveling preacher in Ohio and Indiana, participating in dozens of backwoods camp meetings. He had met and married Letitia in Ohio's Western Reserve, a devout woman in her own right, who had leaped at the chance to go west to minister to the Indians when the Methodist Mission Board made the offer to Hancock. Hancock confessed he had hesitated before accepting, out of concern for his daughter's welfare. The frontier was no place for a frail girl like Eliza. But Letitia had persuaded him. "Our duty to God comes first," she said, explaining it to Gordon and Stewart and the others, "before our own selfish desires." Gordon couldn't figure out how concern for one's own daughter could qualify as selfishness. "If we put ourselves or our child before God we have sinned," she added. "The Lord saw fit to give us our own lives. But does that mean we should shirk our duty to save ourselves? We are the instruments of His will, and that is the only purpose to life, after all." At her husband's urging she sang a hymn, and Gordon was surprised by the richness of her voice.

> In the deserts let me labor,
> On the mountains let me tell
> How He died, the blessed Savior,
> To redeem the world from Hell,
> Let me hasten far in heathen lands to dwell.

So it was that Hancock and his family had traveled to St. Louis last spring, there to meet a man named Parker, who had spent several years as a missionary to the Osage tribe. Parker had made arrangements for them to journey up the Missouri aboard one of the American Fur Company's riverboats, but the Hancocks were delayed and missed the boat. Parker encouraged them to wait until summer, when another boat was scheduled to make the trip upriver to Fort Union, but Hancock was far too impatient for that, and used some of the Mission funds at his disposal to purchase the wagons and oxen teams. Parker introduced them to Jonathan Miller and to the Flathead Indian guide, and they were off. Their progress was slowed by late spring rains that made the rivers swell, and then Letitia had become so ill that Hancock dared not travel for fear it would be the death of her. Then their guide had abandoned them, and the Blackfeet had attacked. Through it all, though, Hancock had trusted in the Lord Almighty to deliver them.

The arrival of the Hancocks—at least the two females—presented Campbell and Sublette with a bit of a problem. With fifty men and a considerable quantity of trade goods to be stored, there wasn't a lot of room for unexpected guests within the walls of the new post. A barracks full of rowdy, unwashed, and profane mountain men was no fit place for ladies, especially the wife and daughter of a man of God. It was decided that another cabin would be built, a small one—with most of the men working at the task it would require but a day or two to erect the structure. The men didn't mind the extra labor. It was something to do. A few of them were already getting bored and restless, even though Campbell was still sending out hunting parties on a daily basis.

In the interim, blankets were hung from rope to block out a corner of one of the barracks, and it was here that Letitia and Eliza Hancock spent their first two nights at the post while the cabin was being constructed. Marcus Hancock and Jonathan Miller mixed with the rest of the men in the barracks—which happened to be the one to which Gordon had been assigned, along with Stewart. Gordon found it somewhat amusing to watch the mountain men try their best to mind their manners, conscious of the tender sensibilities of the womenfolk present—present though rarely seen, as Letitia kept to her partitioned corner, and kept her daughter close at hand. Marcus Hancock, on the other hand, proceeded to save souls, or try to. His attempts to convert the trappers—the most heathen and scoundrelous crew one was ever likely to find— proved another source of amusement for Gordon. Until, that is, Hancock turned on him.

"Have you been washed in the blood of the lamb?" the missionary asked him.

"I was baptized, if that's what you mean."

"And do you know your Scripture?"

"I know a little of it. My mother used to read to me from the Bible."

"And have you seen the Light?"

Gordon was no longer amused. In fact, he was quickly becoming annoyed. "I have not," he said tersely. "Truth be told, I'm not even sure that there *is* a God."

Hancock's eyes blazed. He lifted his hands skyward, Bible clutched tightly in one of them. "Then indeed, Lord, here is a soul I must redeem to You."

"Don't bother," said Gordon. "If there is a God, He has no interest in me."

"You must have faith, or you will be condemned to burn in the fiery torments of everlasting Hell."

"I've been to Hell," said Gordon, his blood running cold as he remembered his voyage aboard the *Penelope*—the epidemic of ship fever that had claimed his father and transformed the emigrants' hold into a pit of death and despair, the opium-induced madness of his mother, the terror-filled weeks he had suffered as the victim of sadistic Captain Warren. Gordon hadn't thought about God much, and now that Hancock had brought up the subject he realized that his experiences aboard the *Penelope* had been such as to make him doubt that a merciful Almighty presided over earthly affairs.

"Take care what you say," admonished the preacher. "The Lord sees and hears all. He will show no mercy to those who scorn him."

"He has shown me no mercy," was Gordon's bitter

reply. "You're wasting your time, Mr. Hancock. Just leave me be."

The next day Gordon was posted to guard duty. It was his least favorite thing to do. He would have much preferred to join the day's hunting party, or thrown in with the rest of the company as they finished up the small cabin. Instead, he was relegated to the west wall of the stockade, pacing the length of the barracks roof and trying to stay alert and scan the brown, lifeless plains. As usual, it was bitterly cold, and after an hour on the wall, buffeted by icy winds that roared down from the north, he was very nearly numb clean through.

Eliza came up so quietly that she startled him, and he realized, abashed, that he'd been gazing at those distant mountains, daydreaming. Some lookout he'd turned out to be! She held a tin cup filled with steaming hot coffee in her hands, and as she held it out to him he noticed how long and slender her fingers were, her skin almost translucent, so that the veins beneath it looked blue, as deep as her eyes. She wore a shawl around her shoulders, but she was barefoot, and Gordon wondered if the poor girl even owned a pair of shoes.

"I brought this for you," she said, and it struck him that this was the first time he had heard her speak. Her voice was very soft, and had a lyrical quality to it.

"For me?" he asked lamely, and looked around, wondering if she had taken coffee to the sentry posted on the far wall.

"Don't you want it?"

"Sure." He put his rifle aside and took the cup with

both hands, so that its warmth could thaw his frozen fingers.

"You need some gloves," she observed.

"And you need some shoes."

"Oh, I have a pair of shoes. But I must make them last. It might be quite a long time before I get another." She glanced over the ramparts at the great wild expanse, and Gordon, watching her eyes, thought he saw some trepidation lurking there, and he felt tremendously sorry for her. This was no place for such a frail creature, and he thought poorly of Marcus Hancock for bringing his daughter out here.

She caught him staring at her, and she turned her head shyly and looked down. "You ought to drink that coffee before it gets cold."

Gordon sipped the coffee, then gave the cup back to her. "Here. Hold this for a minute." She did as he asked, and he shed his blanket coat and draped it over her shoulders, cutting her protest short. "I'm fine," he said. "This weather doesn't bother me." He strove to keep his teeth from chattering as he said it.

She returned the cup to him. "I really ought not to stay. My mother says you are a Godless man, and if she caught me up here talking to you . . . Are you?"

"Godless? I don't know. Maybe I am."

Her gaze was very earnest and forthright. She studied his features for a long moment and shook her head. "No. I don't believe that."

"You ought to be afraid of being anywhere near me," he said. "Isn't that what your mother told you?"

"But I'm not afraid. Especially of you. I've never felt more safe than I do at this moment."

The fact that she was giving him such searching

looks, in spite of her inherent shyness, alarmed Gordon. Could it be that she was—God forbid—infatuated with him? The thought scared him half to death.

"You don't know anything about me," he said briskly, "and believe me, you don't want to."

"But I already know you. You are a brave and decent person."

"I am neither of those things." Gordon was becoming increasingly exasperated. How could he get it across to this girl that he didn't want anybody to get close to him again? That he just wanted to be left alone? That even if he were attracted to her—which he wasn't, particularly—he wouldn't permit himself to get into a situation where he could be hurt. No, he'd had quite enough of that sort of thing to last him a lifetime. Besides, this poor, simple child's attachment to him, if indeed that's what it was, stemmed merely from the fact that he had been one of those who had rescued her, and of all those involved he was the one closest to her age. Yes, that had to be the explanation for her strange behavior. He had shown her a small kindness and she was trying to make something out of it. She probably got little or no affection from her parents—of that Gordon was fairly sure after a few days of observing the Hancock family—which made her all the more desperate for an attachment. So how was he to tell Eliza to leave him be without hurting her feelings?

He didn't have to tell her. Looking away, a pensive expression on her waiflike face, she shrugged out of his coat and gave it back to him.

"I'd better be going," she said, so softly that he could scarcely hear her. "I'm sorry if I bothered you."

"No bother. I mean, you didn't . . ."

But she smiled what was meant to be a brave smile and only half succeeded, and walked away, leaving Gordon with the memory of the hurt in her eyes, and he felt like an absolute heel as he just stood there and watched her go.

II.

The Indians arrived the following day, but the alarm that the sighting elicited was short-lived, as it quickly became apparent that they were not on the warpath. Far from it, in fact. There were women and children in the party, and they had brought all their earthly belongings with them, carried on travois. They pulled up shy of the outpost's walls and one of the warriors rode on ahead. Near the gate he circled his horse several times and then cast his buffalo lance into the frozen earth. Gordon asked Vasquez, who happened to be standing at the parapet beside him, what this performance was supposed to signify, and the old veteran explained that the brave was making it abundantly clear that they had come in peace. Gordon expressed doubt that this should be taken purely on faith. Vasquez quickly put him straight.

"Those be Absaroka Crow, boy, which means that like as not they mean us no harm. You see, the Crow and the Blackfeet are arch enemies. Those two tribes have hated each other for *beaucoup* years. Now they know McKenzie's made a pact with the Blackfoot Nation, and they also know we're no friends of the American Fur Company. The enemy of my enemy is my friend. See what I'm gettin' at?"

Gordon nodded. "But what are they doing here?

What are they up to, then? I remember Mr. Campbell saying all the bands would be in their winter villages by now."

"Reckon we're gonna find out soon enough."

Sublette and Campbell went out to palaver with the Crow warrior. The conversation didn't take long. The partisans returned to the stockade and the warrior rejoined his people. Vasquez left the wall to find out more about what was going on. Gordon stayed where he was, watching the Indians. In short order it became apparent that they had every intention of staying, for in a matter of minutes the squaws and older children were hard at work erecting lodge poles and digging fire pits. This band of Crows was settling down for an extended visit.

Before long Gordon had all the details. The Absaroka had gotten the short end of a falling out with a band of Shoshones who had happened to claim the same valley in yonder mountain range for their winter quarters. It had proven impossible for the two groups to share the valley, and the numerically inferior Crows had been driven out. Worse, they'd lost most of their winter food stores in the process. Knowing that another Absaroka band would have insufficient resources to share with them, these Crows had decided to throw themselves on the mercy of the Rocky Mountain men at the new outpost.

Quick to realize that it was in their best interests to maintain good relations with the Crows—next to the Blackfeet the most powerful tribe in the region—Sublette and Campbell had agreed to let the band make their village in the shadow of the stockade walls. Not that this decision was based solely on considerations of business or High Plains strategy. The Crow women and children were suffering from cold and hunger, and Sublette and Campbell were decent, compassionate men. Which, mused Gordon, might go far toward explaining why they and the Rocky Mountain Fur Company were being bested by McKenzie and his Upper Missouri Outfit; Gordon doubted that humanity ever colored Kenneth McKenzie's decisions.

The band numbered no more than a hundred and twenty souls, with thirty-five men ranked as full-fledged warriors. They erected about twenty-five skin lodges. Their cavallard consisted of nearly two hundred shaggy mountain mustangs. The principal chief of the band was a man named Little Raven, though Gordon would soon learn that the chief's powers were limited unless the band was at war; a council of elders was possessed of a great deal of power, and their words held sway over the members of the band nine times out of ten. Little Raven's influence had dwindled, too, because of the recent debacle in the conflict with the Shoshones.

Many of the men in the company knew a lot about the Crow nation, and from a dozen conversations focused on their new guests Gordon pieced together the story. The earliest white men to visit the High Plains had recorded that the Crows were consistently friendly. Tradition had it that the Crows had advanced up the Yellowstone, pushing the Snake Indians westward. British traders supplied the Snakes and their Flathead allies with guns, allowing those tribes to slow the Crow expansion. Another thing that slowed the Crows was a devastating smallpox epidemic. This epidemic so weakened the Crows that the two tribes—the

River Crows and the Mountain, or Absaroka, Crows—were forced into an alliance to resist a new and formidable enemy. The Blackfeet had been pushing down from the Canadian hinterlands and the threat they posed to all the lesser tribes of the High Plains encouraged the former foes of the Crow tribes—the Snakes, the Bannocks, and the Flatheads—to make their peace with their erstwhile enemies. And though a few clashes had occurred between whites and the Crows, the peace between trappers and the tribes held fast.

Past history, however, did not equate with blind trust, as Gordon soon learned; Sublette and Campbell refused to throw open the gates of the outpost, unwilling to let too many Indians, friendly or no, wander freely within the confines of the stockade. On the other hand, they gave their men the freedom to mingle at will with the Crows in their village—with one caveat. They made it clear that they would tolerate no trouble over women. The men had been celibate for quite a long time now and the Crow maidens were a real temptation.

Another cause for concern from the perspective of the company's leaders was the enthusiasm exhibited by Marcus Hancock for proselytizing these most convenient heathens. In the missionary's opinion it was the Lord who had caused the Crows to be driven from their winter camp and delivered here into his hands. The Crows were accustomed to dealing with mountain men and were familiar with their ways. But how would they react to Hancock, who was a horse of an entirely different color? Campbell and Sublette kept an eagle eye pinned on the Methodist preacher.

Gordon thought it was somewhat comical to watch

Hancock try to convert the Indians. Equally comical was the plight of Louis Vasquez, who had been ordered by Campbell to act as Hancock's interpreter. In this way, reasoned Campbell, he could protect Hancock from himself, for Vasquez was charged with the duty of not translating possibly incendiary remarks by the preacher. Indians could be very touchy about some things, and Hancock didn't know what to say, and not to say, in their presence. This was not a job that Vasquez took much pleasure in, but as usual he did his utmost to carry out his duty, knowing that lives could depend on it.

For himself, Gordon was not all that eager to rub elbows with the Indians. He spent much of his time on the wall, gazing down at the Crow village from a safe distance. He found his ambivalence unusual, and tried to think it through. All he could figure was that it had something to do with his first experience with wild Indians, that night when the Arapahoes had tried to steal horses out of the cavallard—that far-from-pleasant occasion when Gordon, scared out of his wits, had ended up killing an Indian youth. Two times Stewart searched him out; the Scotsman asked that he accompany him into the village. Both times Gordon declined. Perplexed, Stewart remarked that he thought this was what Gordon had been looking forward to all these months. Gordon just shook his head and told the Scotsman to go on without him.

It was on Eliza's account that he finally did venture forth from the outpost. Part of Hancock's performance to draw the attention of the naturally curious Indians was to employ his wife and daughter in the singing of hymns. The singing drew a much larger audience than anything else Hancock could have done—so large an audience, in fact, that Gordon became rather alarmed by the keen interest many of the Crow men took in Eliza. She was quite unlike any woman they had ever seen, and the Indians seemed as beguiled by her yellow hair and pale, translucent skin as they were bewitched by her sweet, clear voice. They closed in around her and touched her hair and peered closely into her deep blue eyes, and while she withstood this unwelcome scrutiny with admirable stoicism, Letitia Hancock became visibly agitated and finally struck one of the braves as he reached out to put his hand on her daughter. The brave jumped back, much offended, and it was Vasquez who stepped quickly into the breach and said something to the warrior that made the Indian laugh, defusing the situation in one deft stroke.

Much to Gordon's dismay, Hancock failed to learn his lesson. A few days later he was back out in the village with his wife and daughter in tow, and Gordon happened to be on the wall again, and he called down to several men in the stockade, telling them to hurry up and find Vasquez because this time Vasquez wasn't with the missionary. Hancock had slipped away from his keeper. The man was a fool, Gordon decided. A gold-plated, first-rate fool, most especially because he couldn't see that the braves gathering around him weren't at all interested in the passages of Scripture he belted out in his best fire-and-brimstone voice, exhorting the copper-skinned sinners to heed the Word and see the Light and save their immortal souls from eternal Hell and damnation. No, the Indian men were drawn like moths to a flame by the presence of Eliza, and this time one warrior stood directly in Hancock's path and put a halt to the missionary's progress through the skin lodges. The Crow put a pile of bearskins at Hancock's feet and then motioned at a pair of horses held by a squaw standing nearby. Finally he gestured at Eliza. At that point one of the trappers, who had joined Gordon on the wall to see what was going on, shook his head with a chuckle.

"I'll be damned," he said. "That buck's tryin' to buy the preacher's daughter. Reckon he's tired of dark-skinned squaws and has a hankerin' to try somethin' different."

Gordon didn't think that was at all amusing. In fact, he had to tamp down an urge to knock the man's teeth down his throat. Instead, he abandoned his post, made the long jump to the ground from the rim of the barracks roof, and was out the gate at a run, a good ten strides ahead of Vasquez and Campbell, who were coming at a dead run.

The Crow brave was becoming agitated because Hancock wasn't responding. The preacher didn't catch on to what was being offered—prime skins and two of the Indian's finest ponies in return for his daughter. So the warrior brushed past him and took hold of Eliza and pulled her toward him as a means of illustrating exactly what it was he wanted, and Letitia let out a cry and started for him, intent on scratching his eyes out, only Gordon got to him first, breaking the Crow's grip on Eliza's arm and giving the man a rude shove.

In the next instant he regretted his rashness, for the Crow warrior's eyes blazed with hot anger and his hand dropped to the knife at his side, and Gordon realized that he might have brought the worst fears of Campbell and Sublette to fruition. But then Vasquez stepped into the middle of the fray and said a few words to the Crow and some of the other warriors who stood nearby looked surprised and laughed. The warrior Gordon had pushed visibly relaxed, and some of the anger left him, with just a residue of resentment as he gave Gordon a long, hard look. Gordon was aware that Letitia had grabbed Eliza and was hustling her toward the stockade, but he kept his attention focused on the warrior.

Vasquez turned to him. "Let's go, Hawkes. It's all over now. Just turn and walk away."

"I don't fancy a knife in the back."

"Won't happen."

"I don't trust this one."

"And he doesn't like you. But that doesn't mean you have to kill each other. It was just a little misunderstanding. Put it behind you."

"I didn't misunderstand anything. I saw what he did and I know what he was after."

"He won't do it again. I told him she was your woman."

Gordon was aghast. "You *what*?"

His reaction brought the glimmer of a smile to the old trapper's face. "I said she belonged to you. That was the only way he would have tolerated what you did. He figures now that you were jealous and just protecting what was yours, and he can understand that."

"I wasn't jealous. That had nothing to do with it."

"Sure, I know that. But he won't accept any other motive for your striking him. Now shut up and come on."

It was no longer a request, and Gordon complied.

Late that day, Marcus Hancock came in search of Gordon and thanked him earnestly for intervening.

"I had no idea what that heathen was after," said the missionary. "Of course I know now. It's quite shocking, how backward they are."

"My guess is they think we're the backward ones," retorted Gordon, still irritated by the day's turn of events. "Take my advice, Mr. Hancock, and go home. This is no place for you or your family. The Indians don't want your religion. They've got one of their own, and from what I've heard they're real happy with it. So just go home before somebody gets hurt."

"I cannot," replied Hancock stiffly. "This is my calling. It is my destiny. If I die while doing God's work, so be it."

Gordon had no more to say to the man. He detested Marcus Hancock, and had no use for him, because the preacher was willing to risk his daughter's life on the altar of his convictions. Hancock and his family would perish. Of that Gordon was certain, and he resolved to wash his hands of the whole affair.

III.

A blizzard came howling down from the north a few days later, blanketing the earth with snow and ice, and for nearly a week everyone huddled in their barracks or skin lodges, waiting out the storm. When at last it had passed and the sun reappeared, several feet of snow had fallen, and the nearby creek and river were covered from bank to bank with ice. Ireland's winters could be pretty severe, but Gordon was convinced that they couldn't compare to this.

He was the brunt of some devilment from his barracks mates as the word spread about what Vasquez had told the Crow warrior regarding his relationship with Eliza Hancock, but he didn't let their remarks get under his skin. He was relieved to see that when Hancock ventured into the Crow village again he did so without his wife or daughter. In fact, Letitia and Eliza stayed in their cabin, and a fortnight passed without Gordon even catching a glimpse of the girl. That suited him just fine. Did she know the details of what had happened? If so, how embarrassed she must be! As for Hancock, he was accompanied, as usual, by Vasquez, and by Jonathan Miller, who had by now fully recovered from his wound. Word got out that Mr. Miller seemed particularly interested in the salvation of the young Indian maidens, but Gordon couldn't say if that was true, and saw no evidence to substantiate it.

The company's horse herd had been brought into the stockade just prior to the norther—once the storm was over they were let out, and every other day or so Gordon and Stewart would ride out to count heads. They never failed to check the timbered hollow, for many of the horses instinctively sought shelter among the trees, and some had taken to eating the bark off the trees. Though the cold made his bones ache down to the marrow, Gordon enjoyed these excursions; after a day or two cooped up in the stockade he would start suffering from a bad case of cabin fever.

It was on one of these forays, just as he reached the trees, that Gordon and his Scottish companion heard a piercing scream of pure terror coming from the direction of the river. They rode to the sound, and upon reaching the embankment were greeted by a sight that made Gordon's skin crawl. The past few days had witnessed a slight warming trend, enough to begin melting the ice on the river. Now Gordon could plainly see that the ice was breaking up into large floes—and he spotted a pair of figures huddled together on one of these rafts of ice. He knew instantly what had transpired. The two Indians had been fishing in the river, cutting holes in the ice for that purpose. They had ventured a bit too far from the bank, and now were trapped on a fragment of ice roughly ten feet in diameter. They had to stay in the center of the floe, for to venture too close to the edge would cause the raft to tilt sharply, spilling them into the freezing waters of the river—and that would spell certain death. As he drew nearer, Gordon could see that it was a woman and a small child, and the woman's shrieks brought many on the run from the stockade and the Crow village. But Gordon wasn't inclined to wait.

"We've got to save them," he told Stewart, dismounting and taking from his saddle the length of rope they sometimes used to "snake out" horses or mules who had floundered in deep drifts of snow. It was a stroke of extreme good fortune that they had the rope, and an idea how to use it had sprung instantly into Gordon's mind. He tied one end of the rope around his waist and tossed the other end to Stewart.

"What are you up to, lad?" asked Stewart.

"You stay as close to the bank as you can. The ice is thickest there."

"Don't be a bloody fool, Gordon. The ice is breaking up. You can't possibly get to them."

"I won't just stand by and do nothing. And I don't believe you're so inclined, either."

"Wait for help."

"There's no time. Are you with me?"

Stewart grinned, shaking his head. "But of course."

Without hesitation Gordon proceeded out onto the ice. The rope was about forty feet long, and Stewart remained on the bank as long as he could, but soon the rope was played out completely and Gordon still had a good twenty or thirty feet to go before he could get anywhere near the two Indians stranded on the floe of ice. At that point Stewart had no choice but to venture further out onto the ice, because there was no holding Gordon back. Men and women from the village had reached the edge of the river now, joined by some of the trappers from the post. Campbell and Vasquez slid across the ice to Stewart, and several more men followed, but Campbell kept his wits about him and yelled an order to them to go back. Though the ice was thicker close to the bank there was no way to be certain how much weight it would sustain.

"Hawkes will fall through," predicted Vasquez, grabbing hold of the rope. "The ice is too thin to hold him out that far. Keep a firm grip, Captain Stewart, or you'll be seeing the last of your friend."

"I know," replied the Scotsman. "And then we would have to name a creek or a mountain after him, wouldn't we?"

Vasquez gave him a funny look. He saw that Stewart was trying to mask his concern with gallows humor.

As he neared the edge of the solid ice, Gordon could see that the thinner ice at midstream was breaking up. In a matter of moments the floe upon which the two Indians huddled in frozen terror would break free from its constraints and be pushed downstream by the current. Seconds later, he was certain, the mother and child would be plunged into the frigid waters, and their fate would be sealed. Time was working against him. But how could he reach them? He could see in a single despairing glance that he could not. If he tried to leap across to the raft of ice it would tip so sharply beneath his weight that the river would surely claim him. If he fell in, and the current swept him under the solid ice—well, there was no profit in dwelling on the horrible death that would await him in that event.

"Let go of the child!" he shouted at the woman, gesturing madly to make himself understood. "Let the child jump!" The woman crouched in place, huddling the youngster to her bosom, and staring with uncomprehending and fear-haunted eyes at Gordon. "For God's sake, it's his only chance!" yelled Gordon. "Let him go!" He looked around, saw Vasquez behind him, and was about to call on the veteran trapper to interpret his words when Vasquez, realizing what Gordon was trying to do and understanding the problem, shouted at the woman in her own tongue. She hesitated, looked about her, and saw that the only hope for her child was to do as she was told. Sobbing, she released the boy and gave him his orders. He, too, hesitated, but she spoke more sternly, more calmly, and the boy left her side, half sliding, half running to the edge of the ice floe. He was six or seven years old, Gordon guessed, and weighed no more than fifty pounds, but fifty pounds was enough to begin to tip the raft of ice, and in the instant before he could make his jump across the four or five feet of water that separated him from Gordon he slipped and fell and slid straight into the river, and Gordon heard the mother's scream, a sound that seemed to slice through his brain like a knife. The boy bobbed to the surface, gasping, and Gordon, knowing it was the only recourse, jumped in to get him.

The coldness of the water forced the air out of Gordon's lungs as he went under. Gripped by panic, he flailed to the surface, collected his wits, reached out just as the Indian boy went under again, and grabbed hold of an arm. He tried to lift the boy over the lip of the solid ice pack, but his strength was failing him. He couldn't seem to control his spasming body. Then he realized that someone else was in the water—the boy's mother. Together they heaved the boy over onto the ice, and Campbell was there, clutching the boy and flinging him shoreward, so that he slid a good twenty feet toward where Vasquez and Stewart were pulling on the rope connected to Gordon's waist. Campbell took hold of the rope, too, and Gordon felt himself being hauled out of the river's grasp, but the Indian woman was going under, and Gordon hooked an arm around her and brought her out with him. Vasquez rushed forward, and swept the half-conscious woman up in his arms, taking her to dry land. Gordon lay on the ice, his body convulsing uncontrollably, and through a darkening haze he dimly saw Campbell leaning over him. Gordon tried to say thanks, but his jaws were locked. Oddly, a sensation of warmth began to spread up through his legs. "Hang on, Hawkes," said Campbell. "Just hang on," and as the partisan began dragging him across the ice, away from the churning maw of the cheated river, Gordon gave up and let the blackness claim him.

IV.

When he came to he was lying on a bed made of bundles of trade blankets, set up close by the fireplace in his barracks, and he was covered with more blankets that were tucked tightly up around him, and all of it topped off with a buffalo robe. This, combined with the heat from a roaring blaze in the hearth, was the reason he was sweating buckets. Groaning, he tried to throw off the covers. But he was too weak to accomplish even so simple a task. He had absolutely no strength in his arms. It was all he could do to raise his head and look about him. The first face he saw belonged to Eliza Hancock. Behind her stood a dozen men, among them Stewart and Vasquez. The latter grinned and expectorated a stream of tobacco juice into the fire.

"There now," exclaimed Vasquez. "Didn't I tell you? He's tougher than my ol' Flathead squaw's homemade biscuits."

Stewart looked vastly relieved. "I thought you were a 'gone beaver,' as they say in these parts, Gordon. It gave me a scare when I saw you go into that river."

It was only then that Gordon remembered what had transpired. "The boy and his mother. Are they . . . ?"

"They're laid up same as you," said Vasquez. "One minute in water that cold and you commence to dyin'. But they'll be fit as a fiddle 'fore long. Same as you. You're the big hero, Hawkes. In one swoop you done made up for all the damage that damned preacher's done with our Crow friends. Sorry, miss, don't mean to talk bad about your pa in your presence."

"You're just the soul of tact, aren't you, Vasquez?" admonished Stewart.

"I'm not offended," said Eliza. "My father has his shortcomings. That I freely admit. Chief among them is his desire to save the souls of those who have not been introduced to the saving grace of our Lord Jesus."

Vasquez was chastened into silence.

Eliza helped Gordon sit up. He clung tightly to the blankets that covered him now, for he had come to realize that every stitch of his clothing had been removed. She held a tin cup half filled with steaming hot coffee, and he sipped from it. The pungent brew went far to restore him. He thanked her, and she answered with a shy smile that for some reason made Gordon a little nervous.

A moment later Campbell appeared, pushing through the throng of men attending to the new hero in their midst. Campbell was wearing a bemused expression as he looked at Gordon.

"I've got an important bit of news for you, Hawkes. So happens that the boy you saved was the youngest son of Little Raven, the chief. That woman was one of his squaws."

"A chief's son!" exclaimed one of the other mountain men. "Hawkes, you done made friends for life with the whole goldurned Crow nation."

"Little Raven wants to show you his appreciation as soon as you're up and around," said Campbell.

Gordon shook his head. "No reason to make a big show of it. I simply did what any other person would have done."

The mountain men exchanged glances, and Gordon thought maybe he was wrong—maybe some of these men wouldn't have risked their lives to save the woman and the child. Wouldn't have because, after all, they were only Indians.

"You've got to accept whatever he gives you as a token of his gratitude," explained Campbell. "You would insult him were you to do otherwise."

Gordon sighed. "These people are awfully sensitive about everything, aren't they?"

"Cheer up, lad," said Stewart. "You'll probably get a pile of plews and a good horse or two for your trouble."

"Well, he's entirely too weak to go anywhere or do anything right now," said Eliza, with more authority than anyone present had ever imagined she possessed. She turned to confront the knot of burly trappers, a frail and feminine Horatio holding the bridge that gave access to her patient. "He needs rest and quiet now, if you please."

Campbell glanced at the others. "You heard the young lady, you big monkeys. Go on about your business. Macawley, Smith, put up some blankets along here so that our hero can have some privacy."

Gordon winced at the word "hero." The last thing he wanted was this kind of attention.

The blankets were put up, hanging from ropes secured to the log rafters, in a fashion similar to what had been done to give Eliza and her mother some privacy when they had stayed in the barracks prior to the construction of their cabin. Gordon wondered idly why Letitia Hancock was letting her daughter act as his nurse, but he didn't think about it too much, because in no time at all he had drifted off into exhausted sleep.

He slept around the clock, waking groggy and

aching from head to toe. It was the middle of the day and the barracks were virtually empty. Three men sat on some blankets playing a Mexican shell game, waging twists of tobacco and rifle cartridges. Gordon was astonished to find that Eliza was still with him. She sat with her back against the wall near the fireplace, a blanket around her shoulders, knees drawn up, head back, eyes closed—and at first he thought she was sleeping, but when she heard his muffled groan as he sat up her eyes snapped open and she got quickly to her feet.

"How do you feel?"

"Better. I think I'll live."

She beamed. Adding a piece of wood to the faltering fire, she prodded the fire with a stick, and Gordon watched her, studying her profile, and the way she brushed her long pale hair back away from her face, curling it behind an ear, and then she glanced at him, caught him staring, and smiled. "Would you like some coffee?"

"God no. But I could eat a horse. I'm starving."

"Good. That means you're going to be fine."

"Of course I'll be fine."

"You had a touch of fever. I was afraid you might catch pneumonia."

"Shoot, a little swim never hurt anybody."

She laughed at that. "I'll bring you something to eat."

Gordon was finishing off the biscuits and venison stew Eliza had produced for him when Campbell and Stewart, having heard that he was awake, came to see him. After asking how he felt, Campbell reminded him that Little Raven was still waiting to see him. Gordon surrendered to the inevitable.

"Let's get it over with, then," he said.

"Fine. Then you're up to going into the Crow village today?"

"I guess."

"I'll pass the word on to Little Raven."

Stewart lingered after Campbell's departure. The Scotsman glanced speculatively at Eliza and then smiled wryly at Gordon.

"My boy, you've got the luck of the Irish."

"What do you mean by that?" asked Gordon crossly. The prospect of having to meet with Little Raven had put him in a poor mood.

"It means not every man can find an angel of mercy when he needs one. I daresay our friend Larpenteur is wishing he had been the one to jump into that river."

"I would have gladly given him the honor."

"That's what you get for being such a hero, lad."

"I'll know better next time."

"No you won't," said Stewart, and with a slight bow to Eliza took his leave.

Eliza brought Gordon his clothes, a neatly folded bundle.

"Eliza," he said as she turned to go.

"Yes?"

"Thank you."

She held his gaze for a moment—then blushed suddenly and fled.

A few hours later, Campbell and Vasquez came to get him. The day was nearly done; as Gordon left the barracks he was startled to see that the sun was setting behind shreds of purple clouds, lending a rosy glow to the blue-shadowed snow that covered the ground. Stewart and Harrison and a number of other men joined them at the outpost's gate. Leaving the stockade, the party marched into the nearby Crow village, in the center of which a huge bonfire was blazing. It seemed to Gordon that the Crows had to have leveled the grove of trees located in the nearby hollow just to feed this immense conflagration. It seemed, too, that the entire village, every man, woman, and child, from the infants to the ancients, had gathered round the blaze. Gordon's arrival was greeted with a great uproar, and the principal chief, Little Raven, stepped forward to escort Gordon to the place of honor in a ring of men, warriors and elders together, that encircled the fire. As Gordon settled on a few layers of buffalo robes spread over the snowy slush that covered the ground, Little Raven took his place to Gordon's right while Vasquez positioned himself to Gordon's left, prepared to fulfill his customary duty as interpreter. Stewart and Campbell and the others gathered around behind Gordon, and more skins and blankets were provided for them to sit on.

When all were in place, Little Raven rose to address the crowd. Vasquez translated for Gordon's benefit. The chief announced that they were gathered to honor a brave man, a friend to the Absaroka Crow, the one who had without regard to his own safety saved the chief's youngest son as well as the boy's mother from the icy embrace of the river. It was a sign, declared Little Raven, that the Great Spirit destined the Absaroka Crow and the Rocky Mountain Fur Company to remain the strongest of allies. Let it be known, said the chief, that the one called Hawkes was now as a son to him, and that, if any harm was ever done to his son, he would not rest until vengeance had been served. The rest of the warriors thereupon loudly and enthusiastically voiced their pledge to act upon Little Raven's vow as though it were their own. The chief then presented Gordon with a beaded belt. Gordon was much impressed by the beauty of the quillwork; the fringed belt was white with blue and red symbols, and Vasquez told him that the symbols would make it clear to all the plains tribes that Gordon was a brother of the Absaroka Crows. "That belt ought to protect you from just about every Injun, 'less he's a Blackfoot, Blood, or Piegan. But then a Blackfoot would kill you with or without that belt." Gordon humbly thanked Little Raven for the gift.

At the chief's gesture, dozens of squaws brought food to the warriors and mountain men circling the great fire. The fare consisted largely of meat—buffalo and deer, some colt and dog—some of it dried, some roasted, some of it in pemmican, and in addition there was plenty of boiled buffalo belly fat, as well as bones to be cracked and harvested of the marrow they contained, and a pasty substance that Gordon found quite good. He learned it was edible roots and berries pounded into a mush. He ate until he thought he would bust a stitch. With a full belly and the heat of the fire, he suddenly became drowsy; soon it was all he could do to keep his eyes open, despite the fact that for the duration of the feast one after another of the warriors would stand before Gordon and Little Raven and launch into a shouting oration punctuated by dramatic gestures. According to Vasquez, the Crow braves were introducing themselves to their new brother, embellishing the introduction with a strong rendition of their exploits in battle or in the hunt. It was all quite entertaining—for a while. Eventually, though, Gordon tired of the spectacle, especially since he couldn't understand a word, and he began to doze off, trying to fend off sleep because he didn't want to offend his hosts. Still, he fervently wished for an end to these festivities so that he could stumble back to his bed next to the fire and sleep for at least a week.

Finally all the introductory performances were over. At Little Raven's command about fifteen Crow maidens clad in long buckskin dresses decorated with elaborate quillwork and adorned with tiny bells entered the circle and proceeded to dance, accompanying themselves with singing while someone nearby beat time on a drum. The maidens circled the fire, each holding on to the waist of the girl in front, and executing in unison a shuffling step. At regular intervals they would break formation and spin completely around and on each of these occasions the men watching would let go with a shout. Then the maidens would slip back into formation and continue their shuffling circuit of the fire. For a few moments at least, Gordon was interested in the performance, but before long he was beginning to nod off again. At least the dance of the maidens, he thought, was more pleasing to the ear and eye than the exhortations and gesticulations of the warriors who had preceded it.

Finally the dance was over, and the maidens came forward to stand in front of Little Raven and Gordon. The chief got to his feet and solemnly spoke to his guest of honor. Vasquez nudged Gordon with an elbow. "He wants you to stand up, younker."

With a weary sigh Gordon got to his feet. Little Raven grasped his right arm just above the wrist, said something briefly in a loud voice which told Gordon that he was speaking to all those present, and then spoke more softly to the maidens. Laughing and giggling, they scattered, leaving only one of their number left standing before Gordon. He thought she was quite possibly the prettiest of the girls, nearly as tall as he, with a narrow waist and graceful carriage, long raven black hair cascading over her shoulders, and framing a heart-shaped face. Her most distinctive feature, in his opinion, were her eyes—very large, dark brown eyes that were bold and inquisitive and, at the moment, piercing in their intensity.

Little Raven said something to her and she stepped forward and extended her left hand, palm up, and as the chief placed Gordon's right hand in hers a shout of acclamation rose up from all the Crows present—such a shout that it made Gordon, in his exhausted and half-attentive state, jump involuntarily. Little Raven stepped back, nodding and smiling at Gordon and the maiden in a very smug way, and Gordon got the distinct feeling that something had just been put over on him.

He looked back at Vasquez, who was standing behind him and grinning like a fox. "What's going on here?" he asked suspiciously.

"Allow me to introduce you to your new squaw, Hawkes," said the old trapper, gleefully. "This here's Little Raven's very own daughter. Her name is Mokamea."

"My *squaw*?" Gordon was stunned. "What are you talking about? You're pulling my leg, Vasquez."

"No, sir, I ain't. Little Raven thinks mighty high of you. 'Course, this match ain't bad for us, either. Is it, Robert?"

Campbell, standing near, nodded and glanced half apologetically at the dumbfounded Gordon. "Can't deny that. This could be the start of a strong alliance between the company and the Crow nation. And with McKenzie and the Blackfeet standing against us, we could surely profit by it."

"And what about me?" asked Gordon, feeling mightily put upon.

"You want to be a surefire mountain man, don't you?" responded Vasquez. "Well now, every mountain man worth his salt's got himself a squaw. And I must say, Hawkes, you got one of the purtiest I've ever laid eyes on."

Gordon realized he was still holding Mokamea's hand, and he very nearly snatched his away. But then he glanced at Little Raven, and at all the Crows around the fire, and kept his wits about him. No doubt such an act on his part, a clear rejection of Mokamea, would be a tremendous insult to the chief and to the band at large. He looked then at Mokamea, and for an odd moment he seemed to be drawn into her eyes, into her core, and everything else going on around him seemed to fade away. The sensation lasted only a few heartbeats, and when it was over he felt a little dizzy.

"So what am I supposed to do now?" he asked Vasquez.

"What any red-blooded man would do with a squaw what looks like her, I reckon." He spoke to Little Raven in the Crow tongue, and at the chief's command the other maidens reappeared, still laughing and giggling, and they clustered around Gordon and Mokamea, singing. Gordon found himself being herded away from the fire. He glanced back once, remembering Stewart, and saw the Scotsman standing there looking after him, arms folded, a faintly troubled expression on his face. Gordon wondered what reason Stewart had to be disturbed. Then he forgot all about his friend. The maidens were pushing him into a skin lodge. A small fire burned in a ring of stones, its smoke a serpentine gray ghost rising to the smoke hole high above. The ground was covered with skins and buffalo robes. Mokamea entered the skin lodge, and her gaze once again held Gordon in thrall, and he forgot about everything else as she slipped out of her long buckskin dress and came to him.

CHAPTER 6

I.

Looking back on that winter, Gordon would remember it as though it had been a dream, an interlude in his life that seemed so different, so far removed from what had happened to him before, and what would come after, that it just took on the trappings of fantasy. This was ironic, because what happened that winter changed him and his life completely. For one thing, he ceased to be a boy and became a man. It went beyond simply exploring the hitherto forbidden realm of sexual pleasure. He did not achieve manhood because he slept with the Crow maiden Mokamea, but because his perceptions of himself and his relations with others changed fundamentally. He was, in every sense of the word, married to Mokamea, and though he had entered into the covenant reluctantly and for all the wrong reasons, and in spite of the fact that it was a covenant that his own religion would not only leave unrecognized but sternly disapprove of, he willingly took on the responsibilities of taking care of Mokamea, and it was in acceptance of his duties as her husband that he made the transformation of boy to man.

Though the subject never came up, Gordon eventually concluded that he was in love with Mokamea. He was attracted to her from the first, and his desire for her was so strong that it consumed him, blocking out all other thoughts and considerations. For the first few days neither one of them strayed from the skin lodge. They made love at all hours of the day and night. Mokamea's sexual appetite was insatiable, and his for her became so. He gave no thought to food or drink or anything else, for that matter. Fortunately, both food and drink were brought to them, always by one of the other Crow girls, one of Mokamea's shy and giggle-prone friends. And so Gordon spent his honeymoon, wrapped in Mokamea's arms and legs beneath the buffalo robes in an Indian village on the frozen high plains near a remote trappers' outpost on the upper reaches of the Missouri River. It was the last place Gordon had expected to find perfect contentment.

After several days of this paradise on earth, Stewart paid him a visit. He brought a tin of English tea as a gift, and he and Gordon sat across the center fire from one another while Mokamea played the role of dutiful wife and brewed the tea and added some sugar to make it sweet and then withdrew to the back of the skin lodge and occupied herself with quillwork. Gordon could scarcely keep his eyes off her, so he was tardy in noticing that Stewart was watching him instead of her.

"I daresay I have never seen you looking so contented, my friend," observed the Scotsman.

"I don't recall ever having reason to be."

Stewart nodded. "Aye, it's been a long and difficult

road for you, lad. I'll give you that. But I would say you've found your place. Suppose you'll be going off with the Crows come spring?"

"I hadn't really given it much thought," confessed Gordon.

"You could stay with the company. Do some trapping in the mountains. Or remain here at the post. I think it's safe to say you could write your own ticket where Campbell and Sublette are concerned. You've become a very valuable asset for the Rocky Mountain Fur Company, you know. And your young bride is pretty well obligated to go with you wherever you choose to go. You'd best learn the language so you can make your wishes known to her when the time comes."

"Yes, I'd better. What about you? What are your plans for the spring?"

"I'll go West. Over the mountains to the sea. Find a ship and book passage to England. I've had my buffalo hunt. I've seen Indians. I've done what I set out to do."

Gordon knew what Stewart was thinking of at that moment—something he himself had forgotten all about until now—the fact that a murder charge still hung over their heads.

"You're welcome to come along with me, of course," added Stewart. "As far as the Pacific, or farther, if you wish. Though I don't know how your bride would take to England."

Gordon looked across at Mokamea and she glanced up and smiled at him, and as always the expression in her smoky eyes turned his insides into mush.

"I don't know," he said. The thought of Stewart taking his leave was a somber one. They had been through a great many adventures together, and the Scotsman was the only true friend he'd ever had.

"Well, plenty of time to make that decision," said Stewart. "Oh, by the way, you should know that the Hancocks and Mr. Miller will be going part of the way with me. They intend to find a suitable site for their mission. it seems that their close call with the Blackfeet didn't dissuade them from their purpose."

Mention of the Hancocks struck Gordon like a soaking with cold water. He suddenly remembered Eliza—and the way she had taken care of him while he recovered from the ill effects of his immersion in the icy Missouri River. Oddly, he felt slightly nauseated—and slightly guilty, too.

"How is . . . um . . . how is Eliza?"

"Ah, yes. Eliza. Well, of course she has asked about you."

Gordon waited, but Stewart sipped his tea, apparently ready to offer nothing more.

"What did you tell her?" asked Gordon. For some reason he dreaded the answer.

"I didn't get a chance to tell her anything. Vasquez and some of the others were there, talking, and it came out that you'd been hitched—that's the way they described it; quite colorful, don't you think?—to the daughter of the chief."

Gordon asked no more questions. He didn't want to know how Eliza had reacted to the news.

"I did make the comment that you'd had rather little choice in the matter," added Stewart.

Gordon nodded. Eliza cared for him, of that much he was fairly certain, and he regretted the hurt the news must have caused her. But there was no help for it. She would get over it in time, he told himself. Still, it was funny how this thought proved to be of such little comfort to him.

Stewart returned to the outpost and Gordon resumed his idyll with Mokamea. As far as the Crows were concerned, nothing more was expected of him. He could wander the village freely, and was treated with unfailing courtesy by all the Indians. Not that he ever wandered far from the skin lodge; Mokamea's desire for him seemed destined never to slacken, and while he appreciated all the attention, he couldn't get Eliza out of his head. This had nothing to do with any feelings for her on his part, except perhaps pity. Of this he was sure.

A few days after Stewart's visit he got up one morning, dressed quickly, and slipped out of the skin lodge before Mokamea had awakened. As usual, a bitterly cold wind was blasting down from the north, cutting through him to the bone, and he shivered uncontrollably as he traipsed through the snow in the direction of the stockade. Though of half a mind to retrace his steps and resume his place beneath the buffalo robes warmed by the slender, naked body of his desirable bride, Gordon pressed resolutely on. The guard at the gate greeted him with a slap on the back and a sly grin. He found Campbell with Vasquez and some of the others, drinking coffee in front of the fireplace in one of the barracks.

"I feel bad," he told Campbell lamely, "not doing my share of hunting and guard duty and all."

"I can't believe you're tired of that Injun gal already," said Vasquez, joking.

"Yeah," chimed in one of the other mountain men.

"A squaw what looked like that would sure enough keep me occupied until summer."

"Now, boys," chided Campbell. "No call to talk like that about Hawkes and his wife."

Gordon grimaced. "I'm right happy with the Crows. Believe me when I say I have no desire to move back into these barracks with a pack of slap ugly, skunk-smelling outcasts like all of you."

That elicited a roar of laughter from the others.

"But don't feel badly," Campbell told him. "We don't think you're a shirker, if that's what you're worried about. Fact is, you've helped us a great deal by accepting Little Raven's gift. Your duty is back there in the Crow village."

"Yep," said Vasquez. "You just keep up the good work, Hawkes."

" 'Course, if the job's too much for you to handle, I reckon any one of us would be glad to take over for you," said one of the others.

They laughed again, and Gordon felt his cheeks burn. "I doubt you'd be welcome. Funny as it may seem, Mokamea's in love with me."

Vasquez leaned forward, eyes narrowed. "You reckon?"

"I do."

"Well, don't be forgettin' that she *is* an Injun gal."

"What's that supposed to mean?"

"Shut up, Vasquez," said Campbell. "He doesn't mean anything, Hawkes. I admire your sense of responsibility to the company. But you are free of any duties here."

Gordon lingered in the stockade for a while, hoping for a glance at Eliza, but she did not emerge from the cabin occupied by the Hancocks. He wasn't sure why he wanted to see her; it really made no sense when he thought about it—in fact, it could only bring her more heartache, so he moved on eventually, returning to the skin lodge and Mokamea.

In the weeks to come Gordon prevailed on Mokamea to teach him some of the sign language that the Plains tribes used to communicate with each other. He'd figured out early on that it was beyond his capabilities to learn much of the Crow language beyond a few simple words—man, woman, food, water, day, night, sun, moon, horse, dog. The sign language was easier for him to grasp, and in a month's time he could express himself fairly well. With a few simple signs he could put together a conceptual phrase; he could "say," for instance, that the man had traveled many days to find food, or that the moon would be full tonight.

During this time he became better acquainted with the Crows, learning a lot about their customs, and about the collective personality of the band, largely from what Mokamea conveyed to him now that they were better able to communicate, but also as a result of his own observations, for as time went on he began to mingle more with the rest of the Indians. He came to know them as a generous and amiable people; he was greeted like a long-lost brother by every warrior, and every woman and child was unsparing with their words and smiles. He was welcome in every skin lodge. He was invited to share every fire and every meal. The fact that his skin was white seemed to be of no consequence to any of them. He was accepted without reservation, and the friendship they offered him was without strings attached. They expected nothing from him in exchange.

The days blended into weeks, the weeks into months. Gordon lost all track of time. In his world time really didn't matter. Though the fare was plain he ate well, and put on some weight. There wasn't much for him to do aside from eat, sleep, and make love to his beautiful bride. Often, when the weather permitted, he and Mokamea took long walks. Occasionally they would ride together across the snow-covered plains. Sometimes she would spend time with her friends, the other young women of the village, and now and then Gordon would join Little Raven and the warriors in a ritual that included a great deal of discussion about past and future conflicts with the hated—and feared— Blackfoot nation. But most of the time Gordon and Mokamea spent alone, together in their skin lodge, and he was quite content to put aside any thoughts about the future. He simply preferred not to think about it, for he knew that the time for decision would come soon enough.

As the winter drew to an end Little Raven and the council of elders made it known that soon the band would be on the move, westward into the mountains, and in the valley of the Wind River they would make their summer encampment. There they would do some hunting and trapping, joining with another Absaroka band, and perhaps there would be a raid or two against the Blackfeet, until such time as the buffalo returned. Then there would be a great buffalo hunt, and then, too, Little Raven would return to the Rocky Mountain Fur Company outpost to trade plews for blankets and muskets, powder and shot, tobacco and beads. Campbell visited the chief, and solicited an earnest commitment from Little Raven on that score. Gordon was present at this meeting, and saw the two principals share a peace pipe, sealing their bargain. As he was leaving, Campbell turned to Gordon and asked him to come into the post at his convenience—they needed to talk. Gordon said he would.

But he procrastinated for several days, reluctant to acknowledge that the time for choosing was almost upon him. Not that the choice itself was a difficult one. He knew already what course he would take. The hard part was telling his friends. Especially Stewart.

Campbell wasn't at all disappointed. He nodded, smiling, when Gordon informed him of his decision to remain with Little Raven's band.

"That suits me, Hawkes. Now don't get me wrong. You're a good man, and we hate to lose good men. But you do us the greatest service by floating your stick with the Crows."

"I'm glad to be of help," replied Gordon. "But that's not the main reason I'm going with them. It so happens that I love Mokamea, and she loves me. But that's not all of it. You see, for the first time I feel like I really belong. I haven't felt this way since I left Ireland. Maybe I never did feel this way, even in the old country. It's hard to explain."

"Whatever your reasons, I wish you well," said Campbell. "Keep your powder dry and the hair on your head."

Gordon went looking for Stewart, and found him at the parapet, gazing at the distant mountains that had so enticed them months ago. But this time Gordon paid scant attention to the distant high reaches; from this vantage point he could see a fair length of the Missouri River, and for the first time in many weeks he saw running water; where the current was strongest the ice was broken up. It was a sure sign that the long winter was well and truly on its last legs.

"So you've told Campbell you'll be going, I take it," said Stewart.

"How did you know?"

Stewart shrugged. "I think I know you fairly well, lad. You've found what you're looking for, haven't you?"

"Yes, I have. And I've never been so happy."

"It is happiness you deserve, my friend, after all the hardships you have endured."

"Once or twice you told me that life doesn't play fair. Seems to me that this time it did. I don't know how to explain it, exactly, but I feel as though this is what I'm meant to do. This is why I had to get through everything that came before. It was as though I were being shoved from one crisis to the next without any will of my own. But now I see a purpose behind all the travail."

"Sounds to me as though your faith in the Almighty has been restored."

"Well, yes," said Gordon, surprised. "I guess maybe that's true."

Stewart put a hand on his shoulder. "I'm truly glad for you, Gordon."

"I just feel bad, parting company with you."

Stewart laughed. "And I'll miss you, as well, have no doubt on that score. But all good things must come to an end. I realized long ago that you would never be going back to Ireland or Scotland. You speak of destiny. It is something in which I put much credence. I've known for some time that you were destined to make your mark on this wild frontier. This is where you belong. You were born to live this kind of life. Just as I was born to lead the life of a wanderer."

"Someday you'll find a place you want to call home."

"Never," said Stewart, with an adamant shake of his head. "No one place and no one woman could for long detain me." He nodded in the direction of the mountains. "You see, I have an insatiable appetite to sample the mysteries of what lies beyond—beyond the next mountain, or beyond the next ocean. I won't be stilled until death claims me. A hole six feet under—that will be my first and last permanent residence."

"I wish it were otherwise for you."

"As I do. But why the long face? This moment was bound to come."

"I suppose." Gordon stuck out a hand. "I won't forget you."

"Nor I you, lad."

There was nothing more to be said. With a heavy heart Gordon started to turn away.

"Will you say your farewells to Eliza?" asked the Scotsman. "Or should I extend them to her in your stead?"

Gordon hesitated a moment. "I guess maybe it would be better if I did it myself," he said, without any enthusiasm.

Stewart nodded approvingly. "You're a brave man—braver than I would be, under the circumstances."

Gordon didn't feel brave at all as he crossed the stockade to the cabin where the Hancocks had spent the winter. In fact, he was petrified with fear. He couldn't think of anything worse than to face Eliza and say good-bye. *I'd rather face a grizzly bear than do this,* he thought. Maybe it would be easier on her if I didn't speak to her at all. After every other step he nearly succumbed to cowardice, nearly turned toward the stockade gate and escape. But every time the urge to shirk his responsibility swept over him he cursed himself for being yellow and forced himself to go on. He felt like a condemned man on that long walk to the gallows.

As it turned out, though, all the agony he suffered in those moments was for naught. Marcus Hancock and Jonathan Miller emerged from the cabin and blocked his path.

"Where do you think you're going?" asked Miller belligerently.

"I've come to say good-bye to Eliza. If that's any business of yours."

"What makes you think she wants to see you?"

Hancock made an impatient gesture. "That's enough, Jonathan. Let me handle this. Young man, I don't want you to call on my daughter."

"Why not? I haven't done anything wrong."

"Nothing wrong?" scoffed Miller. "You've been shacked up with some dirty heathen all winter long. You're not fit company for a pure and innocent child like Eliza."

"Wait a minute," said Gordon, his ire on the rise. "How dare you call my wife a dirty heathen. I ought to punch you in the mouth."

"I invite you to try," said Miller.

"Mr. Miller!" said Hancock sternly. "A godly man

does not resort to violence except in self-defense. He most certainly does not encourage it."

Sullen, Miller clamped his jaws shut and had to satisfy himself with trying to kill Gordon with glowering looks.

"You should let Eliza make up her own mind whether she wants to see me or not," said Gordon.

"My daughter is only a child. She doesn't know her own mind. When she found out you had taken up with that . . . that Indian woman, she was devastated. I have endeavored since to convince her that she was wasting her time pining over you. And I believe that, over time, I have succeeded. Seeing you would undo all my work. I simply won't allow it."

Such revelations served only to convince Gordon that it was imperative he see Eliza and explain. Maybe Hancock was right. Maybe she would be better off not seeing him again. But he had to explain. He owed her that much. Or so he told himself—even as persistent doubts nagged him. Was it possible that what he really sought to do was assuage his own guilt.

"I insist on speaking to her," he said. "She showed me a kindness when I was ailing, and I have a right to say good-bye."

"You do not have that right unless I give it," responded Hancock imperiously. "And I most emphatically do not."

Gordon glanced beyond the two men at the cabin. Eliza was in there—he could call out her name, or try to get past Jonathan Miller. Of course in either case he would have Miller on him like a duck on a June bug. Miller outweighed him, and looked like he could put up a good fight, but such considerations did not enter into Gordon's final decision. He wasn't really afraid of Miller. It was the words Hancock spoke next that made up his mind.

"Listen, son." The missionary's tone was suddenly much more conciliatory. "I know you want to do the right thing. And that would be to leave Eliza be. Don't you see? It would do her no good to see you. That would only cause her more heartache."

"I'm sorry, sir," said Gordon, chastened. "I never meant for that to happen. I didn't encourage her . . ."

"Of course not. As I've said, she is only a child, and it was merely childish infatuation. Given a chance, she will forget all about you, and don't you agree that would be best?"

"Yes, I suppose so."

"Then go. And go with my prayers that you will not take up the ways of the heathens you have chosen to dwell among."

Gordon turned away, saddened, and cast one last look at the cabin. He'd been of a mind to defend his Crow friends, who did not deserve the ill-concealed contempt of these two men. But he wasn't in the mood for it. Depressed by the knowledge that he had caused Eliza Hancock so much hurt, he left the stockade. For the next couple of days he brooded about Eliza, and not even Mokamea's attentions could divert him. And then he awoke early one morning to find the village bustling with activity. The day had come to make the move. In a matter of hours the camp had been dismantled, lodge by lodge, and before midday they were departing the outpost, and the men of the Rocky Mountain Fur Company gathered at the gate or along the parapets to bid them farewell, but Gordon avoided looking at them, never once glancing back as he headed west for the mountains.

II.

Gordon's glum mood prevailed for several days—until they reached the mountains. Then he spent a lot less time thinking about the friends he had left behind. The grandeur of the high country thoroughly preoccupied him.

The mountains were still covered with snow. Great waterfalls careened off sheer cliffs. Hawks and eagles, mere specks in the sky, soared beneath towering crags. Swollen creeks and rivers traversed the great valleys. In the meadows, green patches of new growth could be detected beneath the matting of last year's dead brown grass. Trees and bushes were beginning to put out new buds. If anything, it seemed warmer in the valleys hemmed in by the mountain ranges than on the wind-scoured plains. There was abundant wildlife. Gordon could understand now why the mountain men spoke with such reverence about this country. He was completely taken with this pristine wilderness, where a vista of breathtaking majesty and beauty greeted the eye at every turn. In these mountains, he resolved, he would make his home, safely removed from the dangers and disappointments of the so-called "civilized" world. This would be his sanctuary.

The Crow band with which he traveled passed through one range of peaks, skirted another, and, crossing a rocky saddle by means of a tortuous trail, came finally to a valley several miles across at its widest point and about ten miles in length. At the north end of the valley, four waterfalls cascaded down into a lake which fed a serpentine creek that ran the length of the valley, squeezing through a rocky defile at the south end, to join a river that raged violently within the confines of a deep canyon. Great meadows afforded the horses plenty of graze. Still-leafless aspens formed vast forests on the lower slopes of the mountains, while immense patches of evergreens, interspersed with high meadows yet blanketed in snow, cloaked the upper shoulders. The peaks to the west were particularly rugged, with sheer precipices and towering rock formations jutting skyward. Here and there on the valley floor could be found piles of massive boulders where several of these pinnacles had tumbled down the steep slopes.

Here the band made its summer camp. In a meadow bordered on the north by marshy lowland, to the south by a stand of aspen, and to the west by the creek, the skin lodges went up. Gordon was given to understand that soon at least one other band, perhaps two, would join them. Then it would be time to plan for a raid or two against the Blackfeet, whose territory lay just to the north and east. Gordon wondered if he was expected to participate in this annual war making. He had absolutely no desire to do so. If he declined, would his new friends scorn him as a coward? Fighting the Blackfeet was a very important and apparently perennial business; to strike a blow against them was expected of every band, every warrior.

Of course, a quick strike here or a pinprick raid there would amount to nothing in the larger scheme of things. Such minor actions could not fundamentally alter the balance of power between the Blackfeet, with their allies the Bloods and the Piegans, and the Crows, with their friends the Bannocks and Shoshones. Using sign language, Gordon asked Mokamea why the Crow bands did not unite and attack their enemies in force. She couldn't tell him, for she did not concern herself with such matters. So Gordon asked a young warrior called Five Horses, who had become the closest thing to a friend Gordon had among the Crows, but Five Horses, normally a very thoughtful, helpful, and articulate fellow, merely shrugged and declared that it simply wasn't done. A little while later, Gordon had an opportunity to pose the same question to Little Raven. His father-in-law explained that this was not the way men made war.

Gordon remembered the stories his father had told him about the warlike Scottish clans, which had seldom been able to put aside their differences and join forces to fight the English—a shortcoming that had contributed to Scotland's loss of her independence a century before Gordon had been born. Gordon concluded that a similar situation applied in this circumstance. Would the Indians suffer the same tragic results? He thought about warning Little Raven of the threat that lay east of the Mississippi—a restless, numerous and aggressive people who had conquered half a continent in a few decades. St. Louis seemed like a lifetime away, but the vast expanses of the prairie and the plains would not long deter the American surge westward. The mountain men and the missionaries were already here. The rest would follow in their wake. If the Indians did not join together to resist this inevitable encroachment there would be no stopping the onslaught of civilization. But Gordon opted not to try explaining all this to Little Raven—it exceeded his ability to communicate, and he doubted that the caveat would have any impact on the Absaroka chief. Such a threat, though real, did seem far removed from this idyllic setting so many hundreds of miles from St. Louis's bustling Market Street. *I expect I'll be long gone before civilization reaches this valley,* decided Gordon.

As for the more immediate threat of the Blackfeet, Gordon pushed it to the back of his mind in the coming weeks, as he watched and marveled at spring bringing new life to the mountains. The days grew warmer, the snow receded, the first wildflowers of the season dotted the meadows, the trees put on new foliage. Early in the mornings, a mist would rise from the cold water of the creek, and often in the late afternoon clouds would gather between the jagged peaks and release a gentle rain.

During this period, Gordon's appearance changed. Over the long winter his hair had grown to shoulder length, and he chose not to cut it. He exchanged his trousers for buckskin leggins and a breechclout, but kept his linsey-woolsey shirt, though he cut the sleeves off, as one of them had been badly torn. Mokamea made him some moccasins, which he found much more useful for the life he was leading than the mule-ear boots he'd been wearing since St. Louis.

Still, there was no mistaking him for an Indian. His sandy hair and pale skin that refused to darken made him stand out among his Absaroka friends. They didn't seem to take notice. Little Raven presented him with a bow and a quiver of arrows, and Gordon— much to his surprise—proved to have a real knack for using these weapons for hunting, so that he was very much admired by the Crow warriors. For his part, Gordon was quite happy to contribute to the band's food supply; if he killed a deer he would keep only enough for Mokamea and himself and give the rest away. If, for instance, he gave food to Five Horses and his family, Five Horses would return the favor at the earliest convenience. In addition, his skill with the bow and arrow provided him with an opportunity to save his powder and shot.

Life with Mokamea settled into a predictable routine. No longer did she and Gordon spend every moment together, as they had during the winter. Gordon often went hunting alone or with an Absaroka brave, or set out on his sorrel to explore the valley, again usually with someone like Five Horses accompanying him. Mokamea spent time with her girlfriends. Gordon didn't mind. He still enjoyed her company, and looked forward to their passionate nights together, but in one sense he was relieved—he couldn't have kept up the pace they had maintained over the winter. All in all, he was quite happy with the relationship. He loved Mokamea, and was secure in the knowledge that she loved him. Thoughts of Eliza Hancock faded, and he looked to the future with his Indian bride. He gave some thought to fatherhood. In good time Mokamea would bear him a son or daughter. Though he was only seventeen years old, Gordon felt much older and wiser, and he was ready for the responsibilities inherent in having a child.

Once again, however, Fate intervened.

It began on the day that another band of Crows, about two hundred men, women, and children, arrived

in the valley. They were led by a chief called Broken
Lance, who had arranged with Little Raven the summer before to join forces this spring. Gordon was ambivalent about their arrival, for he feared that it would
mark the beginning of the annual campaign against the
Blackfoot nation. He had another reason to be wary of
the newcomers, for when they learned that a white
man was living among Little Raven's people, they
demonstrated an insatiable curiosity in Gordon, who
became something of a specimen on display. All he
could do was endure their scrutiny. He avoided as
much as possible the village that Broken Lance's people raised on the other side of the creek.

Mokamea, on the other hand, did not avoid the village of the other band. She had friends among Broken
Lance's people, and Gordon accepted that. What he
could not accept so readily was the attention a warrior
from that village began to pay to Mokamea. Gordon
began to see this young Crow brave hanging around
more and more often. Even when it became obvious to
the brave that Mokamea had a mate, he continued to
lurk in the vicinity like a coyote around a night camp.
That annoyed Gordon, and he had to struggle against a
rising tide of jealousy. He was sure he had no reason to
be jealous; Mokamea didn't even seem to realize that
the brave existed. For that reason he chose not to ask
her about him, and instead went to Five Horses for information.

Five Horses knew who Gordon was talking about.
The brave's name was Bearkiller, and he was one of
the most famous Absaroka warriors—even at the
young age of twenty summers. Bearkiller had proven
his prowess—and earned his name—at the callow age

of fifteen, when he had killed a grizzly bear in spite of the fact that he had been armed only with a knife. Of course, the incident very nearly claimed the young man's life. For days he had lingered at death's door; no one had given him much chance of recovering. And then one morning Bearkiller stood up and walked out of the skin lodge. But for the scars he would wear as a badge of honor the rest of his life, he seemed none the worse for his experience. It was widely believed that Bearkiller had taken upon himself the strength and courage of the grizzly he had slain in such heroic fashion. Some also believed he was now invincible, that in battle neither bullet nor lance nor arrow could harm him, and he had been in many fights in the past few years. Though young, he was already a war chief of the Absaroka, which meant that many other braves were willing to follow him into action, convinced that he was endowed with strong medicine. To follow Bearkiller assured a warrior of glory.

Such news did little to soothe Gordon's anxiety; he would have preferred that Mokamea's admirer was not such a heroic champion of his people. In the days to come he was tormented by doubts. Just how strong was Mokamea's love for him? How devoted was she? If Bearkiller tried to win her away, would she be able to resist his entreaties? If Mokamea reached the point of deciding between them, how could he, Gordon Hawkes, possibly match up to a warrior like Bearkiller? It was all he could do to refrain from sharing his doubts with Mokamea, from having it out with her once and for all. But he didn't, because she gave no indication that her feelings for him had faded at all. How then could he admit that he had his doubts about her fidelity, when she had given him no cause to harbor such doubts? So he held his tongue, kept his worries to himself, and tried to be satisfied with watching her closely, sometimes following her into Broken Lance's village when she went there with her girlfriends, feeling like a fool all the while, and yet unable to resist the urge to spy on her. She did nothing to justify his efforts; not once did he see her and Bearkiller together. Bearkiller always kept his distance, and eventually Gordon began to think he had made a mountain out of a molehill.

A fortnight after the arrival of Broken Lance's band a council meeting was called, and Little Raven announced that a raid against their hated foes, the Blackfeet, would be carried out in a few days. Twenty of Broken Lance's warriors would ride north, and Little Raven wanted twenty of his braves to do the same. The two raiding parties would ride together under the joint leadership of Bearkiller and Five Horses. It was up to the latter to choose the warriors who would ride with him. All the young men in the village wanted to be among those chosen. Except Gordon. He much preferred to stay behind, and prayed Five Horses wouldn't select him. But of course Five Horses *did* pick his good friend. Gordon's first instinct was to take Five Horses aside and beg to be let off the hook. He even considered feigning illness. *I am a coward,* he decided. *Too cowardly even to let it be known that I want no part of this war making.* It wasn't his fight. He had no stake in it. But he had to go. Had to, because he was afraid Mokamea would think less of him, and if she thought him a coward then perhaps she might *start* paying attention to Bearkiller. Gordon would disgrace himself, his bride, and Little Raven if he refused to participate in the raid. So he had to go.

Mokamea was thrilled that her husband had been chosen. It was a great honor. She urged him to bring back many Blackfoot horses. A brave's wealth was measured by the number of ponies in his possession. She also implored him to bring her some Blackfoot scalps. Gordon wanted to tell her it was just as likely that his topknot would end up on a Blackfoot scalp pole. He was a little hurt that she didn't act too concerned about the possibility that he might not come back at all. He was so consumed by dark thoughts that on the night before the raiding party's departure he made love to Mokamea without much enthusiasm. She sensed that he was preoccupied, and when he took his leave the next morning she was decidedly cool—and that didn't do much to improve his frame of mind as he rode out of the village alongside Five Horses, with the young maidens and little children and camp dogs running along beside the young warriors going off to strike a blow against the demons of the north country.

III.

They rode for four days—by Gordon's calculations almost due north, and then turned east through a high pass and down into forested foothills, finally reaching the high plains that were greening into full-fledged spring. They crossed two rivers in two days and it was then that Five Horses cheerfully informed his white friend that they were in the land of the Blackfeet. This was hardly happy news for Gordon, but he tried his best to conceal his anxiety.

That night they took the precaution of doing without a cook fire. Though winter was over, it was still plenty cold when the sun went down, but a fire was simply out of the question in enemy country. There was no food except for pemmican, and Gordon passed on that; his stomach was tied up in knots. His companions, on the other hand, appeared to be in high spirits. They were excited by the prospect of playing at war. This was great sport for them. Gordon had spent enough time among Indians to know that a warrior was a person of great faith—even though Marcus Hancock would have refused to believe it. A warrior was convinced that if he died bravely in battle he would pass immediately into the next life, where he could reside forever, wanting for nothing, where the buffalo would always be in abundance, and where his honored ancestors would greet him with open arms and the highest praise. So why worry about death? Everything died. What mattered was the way a man died. And if he died young it would simply mean that he had gained admittance to paradise that much sooner.

Part of the problem, thought Gordon, was that the Indian seldom spent much time thinking about the long-term future. They lived for the moment and left tomorrow to the Great Spirit. But now that he had Mokamea, now that he had something to live for, and to cherish with all his heart, now that he could even begin to contemplate the joys of fatherhood, Gordon wasn't in the least bit ready to give up on this particular life. No matter what lay beyond the grave.

And that was the rest of the problem—Gordon wasn't real sure he believed in an afterlife. He'd told Reverend Hancock that he didn't even know if God existed. If there was no God, then only the cold eternity of the grave lay beyond death. And if there *was* a God, then surely one Gordon Hawkes was destined for eternal damnation. All in all, Gordon couldn't share his companions' ambivalence about death.

Early the next morning they passed through some tree-cloaked hills and saw before them, laid out in a large meadow, a Blackfoot village. Horses grazed in the lush grass, and women were at the meandering creek that traversed the open ground, gathering water or doing washing. His eyes feverish with intense excitement, Five Horses turned to Gordon and needlessly made the sign for Blackfoot. He then joined Bearkiller for a quick conference, while Gordon and the Absaroka warriors waited, well hidden in the trees. Gordon studied the peaceful village. There were about thirty lodges. That meant maybe fifty warriors. But many of them seemed to be absent, perhaps on a raid of their own, because most of the village inhabitants that Gordon could see were women and children and old men. Blackfoot or no, he could muster up no animus toward the villagers. He simply had no heart for this business. Surely these Crow braves, who put such stock in personal honor, would not stoop so low as to attack a defenseless village and wage war on women and children.

He glanced over his shoulder at Five Horses and Bearkiller. Evidently they were engaged in a heated though softly spoken argument. Finally Five Horses returned to his men, fuming. Using sign language as he spoke, so that Gordon could better understand what was going on, he explained to the warriors who had followed him that Bearkiller refused to attack the village and had decided to go on. According to Bearkiller, this village was too small. He was after bigger prey. Five Horses, of course, disagreed with Bearkiller's decision, but he had concluded that it would be better if they remained one raiding party, so they would have to pass this tempting target by and continue north. All the others were keenly disappointed, but they accepted the judgment of Five Horses without debate. For his part, Gordon wasn't disappointed at all.

They left the unsuspecting village behind and rode on. That night they stopped thirty miles away from the village, and Five Horses had brooded through every mile. He called his braves together at dawn and told them that he had changed his mind. Bearkiller was a reckless fool, and thought he was invincible, but Five Horses was just as convinced that he himself was mortal, and if Bearkiller did have great medicine it would not protect him, Five Horses. Not that he was afraid to die, but he wanted to die for a reason. And, too, he wanted to strike a blow against their despised enemy, wanted the Blackfoot nation to taste the same anguish of defeat they had inflicted so many times before on the Absaroka Crow.

So, concluded Five Horses, he had changed his mind about staying with Bearkiller and the warriors from the band of Broken Lance. "We will go back to the village we saw this morning," he said, "and destroy it. We will take many scalps and many ponies."

The others—save for Gordon—evinced their enthusiastic support for their leader's decision. It seemed that Bearkiller was perfectly happy with the arrangement. He didn't much care for the company of Little Raven's warriors, and he was particularly unhappy with Gordon's presence, having voiced the opinion that bringing a white man along was bad medicine. For his part, Gordon didn't mind leaving Bearkiller, either. Five Horses was right about the man; Bearkiller took too many chances because he thought he could not be killed. On the other hand, Gordon reckoned it was the height of insanity for the raiding party to split up so deep in Blackfoot territory.

It took Gordon and Five Horses and the others most of the day to get back to the Blackfoot village they had seen earlier. Five Horses decided they would take the risk of camping nearby so that they could attack early in the morning. He reasoned that after the attack they would have to make fast time back into the mountains, as Blackfoot warriors bent on revenge would soon be on their trail. They would need fresh horses and daylight hours to make good their escape.

Gordon didn't get any sleep that night. His mind was in a turmoil. On the one hand, he was glad the attack had been postponed; that gave the people of the village at least a few more hours to live. But it also gave him all night long to torment himself with images of what the morning would bring. In fact, he was so tormented that he even considered betraying the presence of the raiding party in some way. Yes, that could very likely mean his death, as well as the deaths of his friend, Five Horses, and his other Absaroka brethren. That was something he simply could not bring himself to do— not for his sake but for the others. It was his own fault that he found himself in this predicament, not theirs. He could have refused to come along in the first place, and endured the shame of being considered a coward. But his desire to keep Mokamea happy had made him weak. All in all it was an impossible situation. There was no way out.

As dawn approached, and the warriors prepared their weapons and mounted their ponies, Gordon was seriously thinking about getting on his sorrel and riding away. At the last minute he decided not to. Running away would not save the women and children of the village. He must join in the attack. But his purpose would be not to kill anyone—quite the contrary. He could try to prevent at least one Blackfoot death.

With cold and calculated efficiency, Five Horses prepared the attack. When the raiding party broke from the cover of the trees they formed a single row, the horsemen spread well apart, with Five Horses in the center and Gordon immediately to his right. They held their ponies to a walk, and not a sound was made as they advanced through the gray half-light, in those moments before sunrise when all the color seems to have bled out of the world. A cottony mist rose from the creek as they splashed across the shallows. It was then that a camp dog barked, and kept barking. An arrow was loosed from a taut bow and the dog yelped, then was silent. But someone in the village had heard; an old man emerged from a skin lodge, looked around, and even as he spotted the line of painted warriors advancing, and hoarsely shouted the alarm, another arrow flashed through the air, struck him in the chest, and hurled him backward.

Five Horses raised his rifle and let loose a chilling war cry. The Absarokas surged forward, all screaming like banshees now. "Oh my God," breathed Gordon, and sharply checked the sorrel, hanging back a moment, a horrified spectator as the slaughter he had been dreading began to unfold like a nightmare from which he could not awake. In this colorless limbo between night and day the scene seemed so unreal that for an instant he wondered if it really wasn't a dream. And then, as the villagers began to die, running out of their skin lodges to fall beneath lance or arrow or rifle ball, Gordon came to his senses. The butchery ignited an anger that burned like brimstone in his soul. He kicked the sorrel into a gallop, half mad with rage and grief and confusion. Somehow his enemies had become his friends and his friends had become his enemies.

There were a handful of warriors in the village, and they fought valiantly, laying down their lives in an effort to blunt the Absaroka onslaught and give the women and children and old ones a chance to escape into the nearby woods. They fought—and died—with a savage fury, and several Crow warriors had fallen before this thin line of Blackfoot bravery was shattered. This happened in less than a minute, and by the time Gordon had reached the edge of the village the Absaroka had scattered, galloping through the skin lodges in search of victims. Gordon saw an old woman crumple, shot through the head. A mother with a screaming infant in her arms was chased down and slain with a lance driven completely through her. He saw a Crow warrior galloping after a boy of eight or nine years; realizing he could not outrun the Absaroka pony, the boy swerved to a cold fire, picked up a stout piece of wood, and hurled it at his pursuer. The wood struck the Crow warrior's horse, and the pony reared, throwing its unsuspecting rider. Trying to dodge the horse as it ran away, the Blackfoot boy lost his footing and sprawled on the ground. The Absaroka brave was on his feet now, drawing a knife. He advanced on the boy, snarling like a wolf.

Before he could reach his prey, however, Gordon was there, launching himself from the saddle and hurling his body into the warrior. They went down in a heap. Though stunned, the Crow was quickly back on his feet. But Gordon was a little quicker. The Crow whirled—and hesitated a fraction of a second as he recognized his attacker. That was all the time Gordon needed. He kicked the knife out of the Indian's grasp and moved in with a hard right that connected solidly with the warrior's chin. The Crow went down. Gordon pressed his advantage, pouncing on the Indian, driving a knee into his chest, and hitting him again on the point of the chin, knocking him out cold.

Gordon looked up sharply, saw the Blackfoot boy, on hands and knees, staring at him with wild and hunted eyes. He made the sign for "friend," but the boy kept staring, no comprehension in his eyes. Gordon got up and took a step toward him, and then the boy moved, agile and quick and desperate, lunging for the Crow warrior's fallen knife. Gordon got to the weapon a split second too late; he curled an arm around the boy's waist, wrenching the blade from his grasp. The sorrel stood nearby, waiting for him, and Gordon mounted up, the struggling Blackfoot youth securely in his grasp. Oddly, the village now seemed deserted. The other Crow warriors had chased their prey into the nearby woods. A rifle spoke, then another. A piercing scream, abruptly cut short, made Gordon's skin crawl. He turned the sorrel and left the village the way he had come, looking neither to the left nor to the right, aware of the bodies lying on the bloodstained ground, but not wanting to look too close at the handiwork of his Absaroka brethren, hating them at that moment, hating himself, too. Across the creek and back into the woods where they had camped the night before, he continued for almost a mile into the woods before halting and letting the Blackfoot boy go.

"Go on," he said hoarsely. "Get. Run." He made the sign for "go," but the boy stood there, shivering uncontrollably, and not just from the morning's chill. "Damn it," rasped Gordon, "*get out of here while you can.*"

But the boy would not budge, and Gordon's anger ebbed. The youth could hardly be faulted for fearful indecision, considering what had just befallen him. His whole world had been irreparably shattered. Perhaps he had witnessed the horror of a mother or father killed. And he had barely escaped death himself.

With a sigh Gordon dismounted, ground-hitching the sorrel. He drew his knife—the dirk Stewart had given him long ago, that fateful night at the plantation of Anton Remairie—from his belt, flipped it, and extended it, handle first, to the boy.

"Okay," said Gordon. "Fine. You don't know what to do. I can understand why. But one thing is certain. You can't come with me. Child or not, I don't think they would let you live where I'm going. So here, take this. Go on, take it."

The boy could not comprehend his words, but could tell that Gordon was offering the dirk to him, and he took it. The Spanish blade was unlike any knife he had ever seen before, and he gazed with wonder at its craftsmanship.

Gordon turned to his horse, removing a blanket and

a rawhide pouch from his saddle. He draped the blanket around the boy's shuddering shoulders and hung the pouch by its strap around his neck.

"There's some pemmican in that pouch," said Gordon. He made the sign for "food." "Now here's what you're to do. Lay low until nightfall. I reckon by then it ought to be safe to go back to the village." He grimaced, annoyed by his inability to communicate effectively. He combined several signs—"stay" and "night" and "go," pointing in the direction of the village—and when he was done he was gratified to see the lad nod his head. The boy understood, or thought he did. *I ought to stay with him,* mused Gordon, *until he is back safely among his own kith and kin.* But he wanted to get going. Wanted to get home in a hurry, before the raiding party returned. He needed to explain to Mokamea and Little Raven why he'd done what he had done. At least that way he would get a chance to tell his side of the story.

He wasn't sure what would happen as a result of the actions he had taken to save this boy's life, but he could be pretty sure it would be none too pleasant. Still, as he gazed earnestly into the boy's eyes, he knew he would never regret his actions—only that he hadn't been able, or had the courage, to do more. Sitting on his heels in front of the boy, he put his hand on the Blackfoot youth's shoulder, gave it a squeeze, and nodded.

"You'll get through," he said. "A friend of mine liked to remind me that though life doesn't play fair it's still worth living. I think you'll find that's true. Hope so, anyway."

He left the boy, then, mounting up and riding away,

not looking back, and saying a silent prayer for the lad—even though he wasn't sure that God would be listening. Or even if there was a God.

It took him five days to get back to the valley, across the two rivers, west through the mountain pass, and then south between the towering ranges of snow-capped peaks, making better time than the raiding party had done on its trek north into Blackfoot country. Dawn found him on the move, and he kept going until well after sundown each day. The nights were clear and the moon full, obligingly lighting his path. At one point he came across the sign of a large party on un-shod horses. That meant Indians, forty of them at least, and the tracks were but a day old, heading in the op-posite direction. He wondered how he had missed them, though he was glad that he had, and concluded that he must have passed them in the night. Wondered, too, who they were.

The following morning, as he neared the village of the bands led by Little Raven and Broken Lance, he could tell even at a good distance that something was very wrong. Many of the skin lodges were missing. As he drew closer he realized with growing horror that in fact they had been put to the torch. And where were all the ponies that usually grazed in the lush grass of the meadow north of the villages? A knot of anxiety in his stomach, he spotted several warriors riding out to meet him. They were armed to the teeth. When they recog-nized him their cautious belligerence, which Gordon could sense long before they arrived, fell away; using sign language, they informed him that yesterday morn-ing a large Blackfoot raiding party had struck the vil-lages, killing many people and taking many horses.

"Mokamea!" Gordon nearly choked on the name of his beloved, and kicked the sorrel into a full gallop. Entering the village, he saw that his skin lodge was one of those still standing. Relief flooded over him. Maybe everything was all right; maybe Mokamea was unharmed. She simply had to be. He jumped out of the saddle and entered the lodge at the run. It was empty. Clinging desperately to slender hope, he went back outside. Little Raven was coming toward him.

"Mokamea?" asked Gordon.

Little Raven's expression was etched with grief. "They took my daughter," he said, using sign language to help Gordon understand what he was saying. "They took her and two other of our young women."

Gordon felt as though someone had hit him hard, right between the shoulder blades; he could scarcely breathe. Shocked by the news, he just stood there, gaping at Little Raven, not wanting to believe the truth, denying that it was so.

"Where are the others?" asked Little Raven.

Gordon didn't answer. Instead he turned to the sorrel, climbing into the saddle, gripped by a sudden cold resolve that banished his weariness.

"Wait," counseled the Absaroka chief. "When Five Horses returns we will go after them. You cannot go alone. Alone you will not save Mokamea."

"You wait," snapped Gordon in the Absaroka tongue. "I go." He wheeled his horse around, leaving the village as he had entered it, at the gallop.

CHAPTER 7

I.

The Blackfoot raiders were moving rapidly. Their three Absaroka captives and herd of stolen ponies did not seem to slow them down in the least. They traveled north, roughly following the route Gordon and Five Horses and the Crow raiding party had taken a fortnight earlier. This gave Gordon something of an advantage, as he knew the country quite well. He thought that if he traveled by night as well as by day he could catch up quickly. And if and when he did catch up—then what? Forty against one were very steep odds. He decided that circumstances would have to dictate his actions. He would simply have to play it by ear.

Problem was, the Blackfeet were using the moonlit nights to good advantage as well. They kept moving well after dark, stopping for a few hours in the early morning to sleep and rest their horses. Before daybreak they were on their way again.

Gordon was exhausted. The trek into Blackfoot country and his rush to get back to the village had taken a lot out of him. In addition, he had absolutely nothing to eat, having given all his meager provisions to the Blackfoot boy. He saw sign of game along the way, but didn't want to take the time to track it down. On the morning of the second day fortune smiled on him; a rabbit darted out of the grass directly in front of him, and he brought the Hawken to his shoulder and fired in one smooth motion. That night he skinned and butchered the rabbit, risking a small fire built in a pit he dug out of the ground; that way the fire would remain hidden from hostile eyes.

That day he noticed that the sign was much fresher; he was slowly but surely gaining ground. Yet he wondered if he would catch the raiders before they reached their homeland. Not that it really mattered. He would follow the devils to the end of the earth to get Mokamea back safe and sound. It would just make it a lot more difficult for either one of them to get back alive if the chase took them much further north.

And would she be sound when he found her? Why had the Blackfoot warriors taken her and the other maidens? That seemed fairly obvious. Gordon was constantly tormented by all kinds of vivid images of what the Blackfeet might be doing to his beautiful wife.

On the third day he was dozing off in the saddle, lulled to the verge of sleep by the warmth of the spring sun on his shoulders, when the crackle of distant gunfire startled him to wakefulness. The sound was coming from somewhere up ahead. He kicked the sorrel into a gallop, but had covered less than a mile before the shooting stopped. Checking the horse, he listened for a few minutes. Silence. Whatever had happened, it was over. Hawken rifle in hand, he proceeded cautiously.

About a half mile further on, his heart leaped into his throat as he spotted a group of Indians emerge from a line of trees directly in front of him. He was caught out in the open with no place to hide. Fortunately, they weren't Blackfeet. In fact, they were Absaroka Crows—Five Horses and his raiding party. Gordon could tell by the symbols painted on their war ponies. No, not just Five Horses, but Bearkiller and his braves, as well.

As they drew nearer, Gordon's heart sang with joy as he saw that Mokamea was riding behind Five Horses. Calling out her name, he rushed forward. Dismounting on the run, he helped her down off Five Horses' pony and held her tight.

An angry shout turned him, and he saw the Crow warrior whom he had fought to prevent the Blackfoot boy's murder coming toward him on foot, his features rigid with a cold fury. The warrior spoke angrily to Five Horses. Glancing up at his friend, Gordon could tell that he would get no support from that quarter. In fact, Five Horses refused to even look at him. Putting Mokamea at his back, Gordon leveled his rifle at the advancing warrior and pulled the hammer.

"Stand away," he rasped. "You're lucky I didn't kill you back there. I'll do so now if I have to."

The warrior halted in his tracks, fuming. He didn't understand Gordon's English, but there could be no question that he was in deadly earnest.

"Enough," said Bearkiller, putting himself and his war pony between Gordon and the warrior. "This is a matter for a council to decide."

The warrior had no choice but to accept Bearkiller's decision. He turned back to his horse, every movement conveying his outrage. Gordon took Mokamea to the sorrel, climbed into the saddle, and helped her up behind him. She seemed dazed and distant, as though she were unaware of everything that was going on around her. Gordon could hardly blame her, considering the four-day ordeal she had endured as a captive of the Blackfoot raiders.

On the journey back to the village he learned the details of what had transpired, listening to cook fire conversations and picking up pieces here and there and putting them together into a more or less complete picture.

Bearkiller and his warriors had struck a Blackfoot village the very day that Five Horses and his men had parted company with them. Pure chance had brought the two groups together again as they made their way south, a fortunate happenstance since they had then run straight into the Blackfoot raiders shortly thereafter. The Blackfeet had gotten away with most of the stolen Absaroka ponies. Several braves on both sides had lost their lives—the Crows were bringing their dead home. Also dead was one of the Crow maidens, slain by her captor during the brief fight. Mokamea and the other girl had been saved. There was some speculation that the Blackfoot warriors had come from the village that Five Horses had attacked; if that was the case they were in for quite a shock when they got home.

As for what had happened to Mokamea in the days she had been a prisoner of the Blackfeet, the way she was acting caused Gordon to fear the worst. The

Mokamea he had come to know—cheerful, fun-loving, and affectionate—was gone. She was withdrawn, lost in herself, and plainly hurting. Not just physically, but emotionally as well. He wanted to comfort her, but she flinched when he so much as touched her, and he tried to respect her desire to be left alone. He didn't ask for details. He didn't know how to communicate the questions that tortured him, and what good would it do to broach the subject anyway? The best thing he could do was allow time to do the healing, and let her know by his gentle smile and small kindnesses that he was there for her, that he did not love her any less because of what had happened. Angered, saddened, and apprehensive, all Gordon could do was wait and hope that the old Mokamea would eventually be restored to him. At the same time he prepared himself for the possibility that she would never be the same.

Concerning what he had done at the Blackfoot village, no words were spoken; Bearkiller had made it clear that Gordon's fate would rest in the hands of a council. No question, though, that his actions had cost him the trust and comradeship of the Absaroka warriors. No one, not even Five Horses, spoke a single word to him. Whenever possible they avoided even looking at him. Gordon was hurt by their silent animosity. On the one hand he did not regret the actions he had taken. At least one innocent life had been spared, and he would never apologize for doing what was right. His conscience was clear. On the other hand, he realized that in a matter of days his whole world had been undermined. He had found a place where he belonged, among a people he admired, and he had dreamed of a bright future. Now that dream was shattered. *Look on the bright side,* he told himself. *At least you still have Mokamea. As long as she is with you, you still could have a future.*

When they got back to the village, Gordon decided to concentrate on doing all he could for Mokamea, to make her comfortable and speed her recovery, resolving not to fret about his fate at the hands of the council. He carried her into their skin lodge, covered her with a buffalo robe, bade her rest, and went hunting. She needed nourishment. When he returned, Mokamea's mother and sister were there, and while they bathed Mokamea and applied poultices to her bruised body, he sat outside, skinning and gutting the doe he had shot. When the women left they refused to speak to him. Later, Little Raven came to see his daughter. Again, Gordon afforded them privacy. Again the visitor acted as though Gordon did not even exist.

Slowly the village recovered from the Blackfoot attack. The dead were honored and grieved over and dispatched with somber ceremony to the next life. The skin lodges that had been destroyed were replaced. Many horses had been lost; replacements would be needed soon, for in a few short weeks it would be time to plan for the buffalo hunt. Another raiding party was sent out, with orders to steal ponies, from the Blackfeet if possible, though any horses belonging to anyone were fair game.

As the days passed, Gordon wondered when the council would be called. The warrior he had dishonored would air his grievances, and Gordon would be given the opportunity to defend himself. He decided to set aside his pride and try to excuse his actions. Not that he expected it to do much good. As time dragged on he became increasingly apprehensive. Why was nothing happening? He wanted to get it over with.

Mokamea was young, healthy, and resilient. Physically, she bounced back quickly enough. But her spirit, her smile, did not return. She spent more and more time away from the skin lodge. Gordon was completely isolated. Even when she was with him he seemed to be alone. Exasperated, he tried to talk to her. But she wouldn't open up to him. He came to realize that she was ashamed of him. That cut deep. Resentful, Gordon retreated into himself, and that just made matters worse. He began to entertain notions of leaving. Everyone had spurned him—and for what? Saving a boy's life. It wasn't fair. If they hated him for doing something like that, then to hell with them. Just go, he told himself, a dozen times a day. But he couldn't go, because of the way he felt about Mokamea. He could not bring himself to leave her and he knew she wouldn't go with him. So he was trapped.

Soon Mokamea was leaving the skin lodge early in the morning, not returning until well after sundown. For his part, Gordon spent much of his time roaming the valley in miserable solitude. One day he returned after dark to find Mokamea absent. He walked through the village to Little Raven's skin lodge and lingered outside, listening to the voices from within, and eventually concluded that Mokamea was not inside. Going back to the skin lodge, he found that she had come home during his absence. Resentful, he asked no questions. But the next morning he pretended to be asleep as she rose early and slipped out. He followed her in the gray half-light through the still-sleeping village, using stealth, and she crossed the creek into the village of Broken Lance's band without an inkling that he shadowed her like a starving wolf trailing a solitary elk. Once or twice she glanced over her shoulder, wary as a thief, but Gordon was able to remain unseen.

Once across the creek, she ran to a skin lodge and entered unbidden.

Gordon sat on his heels between a pair of tepees about twenty yards away—and waited. He posed no questions to himself. His mind was blank. Somewhere an infant cried. The sound tore at his heart as he remembered how once he had dreamed of having a child of his own. How foolish that dream! He listened to the birds, singing to summon the sun as they awakened to the new day. The nearby creek gurgled cheerfully. A dog barked on the other side of the camp. He gazed at the scene, taking it all in—the skin lodges in the meadow, the wooded slopes and the craggy peaks, oddly resigned to the fact that this was no longer his world. The emptiness within him made him numb, so that he experienced no self-pity, no wounded pride, no jealous rage—even when, sometime later, as the first light of day caressed the peaks high above, Bearkiller emerged from the skin lodge into which Mokamea had disappeared. The Absaroka warrior checked the sky and then cast a look about him. He didn't see Gordon. A moment later he turned back into the skin lodge.

A serene calm came over Gordon. He stood, crossed over the creek, walked through the village, and retrieved his Hawken Plains rifle, shot pouch, blanket, and buffalo robe from his skin lodge. He left everything else, including the bow and the quiver of arrows—Little Raven's present. He almost left the wampum belt, too, but decided instead to keep it, a sort of memento. Shouldering saddle and pad, he walked out to where the sorrel stood, at the edge of the village, among some of the Absaroka ponies. The sorrel whickered softly as he approached and stood patiently while Gordon saddled up.

As he climbed into the saddle he noticed that an old woman had emerged from a nearby skin lodge. She was staring at him, and then slowly raised a hand in a gesture of farewell. Gordon was moved. He, too, raised a hand, before turning the sorrel and riding away.

II.

For two days he traveled without paying the slightest attention to the direction he was going. He neither ate nor slept. During the night he sat up and let his thoughts wander freely—from the farm in Ireland, where he and his father worked the fields shoulder to shoulder, and where his mother read from her Bible as they gathered around the hearth after dinner had been cleared away; to the Atlantic passage of the brigantine *Penelope,* that accursed ship with its hellish 'tween-deck quarters where his father's life had been snuffed out by ship fever, to images of the crewmen scampering like monkeys up the rigging to the shrouds, to Captain Warren's evil and ugly round red face. He thought about New Orleans and the fight between Gabriel and Joe Lightning, and his meeting with the octoroon beauty, Lorine, and the long trek with Captain Stewart along the river road to the plantation of Anton Remairie. He had vivid images of the Hawken brothers' gun shop in St. Louis, and the way the bounty hunter he had shot sailed through a hotel window. He remembered that night the Arapahoes had tried to steal the company's horse herd, and he recalled the breathtaking excitement of the buffalo hunt. He saw flashes of Eliza Hancock's pale yellow hair and shy blue eyes. Saw, too, the two figures, mother and child, huddled on an ice floe in the wild Missouri River, and the innocent face of the Blackfoot boy he had saved from death at the hands of an Absaroka warrior. And of course he thought about Mokamea, seeing her in his mind's eye as he had first seen her, at the ceremony, standing before him in all her sultry beauty, as radiant as the sun, as mysterious as the moon. And he also saw her as he had last laid eyes on her, moving like a ghost through the gray obscurity of that moment before dawn. All of these memories flowed past his mind's eye—and he was strangely unmoved by them. It was almost as though all those memories belonged to someone else. They caused no turmoil in his heart because his heart was without life. It felt nothing. It was impervious. He was at peace, albeit an odd and hollow peace.

On the third day he gave way to sheer physical and mental exhaustion. Riding for a couple of hours that morning, then stopping at a creek to drink, he stretched out on the sweet-smelling grass and let the warmth of the sun and the song of the brook lull him to sleep. When he awoke, the sun had made its journey across the sky, and the long shadows of late afternoon reached like the blue fingers of night across the earth. He sat there, marveling at the beauty of the high country, watching the day dwindle away into darkness. A deer ventured out of the forest and he shot it without having to move from his spot. He butchered the kill, dug a fire hole, built a fire, and cooked the choice cuts on his rifle's ramrod, while the sorrel grazed contentedly nearby.

For the first time since his departure from the Crow village he gave some thought to where he was and what he would do next. Having journeyed two days north, he was approaching Flathead Indian country. To the northeast were the Blackfeet. Due east lay the headwaters of the Missouri River and, further on, the outpost of the Rocky Mountain Fur Company. To the west lay a series of mountain ranges, chief among them the Bitterroots, and the land of the Shoshone and, beyond, the Nez Percé and Oregon Territory.

And what would he do? The answer was simple, made simple because his options were so limited. He could go west to Oregon. He could go back to the outpost and his friends in the RMFC. Or he could remain in the mountains, alone. The latter option strongly appealed to him. The mountains would provide for him. Had not that deer wandered out of the trees and into his gunsights at just the right time and place? He would search for a likely spot, build his cabin, and live in splendid solitude. There would be no one around to betray him, to lie to him, to break his heart, to threaten his life; there would be no *arrangements* made. He didn't need anybody. All he wanted was to be left alone. To get his wish he would lose himself in this magnificent wild country, and avoid contact with other humans, red or white, like the bloody plague.

Except he needed several things—a good ax, some powder and shot, a few beaver traps—and there was only one place he knew of where he could acquire those items. The RMFC outpost. He had a little hard

money left over from the funds Stewart had given him
in St. Louis, enough to purchase what he required,
even at exorbitant mountain prices. Then he could lose
himself in the high country and trap just enough to provide himself with sufficient plews to exchange for the
necessities he would occasionally need to pick up at
outpost or rendezvous. Yes, that was it—that was how
he would live from this day forward, beholden to no
one, attached to nothing, trusting in himself and no
other, and the rest of the world could go hang.

The next morning he turned eastward. A week later
he rode into the RMFC outpost.

Campbell was there, and Vasquez as well, along
with perhaps eight other company men. Sublette had
returned to St. Louis on the keelboat, intent on bringing up another load of trade goods later in the season.
The rest of the men had set out in two brigades to do
some trapping. There would be a rendezvous in the
summer in the valley of the Green River, and Campbell planned to be there, primarily to announce the
opening of the outpost to the free trappers who would
venture down out of the hills for the annual frolic.

Stewart was long gone, of course, along with the
Hancocks and Jonathan Miller, bound for parts west.
Campbell had turned into an office the small cabin that
had been erected for the missionary and his family last
winter. It was there that the partisan greeted Gordon ef-
fusively, and they talked things over while sharing a
jug of whiskey, with Vasquez coming in a little later to
contribute to the drinking as well as the palaver.

"I believe Marcus Hancock will build his mission
west of the Bitterroots, among the Flatheads or
Shoshones," announced Campbell. "There are some

prime sites along the Clearwater. I drew a map for Captain Stewart and I have no doubt he will get them there safely."

"I hope so," said Gordon, resolutely blocking out unbidden thoughts of Eliza.

"How's that Injun gal of yours?" asked Vasquez, posing the question Campbell had been too circumspect to put forth himself.

"She isn't mine any longer," replied Gordon flatly, and he told them what had happened. "What I did shamed her, I guess. So she moved in with Bearkiller."

"And you didn't put up a fight?" asked Vasquez. "I thought you loved that gal."

"No I didn't put up a fight. What's the use of fighting for something you've already lost?"

"Well," drawled Vasquez, "that's just like an Injun. Women are fickle, but none more so than a squaw. They'll take up with another man as it suits 'em."

"Vasquez has something of a jaundiced view of the gentler sex," said Campbell wryly.

"I ain't sure what 'jaundiced' means. I missed out on the kind of book larnin' you got, Robert, 'fore you had the good sense to put all that behind you and come West. But I've shared my blankets with more than a few squaws, and I can tell you it just won't do to go and get all misty-eyed about a one of 'em. Sorry it happened to you, Hawkes, but I ain't surprised. Not in the least."

Gordon shrugged. "Doesn't matter, really. I reckon I owe you an apology, though, Mr. Campbell, for messing up that alliance you wanted so bad with the Absaroka."

"Especially on account of some snot-nosed Blackfoot kid," said Vasquez, shaking his head in disbelief. "I swear, Hawkes, you have a knack for jumpin' in with both feet 'fore you've thought a thing through."

"Step back, Vasquez," said Campbell. "He did what he figured he had to do."

"Yep, I know it. But that boy'll grow up into a Blackfoot warrior what won't give a second thought to cutting our friend's throat and hangin' his topknot from a scalp pole."

"Pay him no mind, Hawkes," advised Campbell. "You said the Crows never had a council to decide what to do about you? Sounds to me like Little Raven may have had a hand in that. He won't forget that you saved his boy's life. The Crow warriors may not trust you anymore, or ever ride with you again, but you're still under Little Raven's protection. Have you got that wampum belt the chief gave you? Good. Hold on to it. You never know when you may have need for such a thing."

They passed the jug around, and Campbell asked Gordon if he wanted to stay on at the outpost. Gordon thanked him, and said no. Campbell didn't press him about his plans. The jug made the rounds again and finally Vasquez spoke up.

"Well, Robert, are you goin' to tell him or not?"

"Tell me what?" asked Gordon.

Campbell grimaced. "Two men showed up about a week ago. They were looking for you and Stewart. They'd paid McKenzie a call, and so they knew the two of you had been with our outfit. Said you're wanted for murder. A ten-thousand-dollar reward."

The utter calm Gordon experienced in the face of

this news was reflected by the stoicism he displayed to his friends.

"There was no point in denying you'd been with us," continued Campbell. "So I told them that you and Stewart left out of here at green-up. Said the two of you had gone into the mountains on your own."

"Last we seen of 'em, they were ridin' west," added Vasquez.

"Far as I know," said Campbell, "nobody in this outfit told them otherwise."

Gordon nodded. "My thanks to you, then. I guess you're wanting to know if Captain Stewart and I really did murder somebody. The answer is no. We were framed. The man was a Creole planter down New Orleans way. His mistress wanted him dead, so she had him killed and made it look like we did it. At least that's how we figured it."

"I think I know you pretty well, Hawkes," said Campbell earnestly. "Well enough to be sure you didn't murder anyone in cold blood. Besides, what a man has done in the past is no business of mine, long as he doesn't muddy up my water. The men that come out here often as not are trying to get away from something."

"Didn't care a hoot for them two bounty hunters anyways," said Vasquez. "A pair of no-account rascals. But plenty mean and dangerous. One of 'em is named McCree and the other's Kennedy. You watch your back, Hawkes."

"I didn't think anyone would come out this far just to find me."

"Ten thousand dollars will buy a lot of whiskey," said Campbell.

"Every man I know of in this outfit likes his whiskey."

"True. But you're one of us, and we don't turn on our own. Unwritten rule, you might say. One of the few a mountain man lives by."

"All mountain men?"

"I hope to God so."

"I'm grateful," said Gordon, humbled by the loyalty of Campbell and the other members of the Rocky Mountain Fur Company.

"So what are you aimin' to do with yourself now?" asked Vasquez.

"Going back into the mountains, find a place where I can be left alone. It's a big country, so I don't expect to run into those bounty hunters."

"They'll give up sooner or later," predicted Campbell. "I doubt if they have any idea just how big this country is. No better place to get lost in if that's what you have in mind."

Gordon told them what he needed in the way of supplies, and Campbell offered to give them to him for nothing, but he insisted on paying. Campbell also invited him to stay for a day or two, but he declined that offer, too. "I'll be back next summer, if I'm still above snakes," said Gordon.

"We'll pay top dollar for all the plews you can bring in."

They shook hands on it. Vasquez made sure Gordon got everything he required—double-headed ax, powder and shot, some percussion caps, several traps, modest quantities of coffee, sugar, salt, and flour—and then they, too, parted company. Gordon wasted no time in putting the outpost behind him, turning west for the distant mountains; he was eager to be gone from this place. There were entirely too many memories here to suit him.

He gave some thought to the bounty hunters—but not much. It was unlikely that they could find him in the high country. His goal was to steer clear of any human contact. Besides, he had to keep out of the way of the entire Blackfoot nation, so what did it matter if there were a couple more men roaming around who had designs on his life? At least Captain Stewart was in no danger. Gordon figured the Scotsman would be sailing for England by summer's end if he wasn't already on the high seas.

Within days of returning to the mountains he found an ideal spot for a sanctuary.

On a high table of land overlooking a remote canyon he discovered a meadow encircled by timber, with a sweetwater spring near at hand. The spring fed into a creek that plummeted down a steep ravine from the base of a rock slope, and a game trail that paralleled the ravine took him to the table. He looked the situation over, and then went back down to the canyon floor to make certain the meadow could not be seen from below. Satisfied, he made the climb again and set immediately to work. He decided to build a cabin at the base of a cliff, beneath an overhang; from the front door he could look out through the trees and see the meadow, and beyond the meadow, perhaps two hundred yards from the cabin site, was a rocky promontory from which he could survey the length and breadth of the canyon. There was plentiful evidence that the canyon was chock full of game. On the other hand, he had seen absolutely no sign of human visitors.

While the game trail in the ravine was the best route for descent to the canyon floor, there proved to be another way off the table—a passage through a jumble of immense boulders to the north of the ledge, passable for a man on foot, but impossible for someone on horseback. If need be, Gordon could leave by this route, if it happened that uninvited guests were ascending the ravine.

He set to work on the cabin with vigor, and his experience in helping to build the Rocky Mountain Fur Company outpost the winter before stood him in good stead. The cliff itself formed the back wall; he put up the other three, framing out a door and a single window. He pitched the roof low on sturdy beams, made cedar shingles with a hatchet, and put them up. The door he fashioned from half logs, hinged on strips of leather, and did likewise with the window shutters. Half of the cabin floor was stone, the remainder hardpack earth, and that suited him. Gathering the rocks from the base of the cliff and sealing them in place with mud mixed with sticks, he made his fireplace and chimney.

The cabin done, he erected a pen for the sorrel out of sapling poles, adjacent to the cabin's south side. Usually, though, he let the horse graze unattended in the meadow. This done, he went down into the canyon and set his traps in a pond fed by the creek that tumbled down the flank of the mountain. Tracks and markings on nearby trees indicated that a colony of beaver lived here.

The summer days came and went with an uneventful monotony. Still, he managed to keep plenty busy, preparing for winter, knowing that when the heavy snows came he would be trapped in the canyon until the first thaw. He cut a lot of firewood. He cut meadow grass, too, drying it out in the warm sun and putting it up for the sorrel. He went hunting, using the Hawken at first, and then deciding to make himself a bow and some arrows. He killed a half-dozen deer and a solitary elk, jerked and dried the meat, and hung it from the cabin's rafters. Several beaver fell prey to his well-placed traps, and he scraped and cleaned and cured the plews the way he had seen it done by the Absaroka Crow women. He enjoyed that mountain man luxury, roasted beaver tail. In his spare time he built a split log trestle table and bench, the cabin's only furnishings.

Occasionally he went exploring, and by the end of summer he knew the canyon and adjacent valley like the back of his hand. He kept an eye peeled for any sign of human visitation, and was pleased not to find any. In the evenings he often sat at the rim of the promontory and watched the blue shadows lengthen as the sun descended behind the majestic snow-capped peaks to the west. Only then, as he watched night steal across the land, did he ever get lonely, and when that happened he recalled all the wrongs that had been done him by the people in his past. This proved to be a good antidote. A spell of loneliness now and then was a small price to pay for peace of mind.

Later, when he looked back on those days, he realized that he should have known it was too good to last.

III.

One late summer day, sunset caught him on the canyon floor, checking his traps, when he heard the sorrel whicker, looked around at the horse, and noticed that it seemed keenly interested in a stand of white aspen about five hundred yards to the south. The sorrel's ears were standing at attention, and Gordon knew there had to be something, or someone, lurking in those trees. Was it a bear? Maybe a pack of wolves? A Blackfoot raiding party? Standing in the shallows, out in the open, Gordon felt a chill run down his spine. He could almost feel someone's eyes fastened on him.

Forcing himself to act casual, he left the water and walked to the sorrel, scooping up the reins and leading the horse into the nearest cover, a copse of western larch growing in rocky ground on the east side of the pond. The game trail that led to the table high above him was in this direction, but he decided against making the climb until he knew the nature of the danger that had invaded his canyon. Deep in the trees he tethered the sorrel to the stub of a branch jutting up from a hollow log, then moved off about twenty paces to a rock outcropping where he concealed himself, rifle ready. From this vantage point he could see the pond. There he waited, peering through the gloom of the quickly gathering night.

He didn't have long to wait. A few minutes later a lone horseman appeared at the rim of the pond, checking his mount at the spot where Gordon had emerged from the water. The intruder stepped down and knelt to study the ground in the dying light. Gordon couldn't make out the man's features, but it was clear from his attire—buckskins and wolfskin head gear, that he was white, a mountain man. Or maybe a bounty hunter. Whatever he was, his presence annoyed Gordon. In all this huge country, the man had to show up in this particular canyon? It had to be pure chance, and bad luck; Gordon rejected the notion that this man was hunting for him. As far as he knew there was no way anyone could have traced him here.

The man stood up, took a long look around, and climbed back into the saddle, turning his horse into the trees where Gordon was hiding. The remnants of daylight were fast fleeing the sky, and it was now so dark that Gordon could barely see the horseman, who came within twenty paces of the rock outcropping before checking his pony again.

"I reckon you're close by," said the man calmly, "and you've got me in your sights, too. But I'd be obliged if you didn't pull the trigger on me just yet."

The voice sounded familiar, but try as he might Gordon couldn't put a face or a name to it.

"I ain't lookin' for trouble," continued the man. "Lord knows I ain't never had to look for it."

"Just stay where you are," Gordon called out. "Who are you? What are you doing here?"

"Ben Talley's my handle. Is that you, Hawkes?"

Talley! Now Gordon remembered. This was the trapper he had met in the Hawken gun shop in St. Louis about a year ago—the man who had given up the Plains rifle that Jake Hawken had custom made to his specifications, just so a greenhorn kid dead set on going West could carry with him the best firearm known to man.

Gordon left the rocks and moved cautiously closer. He didn't let his guard down. He held the rifle ready. There were still a lot of unanswered questions. Had Talley been looking for him? If so, how had Talley tracked him down? And why? Talley had shown him a kindness, but that had been a long time ago, and it didn't buy Gordon's unequivocal trust.

He pulled up a few paces shy of the horseman, and Talley peered into the darkness—then grinned beneath his sandy red beard.

"By God it is you, Hawkes. I thought it could be when I seen you earlier, but I was a ways off, and these old eyes ain't what they used to be. Truth be known, I get as blind as a bat this time of day. And you've changed quite a bit, boy. You look half Injun. Comes from livin' amongst them red devils, I reckon."

"You know about that?"

"Met up with a brigade of Campbell's boys a fortnight ago, at rendezvous. They told me all about how you took up with the Absaroka."

"You came looking for me?"

"That I did."

"How come?"

"Well, it's a long story. I'm right stiff from being in the saddle all day, and I could sure use some coffee. Reckon you can spare some?"

Gordon thought it over—and lowered the rifle. "Reckon I can do that," he allowed. "Follow me."

He fetched the sorrel and led the way up the game trail to the cabin. Inside, he leaned his rifle against the fireplace, stirred up the morning's embers, and added a log. By the firelight he and Talley looked one another over. Talley grinned again.

"Glad to see you prize that Hawken so much. Leastways you don't stray very far from it."

"Nothing personal, but I've learned not to trust anybody very far."

Talley nodded. "Good rule to live by. I figured all

along you'd make it in the wild country." He settled at the table and took a look around. "You've got yourself a good place here, Hawkes. Prime fixin's."

"It suits me."

"How about that coffee?"

Gordon nodded. He put a tin pot of water near the fire and added a modest portion of his coffee; he had been severely rationing his provisions—luxuries like coffee, sugar, flour, and salt—so that they would last him through the winter. Sharing his meager supplies was something he was loath to do, but he couldn't turn down Talley's small request. After all, the man had been generous in letting Jake Hawken sell his Plains rifle to a wet-behind-the-ears kid he didn't know from Adam.

"Heard some good things about you, Hawkes," said Talley as he watched Gordon prepare the coffee. "Like how you saved the horse herd for Campbell and his outfit when a pack of Injuns tried to steal themselves a few ponies. And how you saved a feller's life during a buffalo hunt. Not to mention the son of an Absaroka chief from drowning in the Big Muddy."

"Where did you hear all that?"

"Trapper by the name of Rusher. Real talker, especially when he's likkered up. A Rocky Mountain Fur Company man. Met up with him and his brigade about a month back, at the rendezvous. Thought you might have been there."

"Guess I missed it," said Gordon, noncommittal.

"Now, me and Johnny Ornsdorff and Three Fingers Batterson—them two you saw me with back in St. Louis—we're free trappers. Means we don't owe allegiance to no one outfit in particular. Of course, we usually do business with Sublette and his crowd, on account we don't trust McKenzie and his bunch. You ever met Kenneth McKenzie?"

"I have."

"He could charm the antlers off a bull elk. But he ain't to be trusted. He's a cold-blooded cuss and he aims to make certain that every trapper in these mountains works for the American Fur Company, and them that don't he aims to see eat dirt. But I'm straying off my story, ain't I? Thing is, we know Rusher and his crew. And they know us. That's how come he told us all about you."

"You haven't told me yet what brought you here."

"Because a few days later we met up with two more fellers at that rendezvous. They were bounty hunters, and they were looking for you and a Scotsman name of Stewart. They had just talked to Rusher. Rusher told them he didn't know where you were, but that last he'd heard you were livin' with the Crow Indians. As for that Stewart feller, Rusher said he'd headed up Oregon way with a family of missionaries."

The coffee was beginning to boil. Gordon poured it into a tin cup and handed the cup across the table to Talley. He stayed near the fireplace, arms folded, the Plains rifle within easy reach. His mind was racing. What was Talley getting at? Gordon couldn't quite figure it out, but he had a hunch he wasn't going to like how the mountain man's story ended.

Talley sipped the coffee, an expression of pure delight on his weathered features. "This hits the spot, Hawkes. You ain't having none of this nectar?"

"Not just yet. Besides, that's my only cup. Wasn't

expecting much company up here. So what did those bounty hunters tell you?"

"Said you and the Scot were wanted for murder down Louisiana way." Talley was peering at him over the cup's rim, watching his reaction.

"That's true. We're wanted. But we didn't murder anybody."

Talley shrugged. "None of my business even if you did."

"No, I'm telling you, I didn't murder anyone, and neither did Captain Stewart."

"Okay, I believe you. But those bounty hunters think different. Or I should say they don't much care if you're innocent or not. Either way they collect the reward if they bring you in."

"So you came all this way to warn me? Well, thanks, but I already knew about those two. Robert Campbell told me about them a couple months ago."

"Not exactly why I'm here. You see, Johnny and Three Fingers decided to join up with them two."

"Join the bounty hunters? That's great," said Gordon dryly. "Why would they go and do a thing like that?"

"Times are hard for trappers, Hawkes. We've been out here doing this for nigh on ten years. Gets harder and harder to find prime beaver. Many a valley's been all but trapped out. It's particular bad for free trappers. Since McKenzie's made a treaty with the Blackfoot, his brigades get to work the best beaver country, which nowadays happens to be up north, where it's damn near too dangerous for the rest of us. So Johnny and Three Fingers sat up and took notice when they found out about that ten-thousand-dollar reward."

"Hadn't figured the bounty hunters would want to share."

"They're going after your friend first, you see. Figure he'll be easier to find. They thought you being with the Crow Indians made it so's it'd be harder to find you—and even if they did find you, well, they don't want to tangle with Injuns if they can help it. So they showed up at the rendezvous, hoping you'd make an appearance. Anyway, there was a rumor floating around that the missionaries had set up shop somewhere up on the Clearwater, amongst the Flathead Indians. They're betting Stewart is still with them Bible thumpers."

Gordon thought it likely that Stewart had moved on by now. But he didn't tell Talley that the Scotsman intended to make for the Pacific Coast, seeking a ship that would carry him home to England.

"More coffee?" he asked Talley.

"Obliged."

Gordon filled the cup. "You haven't told me how you managed to track me down."

"Wasn't easy. I knew from what Rusher said that it was Little Raven's bunch that you'd taken up with, and I also knew where Little Raven had made his summer camp last year. Figured he might be there again this year, and sure enough he was. 'Course by that time you'd lit out on your own. But, lucky for me, they had a pretty good idea where you were. A buck callin' himself Five Horses had followed your trail for several days. Seems like they still consider you their brother in spite of everything that happened. I told 'em I was a friend of yours, and they pointed the way. So here I am."

Gordon nodded. "So you just like being poor, is that it?"

Talley sipped the coffee, wiped a sleeve across his beard, and acted like he didn't understand what Gordon was getting at.

"I don't reckon I'm all that poor," he replied. "I get to live in this here high country where I'm my own boss. I don't have two coins to rub together, but then I don't have to answer to nobody."

"Why aren't you interested in sharing that reward?"

"Oh, so that's what you're fishin' for. I guess 'cause I got my pride. I won't turn against one of my own kind. Now Johnny and Three Fingers, they ain't so particular. I'm right disappointed in them. Disappointed in you, too, come to think of it."

"Sorry. You did me a big favor once and I guess this is no way to repay you."

"Forget it. A feller in your position don't live long if he's too trustin'."

"I see you've got yourself a Plains rifle, even though you gave that one Jake Hawken made for you to me."

Talley glanced admiringly at the rifle he had carried into the cabin and leaned against the table. "Bought it at rendezvous. I'm right proud of it."

"Mind if I take a look?"

"Go ahead." Talley picked the rifle up and tossed it to Gordon, who half turned toward the fire so that he could get a better look at the weapon.

"Every bit as fine as the one you gave me," said Gordon, turning back and laying the rifle on the table. "I owe you a mighty large debt, Mr. Talley. Don't know how I can ever repay you. First the rifle and now the warning."

"What did you aim to do?"

Gordon had already made up his mind. "Go find those missionaries. Make sure my friend isn't still with them. If he is, I've got to get to him before those bounty hunters do."

"You know where to find those folks, exactly?"

"Not exactly. But I'll find them. Got a little more coffee left, Mr. Talley. You might as well finish it off."

"Don't mind if I do."

Gordon turned to the fire, bent over to pick up the pot—and heard Talley stand up in a hurry, and then the telltale double click of a rifle's hammer being cocked all the way back. Gordon put the pot down, straightened slowly, and turned around to face the free trapper. Talley was aiming the rifle at him and shaking his head.

"I don't think you really learned your lessons after all, Hawkes."

"Might surprise you, but I thought you were lying from the start."

"How so?"

"Way I see it, your friends and those bounty hunters are bound to be real close by. You came in alone to try to find out if I knew where Captain Stewart was—exactly. You see, it didn't make any sense, what you said about the others giving up on finding me and heading out to Oregon. All of you knew I'd been living with the Absaroka. Johnny or Three Fingers could have figured out to ask them just like you did. So how much did those bounty men offer to pay you?"

"What does that matter?"

"I just want to know how much your pride is going for these days."

"You can go straight to Hell, boy. I liked you when I met you in St. Louis. Was right sure you had the makin's to be a mountain man. I like you still. But not well enough to turn up my nose at one thousand dollars American. Sorry, Hawkes. Believe it or not, this ain't personal."

"That's okay," said Gordon, reaching slowly for his own rifle. "Neither is what I'm about to do."

"Don't be a fool," rasped Talley. "Lay a hand on that Hawken and I'll put a hole clean through your heart."

"I doubt that. You see, I took the cap out of your rifle while I was looking at it."

Disbelief flashed in Talley's eyes as he checked his gun. Seeing that Gordon was telling the truth, he let out a roar and hurled the rifle away. In the next instant, as Gordon grabbed his own Hawken, Talley whipped a Green River knife out of his belt and launched himself over the table with remarkable speed and agility for a man of his size. Gordon didn't have time to level his rifle and shoot, so he used it instead to block the downward sweep of the knife. Talley's bulk slammed him into the hearthstones, and he kneed his assailant in the groin. The air wheezed out of Talley's lungs as he staggered, doubling over. Gordon struck at Talley's knife hand with the butt of the Hawken, hard enough to crack the bones in the man's wrist, and the blade fell to the ground. But Talley recovered quickly, grabbing the Hawken with both hands, trying to wrench it from Gordon's grasp. He was bigger and stronger than Gordon, and Gordon knew he would succeed in gaining possession of the rifle—so he squeezed the trigger. If Talley got the gun it was going to be empty.

The muzzle flash was blinding as the Hawken went

off between them. The ball plowed into a wall. In the next instant Gordon was falling backward, bringing a foot up into Talley's midsection, arching his back as he hit the ground, and catapulting Talley over his head, letting the trapper take the empty rifle with him as he went flying, head over heels. Gordon bounced to his feet, scooped up Talley's fallen knife, and whirled as Talley came charging at him like a bull buffalo, swinging the Hawken like a club. Timing it perfectly, Gordon went in under the Hawken and drove the knife into Talley's chest, turning it so that the blade would slip between the ribs. Talley went rigid, his eyes wide and staring. He made an awful guttural sound and then collapsed as though all the bones in his lifeless body had simply disintegrated. Gordon stepped back, shaking, leaving the knife buried in the mountain man's heart.

He stood there a few minutes, breathing hard, waiting for the shakes to leave him, waiting, too, for his mind to start working again. Then he snatched up his rifle and quickly reloaded it. Checked Talley's Hawken, too, putting a new cap in place. Taking a look around, he figured there was nothing in the cabin he needed to bring with him, so he kicked the fire in the fireplace to death, plunging the room into darkness. Moving to the door, he threw it open, half expecting a volley of gunfire, a hail of bullets. But the night was quiet. Too quiet. He was convinced they were out there. Question was, were they nearby, or far away? Counting to thirty, he steeled himself and went out in a crouching run, making for the pen where his sorrel and Talley's horse were located. He hit the ground when he got there and crawled under the pole fence into the corral and lay there for another count of thirty, listening hard. Catching his scent, the sorrel walked over to him, whickered softly, and nudged him with its soft nose.

With each passing minute he became more and more convinced that he was alone up here on the high table—and if that were so he was wasting precious time lying on his belly in horse puckey. His saddle and pad were near at hand, draped over the corral's top pole. At length he moved, throwing the pad on the sorrel's back, then the saddle, working quickly to buckle and tighten the cinch strap. He put a bridle on the sorrel and bridled Talley's horse as well. Then he tied Talley's Hawken to one side of his saddle and his own Plains rifle to the other, dropped the gate pole, and led both horses out of the corral. He walked them to the bottom of the game trail—the going was too treacherous for a rider at night. As he reached the bottom he heard someone—no, make that several someones— coming through the woods, heading for the ravine.

Leading the horses off the game trail, Gordon scrambled up a sharp incline to the base of the cliff that supported the ledge where he'd built his sanctuary. Here there was a cave, and though it was shallow Gordon could only hope the shadows were deep enough to mask his presence. Taking the horses to the very back of the cave, he laid a hand across the sorrel's muzzle to keep it quiet. A few minutes later he saw the shadowy shapes of four men moving up the game trail, leading their ponies and moving single file. They were maybe forty feet away, but Gordon could not see well enough to identify any of them. Still, it was pretty clear in his mind who they were—Ornsdorff and Batterson and the two bounty hunters. Ben Talley's partners. Gordon scarcely dared breathe. If they spotted him he would be trapped—"gone beaver" for sure.

Once they were well past he left the cave and, mounting the sorrel, rode away, leading Talley's horse. He figured if the four men chased him he might need a fresh mount. It would take the men about twenty minutes to reach the cabin; then he could only hope it would take them a little more time to figure out what had happened and that their prey was nowhere in the vicinity. He could reasonably expect at least an hour's head start.

He traveled through the night, pausing just prior to dawn on high ground and watching his back trail for about an hour after day broke. No sign of pursuit. But they would be along eventually. He just had a bigger lead than he had hoped for. Unwilling to squander any more of it than he had to, he pressed on.

In the days that followed he traversed the valley of the Thompson River, past the falls and to the north end, with the Cabinet Mountains on his right hand and the Bitterroot range on his left. There he found the famous Lolo Pass, the passage that the Lewis and Clark expedition had used to cross the formidable Bitterroots. He was in Flathead country now. Sixty miles west lay a great valley formed by several major rivers—the Kootenai, the St. Marie, the Salmon, and the Clearwater. The north fork of the latter curled eastward, in the vicinity of the Bitterroots, and Gordon figured the easiest way to find the best route to the great valley would be by following the Clearwater's north fork.

He had no trouble finding the river—but following it was something else entirely. This country was as rough as any he had ever seen—rocky ridges, steep ravines, and occasional canyons, labyrinths of dead-falls and jumbles of boulders. He picked his way with care, often leading the horses. In this kind of terrain he no longer risked travel by night, settling down into fireless camps at day's end. Always he kept an eye on his back trail. Yet his pursuers never made an appearance. Could it be that they had given up the hunt for some reason? Perhaps had a falling-out? Maybe seeing their friend Ben Talley dead had bled some of the enthusiasm out of Batterson and Ornsdorff. Maybe they were thinking twice about their new vocation of man-hunting. Gordon gave all this more thought than it deserved and ended up with a conclusion that it was mostly wishful thinking on his part.

At least he was still ahead of them. A few hours, or even a day ahead, but that was plenty of time, if he could just locate the Hancock mission and determine whether Captain Stewart was there. If so, he would warn his friend and they would make a run for it together. If not, he would not linger. There was no point in that. Besides, he doubted that he would be welcome.

On the second day west of Lolo Pass, the men hunting him made their presence known.

The first bullet missed him by inches. Hearing its angry *crack*! as it passed, Gordon knew exactly what it was a split second before he heard the gun's report echoing off the canyon's steep walls. He was caught in a bad spot—a sheer rock face on his right, a shale slope leading down to the raging, rock-strewn river below. Making a snap decision, he let go of the extra horse, bent low, and kicked the sorrel into a gallop—a desperate measure on a narrow, winding trail.

The next bullet found its mark, hitting him in the left shoulder, and the impact nearly pitched Gordon out of the saddle. As his weight shifted, the sorrel lost its footing on the trail and toppled sideways onto the shale slope. Gordon kicked his feet out of the stirrups, got a good grip on his Hawken, and tried to jump clear. He landed poorly, nearly blacked out, and began to roll down the steep incline, fetching up about thirty yards later against a log. Before he could collect himself a bullet splintered the dead wood a foot to one side of him. Cursing, he crawled over the log and flopped down on the other side, in a world of hurt. From this cover he got his first sighting of them—less than four hundred yards down the trail he had been on. How had they gotten so damned close without his seeing them? He reminded himself that two of his pursuers had made manhunting a living, while the other two were trappers accustomed to getting around unseen if it suited them.

He looked around for the sorrel. The horse was halfway up the slope, lying on its side, legs thrashing, and in a glance Gordon could see that one of its legs was shattered. Heartbroken, he laid the Hawken across the log, aimed, and fired. The faithful horse was dead. Talley's horse was nowhere to be seen. There was only one way out of the canyon now. Once the decision was made Gordon wasted no time. He got up and took off, running for the river. A bullet splashed into the water in front of him. Another grazed his side, burning like a white-hot branding iron, and spinning him around. In the shallows, he slipped and sprawled into the current which swept him away with breathtaking force. He managed to get turned around so that he was floating on his back, legs pointed downstream, and rifle held above the churning surface of the river. The river careened him off a few half-submerged boulders, hurled him pell-mell down a chute, and tossed him over the brink of fifteen-foot falls. Treading water in a relatively deep, calm pool below the falls, he noticed a ledge beneath the cascade. He swam under the falls, found firm footing, and waited there, all but his head and shoulders still submerged, peering through the curtain of falling water, shivering uncontrollably, and deafened by the roar of the falls.

He didn't have long to wait. The four men on the trail came into view, their shapes distorted by the veil of water behind which Gordon had concealed himself. They were on foot, leading their horses, scanning the river and its banks, looking for some sign of him. Long after their search had taken them further downriver, Gordon waited behind the waterfall. It was all he could do to stay conscious. His blood made a pink mist in the crystal clear water swirling around him. The bullet had passed completely through his shoulder, so in that respect he had been fortunate. But he was losing a lot of blood.

Nonetheless, he waited for nearly an hour before emerging from his place of concealment. He swam to the shore opposite the trail. It took his last ounce of strength to crawl out of the river. For a long spell he just lay there, hurting and exhausted, and let the afternoon sun warm him.

Later he made a poultice out of elm bark, mud, and moss and applied it to his wounds. He tore his linsey-woolsey shirt into strips and used these as bandages to hold the poultices in place. He dried and cleaned and reloaded the Hawken rifle. Though he felt the need to get moving that night, there just wasn't enough strength left in his body. He lay down in a thicket of serviceberry bushes and slept like a dead man until the sun on his face awakened him. His punished body howled in protest as he struggled to his feet. But he had to get started. The bounty hunters were in front of him now. If they got to the Hancock mission first and Stewart happened to be there—well, Gordon had a good idea what would happen then. Obviously the four hunters were planning to bring their prey back dead rather than alive. A whole lot less trouble that way.

He followed the river all day, and in his weakened condition made poor time. In addition, he had to keep an eye peeled for danger now that the bounty men lurked somewhere up ahead. His strength and stamina slowly but surely ebbed out of him, so that by the afternoon of the second day he had to stop and rest—just for a little while, he told himself. But when he opened his eyes it was night. The stars told him that it was early in the morning of the next day, so he went back to sleep. It was again the sun on his face that wakened him, blinding him momentarily—and then something moved across the sun, briefly blocking it and throwing a shadow across Gordon, and he groped in panic for the Plains rifle, his heart lurching in his chest. The Hawken was gone! He sat up, squinting at the Indian who sat on his heels nearby, admiring the rifle that lay across his knees.

"Hey," said Gordon, perturbed. "I'd like that back, if you don't mind. Damn it, I've been through a lot lately and I'm in no mood to tolerate a thief."

The Indian looked up at him, unperturbed, and smiled.

Grimacing, Gordon made the sign for "friend." He added, muttering, "Now give me that rifle back."

The Indian stood up, stepped forward, and presented the Hawken to Gordon. Startled, Gordon took it.

"You . . . understand English?"

The Indian nodded. "Joseph speak English, too. Joseph is half-breed. A missionary man, Dr. Lee, take me East to white man's school."

That stirred the embers of Gordon's memory. "Wait just a minute. Do you happen to know a Marcus Hancock?"

Joseph nodded. "Joseph was guide for Hancock."

"He says you ran off and left them when the going got rough."

Joseph studied the ground between his moccasins, arms folded, brows knit in thought. "This is true," he conceded, finally. "Feel bad. But Joseph warned them to go different way. Hancock would not listen. Say Almighty God protect him from Blackfoot. Joseph say no one protect *him* from Blackfoot, so Joseph went away. What good is a guide if you don't listen to him?"

Gordon smiled. "Can't argue with that. And it certainly sounds like Reverend Hancock. Look here, Joseph. I've got to find the Hancocks. I think they have a mission set up somewhere nearby. Can you help me?"

Joseph pondered the request for a moment. "Yesterday Joseph see four white men. They look very hard for something. Looking for you, maybe."

Gordon nodded. "That's right. And they're bad men."

"Hmm. Are you a bad man, too?"

"I'll explain everything to you—later. Can you take me to the Hancocks or not?"

Joseph turned away. "Wait here."

Gordon lay down, exhausted from the effort it had required just to sit up. "Don't worry. I'm not going anywhere."

A few minutes later Joseph reappeared astride a shaggy mountain mustang. He dismounted, helped Gordon get aboard the pony, and took up the reins.

"Why are you helping me?" Gordon asked.

Joseph fingered the wampum dangling from Gordon's belt, the one Little Raven had given him.

"You are brother to the Absaroka. The Absaroka and the Flatheads are friends. That makes you Joseph's friend. Joseph will call you White Crow."

He walked north, leading the pony, and Gordon asked no more questions.

CHAPTER 8

I.

By the middle of the morning of the following day Gordon was gazing down into a beautiful valley hemmed in by wooded hills, where a cabin had been recently built on the banks of a swift-moving stream. Beyond the hills to the north stood a row of magnificent snow-covered peaks. Smoke curled from the cabin's chimney, as it did from the smoke holes of six skin lodges that stood nearby. A large wooden cross, at least fifteen feet high, had been erected in front of the cabin. A few horses and mules—probably the ones donated to the Hancock party by the Rocky Mountain Fur Company so that the missionaries could continue on their journey—were contained in a small corral adjacent to the cabin. At this distance Gordon couldn't tell whether Captain Stewart's buckskin was among the livestock.

"This is the place," said Gordon. "What are we waiting for, Joseph? Let's get down there."

"This as far as Joseph can go."

"I'm no more welcome than you are, Joseph. So we'll face them together."

Joseph, as was his wont, gave this suggestion a moment of profound study—then adamantly shook his head. "Joseph will go no further. When you are done with the Hancocks you will be welcome in Joseph's lodge. Flathead village at east end of valley." He pointed off to the right.

"What are Indians doing down there?"

Joseph grimaced. "Christian Indians."

"Aren't you a Christian Indian, Joseph? You've sure been a Good Samaritan in my book."

"Joseph is a Christian in spite of Hancock and his friend Miller," replied the Flathead gravely. "Not because of them. Jason Lee was a great man. All Indians knew his word was good. He was true friend to all Indians. With Hancock this is not so. And Hancock's friend, Miller . . ." Joseph just shook his head. "They do not belong here. They will not stay long."

"What do you mean? Looks like they're pretty well settled in."

Joseph shrugged, and changed the subject. "Take the pony. Joseph will send someone to get it."

Gordon put out his hand. "If there is anything I can ever do to repay you, Joseph, just let me know."

Joseph reached up and shook the proffered hand. Then he was gone, disappearing into the trees at an easy lope.

The faint sound of a distant bell brought Gordon's attention back to the mission. People were moving about among the skin lodges and in front of the cabin. He wondered if the bounty hunters had been here before him. Could they still be here? He couldn't be certain until he got closer. But a closer look meant going out into the open. He could see no way around that. It was a chance he would have to take.

Yet he hesitated. Not for fear of his life, but rather out of concern for Eliza Hancock's feelings. It would do her absolutely no good to see him again. By now she had probably recovered from her heartbreak. How cruel it would be for him to show up again like this. There was nothing he could say or do now by way of explaining his actions. No, it was entirely too late for that. So, out of respect for her, he would not linger here. He would make certain of Captain Stewart's whereabouts and then he would go. He needed a place to recuperate from his wounds, but the mission was not that place, especially with those bounty hunters in the vicinity.

As he drew near he could better see what all the commotion was about. Twenty or so Indians were congregating beneath the big wooden cross—men, women, and children sitting cross-legged on the ground. Marcus Hancock's black-clad figure emerged from the cabin, followed by Jonathan Miller and Letitia, she dressed all in gray as was her custom. Eliza came out last of all, clad in a plain white dress. Gordon got a funny feeling in the pit of his stomach when he saw her. Eliza and her mother were singing as they marched in a single-file procession behind the men, moving toward the cross. Gordon realized then that this was a service. Was it Sunday? Hell, he didn't even know what month of the year it was.

They didn't see him at first. He was coming in from the southeast, which put him at the backs of Hancock and his group as they stood facing the Indian congre-

gation. When the hymn singing was finished Hancock
proceeded to sermon, standing with legs spread apart,
the wind pulling at his black frock coat. He gestured
dramatically with a Bible in one hand. He wielded the
Good Book like a sword. As Gordon got closer some
of the Indians began to pay some attention to his approach, wondering who he was. Miller noticed, and
looked over his shoulder, but he spared Gordon a mere
glance. Gordon figured that Miller mistook him for
just another Indian. Ben Talley had said he looked half
Indian, and he was riding a Flathead pony.

Nearing the shallow stream he could hear Hancock's
stentorian voice as he quoted from Scripture.

" 'We know that the law is spiritual, but I am un-
spiritual, sold as a slave to sin. I do not understand
what I do. For what I want to do I do not do, but what
I hate to do I do. And if I do what I do not want to do,
I agree that the law is good. As it is, it is no longer I
myself who do it, but it is sin living in me. I know that
nothing good lives in me, that is, in my sinful nature.
For I have the desire to do what is good, but I cannot
carry it out. For what I do is not the good I want to do;
no, the evil I do not want to do—this I keep on doing.
Now if I do what I do not want to do, it is no longer I
who do it, but it is sin living in me that does it.' "

Gordon crossed the creek. The sound of the pony
splashing through the rocky shallows reached Eliza's
ears; she turned her head slowly and looked at him,
and she seemed to recognize him at once, and gazed at
him without looking away.

" 'Those who live according to the sinful nature
have their minds set on what their nature desires; but
those who live in accordance with the Spirit have their

minds set on what the Spirit desires. The mind of sinful man is death, but the mind controlled by the Spirit is life and peace. The sinful mind is hostile to God. It does not submit to God's law, nor can it do so.' "

Gordon checked the Flathead pony about thirty paces away and returned Eliza's gaze, wondering what she was thinking, unable to read her expression as the wind blew her pale blond hair like a veil across her blue eyes.

" 'Therefore, brothers, we have an obligation—but it is not to the sinful nature, to live according to it. For if you live according to the sinful nature you will die, but if by the Spirit you put to death the misdeeds of the body you will live, because those who are led by the Spirit of God are the children of God. The Spirit himself testifies with our spirit that we are God's children. Now if we are children, then we are heirs—heirs of God and coheirs with Christ, if indeed we share in his sufferings . . .' "

Miller had glanced at Eliza, following her gaze to Gordon, and he clutched at Hancock's arm. The preacher looked over his shoulder and gaped at Gordon as he finished, his voice faltering: " '. . . in order that we may also share in His glory.' "

"Amen," said Letitia—but when no one joined in with her she looked up from her Bible and realized that all the others were watching the lone horseman.

Miller was the first to move. He started toward Gordon with quick, angry strides, ignoring Hancock as the missionary called out for him to wait. As he drew near, Miller reached under his frock coat and brandished a pistol, his features knotted with fury. Until that moment Gordon had been ignoring him, caught up in looking at Eliza, but when he saw the pistol Gordon calmly brought his Hawken to bear, aiming the rifle at Miller's chest and stopping him dead in his tracks.

Sensing that violence was imminent, one of the Flathead women cried out in alarm, and in an instant the entire congregation was up, the women herding their children back to the skin lodges, the men bringing up the rear, shielding their families with their bodies. Gordon noticed that none of them were armed.

"What in the hell are you doing here?" rasped Miller.

"That's no way for a missionary to talk."

Letitia was trying to steer her daughter to the safety of the cabin, but Eliza would have none of it; she slipped away and ran toward Gordon, pulling up short a few paces shy of him, still gazing raptly at his face as though trying to make certain he wasn't a ghost.

"Hello, Eliza," he said.

"Don't speak to my daughter!" roared Hancock, outraged. "Who do you think you are, coming here like this? Have you no respect? No decency?"

Gordon drew a deep breath, trying to calm himself, but before he could reply, Hancock noticed for the first time the pistol in Miller's grasp, and he turned ashen.

"God in heaven, Jonathan—what are you doing with that pistol? You—you carried a pistol to services?"

"You're such a fool, Marcus," was Miller's contemptuous reply.

Eliza stepped closer to Gordon. "You're badly hurt," she said, seeing the blood on his chest, the bullet holes in his side and his shoulder.

"I'll deal with you later," Hancock told Miller, and went to Eliza, taking his daughter by the shoulders and trying to turn her away from Gordon. "Come away from him, child. He is unworthy of your compassion."

"That's a funny thing for a Christian to say, Father."

"I am simply concerned for your own well-being, child. I don't want to see you hurt."

"Look," said Gordon, exasperated. "I've come all this way just to find out about Captain Stewart. I have no intentions of staying."

"Stewart is gone," said Hancock tersely. "He left a fortnight ago, bound for Oregon, I believe."

Gordon breathed a sigh of relief. A two-week head start on the bounty hunters should be plenty for the Scotsman.

"Why do you want to know?" asked Miller.

Gordon decided he might as well tell them the whole truth. Sooner or later the bounty hunters would show up, and these folks would be better off knowing what to expect. So he gave them the unvarnished story, without embellishments, nothing but the plain facts. He explained how he and Stewart had been framed for Anton Remairie's murder, how the bounty hunters had tracked him down, and that they were on their way here, searching for Captain Stewart.

"I don't believe you," said Miller, truculent. "I don't believe you were framed at all."

Gordon's smile was wintry. "I don't care what you think. But what I can't quite work out is why you've got it in for me. Only thing I can think of is that it must have something to do with Eliza."

Miller glanced at Eliza, then at Hancock, and there was guilt written all over his face—but Hancock wasn't paying him any attention. All the minister could think about at this moment was getting rid of Gordon.

"You've done what you came here to do," he told Gordon. "You've found out about your friend. Now you should be on your way."

"No," said Eliza. "We cannot turn him away. Look at him, Father. He needs our care."

"If what he has said is true, and the bounty hunters are on their way here, he *must* leave," reasoned Hancock. "Think with your head for a change, child, and not your heart. If they find him here they may kill him—and us as well. I will not have my family put at risk for the likes of this, this . . ."

"Murderer?" offered Gordon dryly.

"Oh, but you don't mind putting our lives in danger to bring God's message to these Indians," snapped Eliza.

"Daughter!" snapped Letitia. "Do not speak to your father in that manner!"

"If you send him away I will go with him."

"Eliza, you can't mean that! Think about what you're saying."

"I know what I'm saying, Mother. He needs our help and I for one will give it to him."

"Eliza," said Gordon, "your parents are right. I can't stay. It isn't safe."

She came up to the Flathead pony, entreating him with her eyes. "Are you really going to leave me twice, Gordon Hawkes?"

He was stunned, and didn't know how to respond. How could she still have such strong feelings for him after all the heartache he had caused her? No matter what he did, Eliza Hancock still cared for him. This was a truly extraordinary revelation, and he couldn't take it all in at once. One thing was certain: she was quite right about his leaving her again. He couldn't do it, regardless of the consequences. If he stayed, the bounty hunters would find him and, in all likelihood, he would die. But better that than to cause Eliza any more hurt.

He slid off the back of the Flathead pony, and his knees buckled. Eliza rushed to his side.

"Daughter!" roared Hancock. "I forbid—"

"Be silent, Marcus," said Letitia, with a quiet resignation.

Hancock stared at his wife in utter disbelief.

"This is God's will," said Letitia sadly. "Let it be done."

Eliza was trying to help Gordon to the cabin, putting his arm around her shoulder and placing her own around his waist. Hancock looked at her—and his expression softened. He stepped up to Gordon's other side and together they walked the wounded man inside.

II.

He awoke with the morning sunlight streaming through gingham curtains hanging on a window without glass, and the warm breeze moving the curtains brought the scent of the mountains to him. It was the scent of home, and yet it was overpowered by another. This was Eliza's room—he knew it immediately. Her scent was very pervasive here, a clean smell of lye soap and wildflowers and warm skin. He was lying on a narrow bunk, on a thin straw mattress, covered by a quilt, and a thin woolen blanket was rolled up beneath his head. This was a small room, with only the one window, and a door leading to the rest of the cabin. It contained, in addition to the bed, a rocking chair and a trunk. These last two items Gordon remembered; they had been among the belongings taken to the RMFC outpost on a travois after he and Stewart and the others had found the Hancocks and Jonathan Miller stranded out on the prairie.

He was alone in the room. Sitting up, he winced at the aches in his body. His side and shoulder had been dressed. Then he remembered how he had come by those injuries, and thought of the bounty hunters got his heart racing. At least his Hawken was near at hand, leaning against the wall beside the bed. *What are you doing here?* he asked himself, disgusted. *You're a bloody fool for putting Eliza and her family in danger like this. Hancock was right. You've got to go.*

One problem—he didn't have any clothes. His moccasins and buckskin pants were nowhere to be seen. Over on top of the trunk were a pair of brown stroud trousers and a white muslin shirt, both garments neatly folded. Were they for his use? He assumed this was the case. Throwing the quilt aside, he swung his legs out of bed and stood up. He was stiff as a board; there wasn't a square inch of his body that didn't hurt like the dickens. But he could rest and recuperate later. Right now he had only one thing to worry about—getting as far away from the mission as he could before the men who were out to kill him showed up.

Putting on the shirt and trousers—they were much too large for his frame, but at least the pants had suspenders—he glanced anxiously out the window. A beautiful late summer day greeted. He didn't have the eyes to see the beauty, though. He scanned the broad expanse of open valley, wondering where the bounty hunters were at this moment. They had gotten ahead of him after the ambush on the north fork of the Clearwater. He could only assume that somehow they had gotten off course. Still, it was surely only a matter of time before they found this mission.

The door opened and he turned away from the window as Eliza entered the room.

"You really ought not to be out of bed," she said, a gentle admonishment. "Your wounds need time to heal."

"You always end up looking after me, don't you?"

"I don't mind. I came to see if you would like some breakfast."

"Eliza . . ."

"You don't have to go."

"Yes I do. You just don't understand about those men . . ."

"Joseph sent someone last night to fetch his horse."

"Then your father will have to loan me a mount. I'm sure he won't mind, if it means seeing the last of me."

"But I don't want to see the last of you," she replied—and blushed. "Come along and at least have some coffee and biscuits." She turned and fled the room.

Gordon sighed, took up the Hawken, and followed her. Marcus Hancock was sitting at a table, the centerpiece of the cabin's common room. He had finished his breakfast and was firing up a briar pipe to go with his last cup of coffee. Letitia was toiling over a dutch oven hanging from an iron hook imbedded in the hearth, a brisk fire licking at its blackened belly. The aroma of whatever she was cooking—was it venison stew?—

made Gordon's stomach growl. How long had it been since he had last eaten? He honestly couldn't remember. At Eliza's bidding he sat at the table across from Hancock. She put a cup of steaming hot coffee in front of him, accompanied by a plate of biscuits smothered in white flour gravy. He thanked her and dug in. Hancock watched him with a critical eye.

"You're not in the habit of giving thanks to God for your food, I see," remarked the minister.

Gordon was taken aback. "I've—I've forgotten how."

Hancock grunted. "I'm not surprised. Bow your head. 'Lord, we give thanks to Thee for these Thy blessings which we are about to receive, in the name of our Lord Jesus Christ, Amen.' Think you can remember that? It should be simple enough."

Gordon glanced sheepishly at Eliza, who was watching him with that warm, gentle, affectionate smile of hers.

"I'll do my best," he promised.

Puffing on the pipe, Hancock got up and went to the door, which was opened to the summer breeze. Eliza and her mother busied themselves with other things, leaving Gordon in peace, and he commenced to eat, ravenously consuming the biscuits and washing the meal down with coffee.

"I'm obliged for the food and clothing," he said as Eliza refilled his cup from a coffeepot taken off the fire.

"I'm afraid your father's things are a bit too large for his frame, child," Letitia told her daughter. "You'll have to take them up, I think."

"I will, Mother."

Gordon wondered if he was dreaming. He felt completely out of place in this blissful domestic scene. What could explain Letitia Hancock's sudden acceptance of him? Why were they treating him almost as one of the family? This was the last thing he had expected from the Hancocks.

"When you're done we had best have a talk," said Marcus Hancock.

"Yes, we'd better." Gordon took a long breath. "I've got a problem, sir. I can't stay. But I can't go. I don't know what to do."

"We've already decided what you must do," Letitia told him. "You're going to stay."

"What about the bounty hunters?"

"We'll worry about that when the time comes," said Hancock. " 'I sought the Lord, and he answered me; He delivers me from all my fears.' "

"These are very dangerous men, sir. I don't want to see harm come to any of you." *With the possible exception of Jonathan Miller,* he thought.

"It won't," said Eliza. "You must have faith."

"Much as I hate to admit it," said Hancock sternly, "my daughter is in love with you, Hawkes."

"Father!" gasped Eliza, blushing.

"Well? Isn't that the truth? Do you deny it?"

"No," she whispered, avoiding Gordon's gaze. "No, I cannot deny it."

"Very well, then. I won't lie to you, son. I had hoped she would give her heart to a more God-fearing man. You fall short of the ideal I had in mind. You've lived in sin with an Indian woman. As far as I know you may have killed that fellow in Louisiana. I'm sure you've killed other men. You live a wild and reckless life. You told me once that you doubt even that the Lord Almighty exists."

"Marcus," said Letitia.

"Just let me finish, wife. In spite of all that, you have one saving grace, in my opinion. I am convinced that you care as deeply for my daughter as she cares for you. That may come as something of a surprise to you. You're probably asking yourself how I've come to that conclusion. I knew it on the day you left the outpost to live among the Crow Indians. You agreed with me that it would be better for Eliza if you went away without saying good-bye. That required sacrifice on your part."

"I shouldn't have gone away," admitted Gordon. "I made a big mistake."

Hancock nodded. " 'Each one is tempted when, by his own desire, he is dragged away and enticed. Then, after desire has conceived, it gives birth to sin, and sin, when it is full-grown, gives birth to death.' You were tempted, Hawkes, and you surrendered to temptation. I expect you have paid the price for your transgressions. Now here you are, and, as my wife has said, it must be God's will. At least now my mind can be at ease. If something should happen to me and Mrs. Hancock, I know that you will provide for our daughter. Once upon a time I'd thought I might rely on Jonathan Miller in that respect." Brows furrowed, Hancock glanced outside. "I realize now that I could not have been more wrong."

"Sounds like to me you *expect* something bad to happen," said Gordon.

"I have no expectations. My future rests in God's hands. My daughter's future now rests in yours."

Gordon looked at Eliza—and it was as though he

were seeing her for the first time, in a wholly different light. He began to think that he had been wrong all this time in looking for a place where he could belong. His quest had not been for a *place* at all, but for a person— a person who accepted him for who and what he was, who was devoted to him without expecting any payment in kind; someone who made commitments rather than *arrangements*. It was a good feeling—a wonderful feeling—to know that you had found someone who would not hurt you, or betray you, or ask you to be someone that you could not be.

Looking back, he thought he could discern a pattern in all that had befallen him since leaving Dublin's harbor aboard the *Penelope*. If there was such a thing as destiny then surely here was a perfect example. Had his father not perished of ship fever he would never have become Captain Stewart's traveling companion, and if he hadn't been with Stewart he would never have ended up in New Orleans and met the octoroon vixen, Lorine, and been framed for the murder of Anton Remairie. And if all those things had not happened he would not now be the prey of a pack of bounty hunters, and would not have come here to this valley to make certain that his friend Stewart was out of harm's way. Then, too, if he hadn't gone off to live with the Crows, to be with Mokamea, and to be betrayed by her, he could not have learned a valuable lesson about true love, and would not now be able to fully appreciate just how lucky he was to *be* truly loved by someone like Eliza Hancock. Was all of that just a random sequence of unconnected circumstance? Or was it his destiny? Was it the perfectly fitted pieces of a master plan which he could only now, at this moment, perceive in its entirety? Did everything happen for a reason, as his mother had often told him? She had believed that every person was subject to God's will. At this moment Gordon was inclined to think she had been right. Which meant he had been terribly wrong all along about whether there was a God.

"No harm will come to her, sir," Gordon told Hancock. "Not as long as I'm alive."

Hancock cleared his throat and nodded briskly. "Fine. Then that's settled." He looked sadly at Eliza— a father who has just surrendered the care of his child, now all grown up, to another man. "This is an unusual way to go about such things," he muttered. "But out here, in this wild country, I suppose one must cut corners every now and then."

Uncomfortable under all this scrutiny, Eliza sought an avenue of escape, and seized upon the presence of a nearly empty water bucket that stood near at hand. "I'll go down to the creek and get some fresh water," she said.

"I'll go with you," offered Gordon.

"You had better stay out of sight," advised Letitia.

Gordon reluctantly concurred. He went as far as the cabin door, stood there watching her as she went down to the creek. Behind him, Letitia turned her attention to seasoning the venison stew, while Hancock looked to his Bible for solace.

A lone horseman was riding along the creek, coming in from the east. It was Jonathan Miller. Gordon had wondered where the man had been this morning—and what he was up to now as he checked his horse near Eliza and spoke to her. It came as a surprise to Gordon that he did not feel so much as a twinge of jealousy, even though he'd known almost from the first that Miller had had his eye on Eliza. But of course there was no reason for him to be jealous. Not with her.

Whatever Miller was saying upset her, though—she turned and ran back to the cabin, leaving the forgotten bucket lying on its side in the dirt, and Miller dismounted and followed her, leading his horse. Eliza reached the doorway, and Gordon read the truth in her expression, and put an arm around her and drew her to him, glancing up in time to see the flash of resentment this embrace engendered in Miller.

"Your friends are coming," Miller said, and he couldn't quite manage to conceal his pleasure.

Gordon turned inside, taking Eliza with him. Miller frowned. Hancock was on his feet, glowering at his associate. "Where have you been, Jonathan?"

"At the Flathead village. Looking for converts." There was a faint sneer in Miller's voice. An undeniable current of discord was running just below the surface of the relationship between Hancock and Miller, and Gordon didn't have a clue as to its source. The two men had had a falling-out about something—or were on their way to having one. "As I was leaving the village a hunter rode in to say there were four white men coming in. I didn't wait around to get a look at them. I guess we all know who they are. They'll be along soon enough."

"Lend me a horse," Gordon told Hancock. "I'll lead them away from here."

"No!" exclaimed Eliza. "You are in no condition to ride." That wasn't what really scared her though—rather, it was the certainty that if Gordon left under these circumstances he would never return. Gordon knew in his heart that her fears were well founded. His chances of eluding the bounty hunters were slim indeed. But these men were killers; they would let no one stand in their way, and he could not bear the thought of Eliza getting hurt.

"It's too dangerous for you if I stay," he told her. "I'll lead them a merry chase and then lose them. I'll come back. You'll see."

"No," she said, more quietly this time, but no less fervently. "Father, you can't let him go. They'll kill him."

"I know, Eliza, I know. Hawkes, you're staying right here."

"But, sir . . ."

Hancock held up a hand. "No time for arguments. It's your only hope."

"This is madness," said Miller, in disbelief. "Here stands a cold-blooded murderer—and you're all protecting him!"

"I am not his judge," replied Hancock coldly, "and I will not stand by while those manhunters act as his executioners. Eliza, the cellar."

Eliza threw back a threadbare hemp rug to expose a hatch in the common room's puncheon floor. Gordon helped her lift the hatch. A ladder led down into darkness.

"Your friend Stewart's idea," Hancock told him. "There is another hatch at the rear of the cellar—it leads out behind the cabin. The good captain thought it might come in handy in the event of Indian attack. You will note also that there is a bolt on the underside of this door. Be sure to throw that bolt once you are down below, Hawkes. If they find the cellar you'll have a little time that way—hopefully *enough* time to get out the back way and to the horse pen. Eliza, you go with him."

"Yes, Father." Before descending the ladder she turned to Miller. "You won't give our presence away, will you? You know how to keep a secret, I'm sure."

Once again Gordon got the distinct impression that there was more to what was being said than the words alone conveyed. Miller got the message she was trying to send him—he looked shocked and guilty, and appeared quite happy that Hancock wasn't paying any attention. The minister had gone to the cabin door, and Letitia had rushed into another room on some urgent errand.

Miller nodded. "I can keep a secret as well as you, Eliza."

"Good. I'm glad we understand each other."

She went down the ladder into the root cellar. Gordon picked up his Plains rifle and followed her down. She had lit a lantern, and he took stock of his surroundings—a small space with earthen walls, some scraps of lumber, a hatch at the rear of the cabin, accessible by means of another ladder. He looked up as Miller closed the hatch, then climbed a few rungs of the ladder until he could reach the bolt, and threw it. He heard the rug being put back into place to conceal the hatch. Climbing down, he turned to Eliza.

"I'm sorry to have brought all this trouble on you and your folks."

"Don't be. I'm just glad you're here." Thinking that she had spoken too forthrightly, she quickly changed the subject. "This is the first time I've actually been down here. It's kind of like being buried alive, isn't it?" She shivered.

"Do you think Miller will keep his mouth shut?"

"Yes, I'm sure he will. Don't worry about that."

"But why should he? What's going on around here, Eliza?"

"Nothing."

"Something is going on."

"It isn't important. Really. Just trust me."

"I do. Believe me, I do."

He let it go, and sat with his back to one of the cellar's earthen walls, directly below the hatch leading to the cabin's common room. She came to sit beside him, and there they waited for what seemed to Gordon like an eternity, but was really only an hour or two. Eventually she lay her head on his chest and he held her close, an arm around her, the fragrance of her hair and the warmth of her slender frame filling his senses. He could tell she was uncomfortable in the closed confines of the cellar. He wasn't. In spite of the circumstances, he found himself quite happy to be right where he was at that moment. He couldn't think of any place he'd rather be, or anyone he would rather be with—he was right where he belonged.

III.

Gordon was dozing off when the sound of horses at the gallop stirred him. The tension that shot through his body seemed to leap into Eliza's frame, and she woke with a start. Gordon put a finger to his lips and pointed at the lantern. She understood, and turned the lantern down, plunging the cellar into darkness. A little daylight leaked through the seams of the puncheon floor overhead. Listening hard, Gordon tried to envision the scene as it unfolded up above; he heard Marcus Hancock's heavy tread as he moved to the cabin's doorway to greet the visitors.

"Good morning, strangers," said the minister. "Just passing through?"

"Name's McCree," came the gruff, no-nonsense reply. "This here is my partner, Kennedy. Them two is Johnny Ornsdorff and Bill 'Three Fingers' Batterson. You must be Hancock."

"That I am. May I introduce my wife, Letitia. And this is my associate, Mr. Jonathan Miller. Please come in. Would you care for some coffee?"

"No. You two wait out here. Keep your eyes open. Come on, Kennedy."

Gordon listened to the thud of boot heels on the floor as McCree and Kennedy entered the cabin, leaving Ornsdorff and Batterson outside.

"We're looking for two men," said McCree—Gordon heard the crackle of stiff parchment. "Take a good look at this here broadside. Ever seen either one of them two?"

"Why, certainly," said Hancock. "I believe that to be a fair rendering of Captain William Drummond Stewart. The other one is Gordon Hawkes."

"So you do know them."

"But of course. My family and I were attacked by Blackfoot Indians. These two men, with some others, came to our rescue. More recently, Captain Stewart helped us build this mission. He only recently set out for the Oregon coast. It was my understanding that he intended to take passage on a ship bound for England.

It says here that they are wanted for murder. Frankly, I find that hard to believe."

"You do, huh?" McCree obviously didn't care if Hancock believed it or not. "This fellow Stewart—how long ago did he leave here?"

"About two weeks ago."

"Damn it," growled a new voice—Gordon assumed this to be Kennedy, McCree's partner in manhunting.

"What about the other one?" asked McCree. "Hawkes. When did you see him last?"

"That was earlier this year," was Hancock's ready reply. "He was at the Rocky Mountain Fur Company outpost on the Missouri over the winter. Then he went off to live with a band of Absaroka Crows. As far as I know he is still with them."

"I think you're lying, Reverend," said McCree flatly.

A moment of tense silence followed in the wake of this curt accusation. Gordon realized his palms were sweating. He wiped them on his shirt. Someone was pacing the floor, passing directly over the rug-covered hatch.

"I assure you, sir . . ."

"Save it. We tracked Hawkes to this valley. Thought we had him dead to rights, but he got away somehow. If he's still alive, he's somewhere nearby. Figured he might come here, or to the Flathead village, on account of he was shot."

"You shot him?"

"Hit him at least once. Maybe twice."

"Maybe he's dead." This was Miller. "Maybe he crawled into a hole and died. Bad luck for you if that's what happened, huh, Mr. McCree? Since you need a body to turn in to collect that reward."

"You look like a smart feller. Could be you know more than you're letting on."

Gordon stopped breathing. This was Miller's chance to betray him. And why wouldn't he? He wanted Gordon out of the way, out of Eliza's life, once and for all, and here was the perfect opportunity to achieve that goal. As far as Gordon could see, there was no good reason for Miller to protect him by playing along with the deception.

"I can't help you," Miller replied. "I haven't seen Gordon Hawkes since last winter. Don't care to. I never liked him. I'm not surprised that he murdered someone. No, that doesn't surprise me in the least. I hope you do catch him, Mr. McCree, because we'll all be better off if he's brought to justice."

Gordon was amazed. It was a perfect response. There could be no doubting the sincerity in Miller's voice, and McCree had no choice but to believe that he was telling the whole truth, and not just half of it.

"So what are we going to do?" This was the second bounty hunter, Kennedy, and he was posing the question to McCree, who was obviously the leader.

"Search this cabin, top to bottom. Nothing personal, Reverend, but I've got to make sure."

"Be my guest," said Hancock coolly. "But you're wasting your time."

For the next few minutes all Gordon could hear were footfalls on the floor as the two bounty hunters checked the cabin's other two rooms. Was there anything up there that might give the game away? Gordon wracked his brain, trying to remember if he had left any evidence of his presence in the cabin. Then he thought about the buckskins, and the moccasins Mokamea had made for him. What had been done with them? He wanted to ask Eliza, but he dared make no sound.

Finally McCree and Kennedy were back in the common room—in fact, one of them was standing on the hatch directly over Gordon's head.

"I guess you're telling the truth," said McCree. "We'll be moving on, then. Apologize for the inconvenience." He didn't sound very sincere.

"If you don't mind my asking," said Hancock, "what are you going to do now? Go after Captain Stewart?"

"I'm not giving up just yet. Ten thousand dollars American—that's an awful lot of money. Leastways we know the Scotsman is still alive, and we know where to find him."

"I think we're just wasting our time," said Kennedy glumly.

"Think whatever the hell you like," rasped McCree. "I don't aim to go back to St. Louis empty-handed. Now let's go."

"God speed your journey," said Hancock.

McCree laughed, a harsh sound, and walked out of the cabin, followed by his associate.

Gordon felt Eliza stir beside him, but he held her tight, and she went very still. He knew she wanted to get out of the cellar as quickly as possible, but they had to bide their time. The minutes crawled like hours. At one point he heard Hancock tell Miller and Letitia that the bounty hunters were still among the skin lodges of the Christian Flatheads. Then, at last, Hancock said, "There they go. They're gone now." Gordon let Eliza go. She threw her arms around his neck and hugged him, almost giddy with relief. Gordon was cautiously optimistic. Was the chase really over? Was he rid of the bounty hunters once and for all? He was satisfied that Captain Stewart had a big enough lead to make good his escape. McCree sounded like a determined sort, a man who would not give up easily, but he wasn't going to chase Stewart all the way back to merry old England. And Gordon seriously doubted if McCree and his crew would swing back through this valley.

The rug was thrown aside, and he heard Hancock say, "It's all clear. You can come up." Gordon threw back the bolt and Hancock lifted the hatch and grinned down at them. "Praise the Lord," he said.

"Amen," said Gordon.

IV.

He spent the next few days recovering from his wounds and finding out just how much his world revolved around Eliza Hancock. He often went with her when she made her daily visit to the skin lodges of the Christian Flatheads, there to give the Indians their instructions in English. This was a frustrating task, but she never became discouraged or exasperated. Her patience knew no limits, and her kindness and compassionate nature were evident to one and all. The Indians loved her—and who could blame them? They were afraid of Marcus Hancock, with his booming voice and fierce, flashing eyes. They were respectfully withdrawn around the stern, aloof Letitia. But with Eliza they were openly friendly, even familiar. The children especially were drawn to her.

A service was held every day, and Hancock was unfailing in delivery of a fire-and-brimstone sermon—much of his fervor wasted, though, since at this stage the majority of the converts had an insufficient grasp of the language to comprehend the missionary's message of sin and salvation. That, mused Gordon, was probably just as well, since Hancock's main theme was the likelihood that their everlasting souls were doomed to eternal agony if they failed to live their lives in a Christ-like manner. They seemed to enjoy the ritual well enough, even if they didn't fully understand the meaning. Still, Gordon couldn't quite figure out what it was about Hancock's new religion that compelled these Indians to forsake their old ways. For it soon became clear to him that they were paying a price for their conversion.

During one service Gordon noticed three Indians on horseback, watching the proceedings from the other side of the creek, about a hundred yards away. When Hancock began to sermonize, one of the Indians, all done up in an outfit adorned with feathers and fur, and with a rattle in one hand and a scalp-adorned staff in the other, dismounted and proceeded to perform a shuffling dance, accompanying his movements with guttural chanting interspersed with sudden, nerve-wracking shouts. Hancock studiously ignored the Indian, but some of the flock were distracted, and Gordon thought they looked more than a little worried. Later, he asked the minister about the dancing Indian.

"That happens to be the village shaman," explained Hancock. "He is my rival for the souls of these people. I suppose he was using his medicine against me. But his pagan practices hold no dread for me."

Gordon didn't bother pointing out that the shaman's antics seemed to trouble some of the Christian Indians. He didn't need to—Hancock was fully aware of that fact.

Occasionally a Flathead warrior or two would show up among the skin lodges of the converts, trying to stir up trouble, chastising those who had turned their backs on the ways of their ancestors to embrace the religion of the white man. Their hostility to the missionaries was poorly concealed, but they made no overt threats.

As for Jonathan Miller, he avoided Gordon when at all possible, and spent much of his time away from the mission. Gordon assumed he was visiting the Flathead village. Where else was there for a man to go around here? Now it was clear why Miller insisted on carrying a pistol at all times. The mission was a tinderbox, waiting for a spark.

On those languorous summer evenings, when they were done with supper, Gordon and Eliza would take long walks along the creek, as the sunset painted the high snows purple and pink, and the first stars flickered in the blue velvet sky. Sometimes a few of the Flathead children would traipse along behind them, keeping a respectful distance. Gordon hardly noticed them. Eliza occupied his mind and senses completely. They didn't talk very much. There wasn't much reason to. They were both content to treasure the moment. Gordon didn't worry about the future. Tomorrow would take care of itself. It was enough for him just to be here with Eliza—where he belonged.

A week after the visit by the bounty hunters, Joseph came to call, extending an invitation to White Crow, as he called Gordon, to visit the Flathead village. He brought with him a mountain mustang, a quick-stepping, half wild-looking coyote dun, which he presented to Gordon as a gift. Gordon was reluctant to accept the horse, as he had nothing of value to give in return. Joseph assured him that nothing was expected in exchange for the horse. "You are the adopted son of a chief of the Absarokas, our friends," he explained. "You are a Crow warrior, and who ever heard of a Crow warrior being without a good horse?"

Gordon offered no further protest, and honored Joseph by accepting the gift. He had lived among the Indians long enough to know that to do otherwise would only offend the giver. Joseph said that he would expect a visit from White Crow tomorrow or the next day, and Gordon assured him that he would come calling very soon.

The coyote dun proved not to be the troublemaker his appearance had seemed to indicate. The Flathead pony didn't look as good as the sorrel Gordon had been riding since leaving St. Louis, and he lacked the sorrel's smooth gait and even disposition. Whether he was as reliable as the other horse, only time would tell. But Gordon had heard that Indian ponies were bred for speed and stamina, if not manners, and he was satisfied with his new mount—although riding bareback took some getting used to.

The day after Joseph's visit, Gordon set out for the Flathead village. As soon as he was spotted, several young braves ran to their ponies and rode out to meet him at the gallop, yelling like lunatics and stabbing at the sky with their buffalo lances. Gordon pulled up short, uncertain what to make of this reception. Knowing that there was some bad blood between a few of the Flatheads and the Hancock party, he didn't know what to expect. But he kept his wits about him, and did not overreact. The braves rode circles around him, yipping like coyotes. Then Joseph rode out from the village, dispersed the youths with a few stern words, and turned a wide grin on Gordon.

"What was all that about?" asked Gordon, breathing a sigh of relief.

"They honor you, White Crow, as a great Absaroka warrior."

"Joseph, maybe you ought to know the truth. I'm not a warrior. I'm nothing of the sort. I went on one raid with the Absaroka, and they wanted nothing more to do with me when it was over."

Joseph didn't seem at all interested. "Come. You are welcome among my people."

"Am I?" asked Gordon as they rode side by side toward the village. "I get the feeling there are some among your people who don't want any whites in this valley."

"We will speak of that later."

A crowd had gathered to witness Gordon's arrival. Among the many smiling faces there were a few with expressions of a more somber cast. Joseph took his guest to his skin lodge and bade him enter; he was introduced to the family—wife, son, and infant daughter. Joseph's wife provided them with some hump meat and belly fat, and as they ate, Joseph related his experiences during a recent buffalo hunt. The meal done, they went outside to sit in the sun and share a pipe.

A moment later a woman walked by, and Gordon noticed that Joseph was watching her with keen interest as she passed, looking neither to the left nor to the right, her chin held defiantly high. An older woman who was cleaning a buffalo hide in front of a nearby skin lodge saw her and spat in her direction. The young woman did not seem to notice. A warrior saw her next, and took a few menacing steps in her direction, and the woman veered away, clearly afraid, and the warrior shouted something at her that wasn't, by the sound of it, too pleasant.

"Who is she?" Gordon asked Joseph.

"She is part of the problem you spoke of earlier. Her man died not long ago, killed by the Blackfeet. Now she has taken up with the one called Miller. It is bad enough that she lays with another man so soon after her husband's death. But it is worse because the man is a white missionary who treats all Indians with contempt."

"So that's it," said Gordon. "I was wondering why Miller spent so much time away from the mission."

"She has shamed her entire family. Her brother is one of those who speaks out most strongly for driving the missionaries away."

"And your shaman wants to do the same, I reckon."

"Joseph's people have always been friends to the white man. We need the white man's guns and powder to fight our enemy, the Blackfoot. We do not mind when the white man comes and gives us gifts. But we do not like it when he tries to steal our souls."

"Joseph, I thought you were a Christian."

"Joseph is a Christian, when he is among other Christians. But he is a Flathead Indian at all other times. Is there much difference between the Great Spirit and Hancock's God? Joseph does not think so. He does not break his faith. He lives here, among his people, and not at the mission. What more needs to be said?"

Gordon nodded. "I think I understand. So what do you think is going to happen here?"

"Joseph cannot say."

"But you have a pretty good idea, I bet."

Joseph gave him a searching look. "Will you stay with the missionaries, White Crow?"

"For a while, I reckon." Gordon hadn't given the future much thought beyond the certainty that he could be with Eliza. What they would do in the long run presented something of a dilemma. The mountains were his home. They were his sanctuary. With a murder charge hanging over his head he could not return to the civilized world, but even if he weren't a wanted man he wouldn't have wanted to go back. And yet now he had to think about what was best for Eliza. Was she suited to a life in the high country? Would she leave her parents? How committed was she to the crusade that had brought her out here in the first place? Gordon had no answers, only questions.

"Then you must be watchful," advised Joseph gravely. "If trouble comes, it will be as the whirlwind, and no man will be able to stand against it."

A few young warriors walked up and issued a good-natured challenge to Gordon—would the great white warrior of the Absaroka compete with them in a contest to determine who among them was the best shot with bow and arrow? Gordon was happy to oblige, and impressed all concerned with his skill. Then it was time to go, if he expected to get back to the mission before nightfall. He thanked Joseph for his hospitality and took his leave, pleased with the way the visit had gone, and yet troubled by a premonition that disaster lurked just around the corner.

CHAPTER 9

I.

After a sleepless night mulling over several related problems, Gordon bided his time the next morning, waiting for an opportunity to talk to Marcus Hancock alone. As was his custom, Jonathan Miller rode out early—no doubt bound for the Flathead village and the young widow who had taken him to her bed. For the first time, Gordon chose not to accompany Eliza on her daily visit among the Christian Indians. Fortunately for him, Letitia joined her daughter, carrying a basket of fresh-baked bread and some medicines; there was a sickness among the skin lodges. Several of the converts had been afflicted by an ailment with symptoms that included fever, vomiting, and a croupy cough. There was a rumor floating around among the Hancocks' Indian flock that the Flathead shaman had put some kind of curse on them, so Marcus and his wife had agreed that it was doubly important to do everything possible in order to heal those who were sick. In so doing they would prove that prayer and the white man's medicines were more powerful than the shaman's spells and potions.

Gordon found himself alone, then, with Hancock. He interrupted the minister's perusal of the Bible to ask if he might have a word, and Hancock laid the Good Book aside.

"I don't know any other way to say this except straight out," said Gordon. "I think you should leave this place, sir. At once."

"Leave?" Hancock was astonished. "And go where?"

"I don't know where, but you can't stay here. It isn't safe."

Hancock leaned forward. "I never expected it to be safe. Tell me, young man, what it is that you know."

Gordon grimaced. "Ordinarily, I'd say this was none of my business. But since Eliza's life may be at stake, I've got to speak out. There is a growing sentiment among the Flatheads that you should get out of this valley. If you don't go on your own, sooner or later they'll drive you out. Or kill you. To make things worse, Miller is seeing an Indian woman in the Flathead village. That's causing even more hard feelings."

Slamming his fist on the common room table so hard it made Gordon jump, Hancock shot to his feet. "This can't be true. Miller wouldn't commit such a . . . such a vile act."

"You know he would. Admit it, sir. You made a mistake bringing him out here. Why do you think he carries that pistol around all the time? Because he knows that there will be hell to pay on account of what he's doing."

Hancock turned away with a dismissive gesture. He

moved to the cabin door and looked out across the sun-drenched valley, and then bowed his head, and Gordon, thinking he must be praying, kept silent. Finally, head still bowed, Hancock spoke.

"This is my calling, Hawkes. I have come too far, endured too much, to give up now. I'm staying, come what may."

"I kind of figured that would be your decision," said Gordon quietly. "So I have two requests to make of you. I would like to marry your daughter. And then I would like to take her away from here."

Hancock turned and stared at him, and by the expression on the minister's face Gordon just knew that Hancock would turn him down. But then the missionary's scowl melted away.

"Have you spoken to Eliza about this?"

"No, sir. I haven't yet."

"What makes you think she will consent to your proposal of marriage?"

"I don't know if she will or not."

"And if she did, why do you think she would go away with you?"

"She probably wouldn't—unless you told her to."

"I see." Hancock came back to the table and sat down, shoulders slumped. "You expect me to send my only child away from me. And that is what she is, you know—a mere child."

"It might save her life."

" 'There is a time for everything, and a reason for every activity under heaven, a time to plant and a time to uproot, a time to weep and a time to laugh, a time to keep and a time to throw away—a time to be born and a time to die.' "

"But I don't want Eliza to die. I want her to live. I love her, sir, and I know you do, too. So prove it. You don't care if you die a martyr to your faith, but think like a father before you decide Eliza has to die a martyr, too."

Hancock looked at the Bible lying on the table between them. "And where would you take my daughter, Hawkes? What would you do? How would you provide for her?"

"I don't know. But I will take good care of her. You know I will. You know you can depend on me. You as much as said so."

Hancock made up his mind. "Very well. You had better go ahead and make your proposal, young man. If Eliza accepts, you will be wed in the morning."

He opened the Bible to the place he had marked and resumed reading, his expression a stoic mask.

"Thank you," said Gordon, but Hancock did not seem to hear him, and he got up and walked out of the cabin and felt the warmth of the sun on his face and looked at the valley, and the mountains beyond, and decided that the world had never been more beautiful. He turned his steps in the direction of the skin lodges, found Eliza in a circle of Indians, most of them children, and she looked up from the primer in her hand when she felt his eyes dwelling upon her, and returned his smile. Brushing a stray tendril of pale yellow hair from her cheek, curling it behind an ear, she could sense that something important was about to happen, and stood up.

"What is it, Gordon?" she asked.

He struggled to get the words out. "Eliza, will you . . . will you marry me?"

"Of course I will," she said, without hesitation, and only a trace of shyness. She came to him and put her arms around his neck and stood on tiptoe as he kissed her on the lips, and some of the Indian children encircled them, laughing and tugging at their clothes, but Gordon didn't even notice. The whole beautiful world just seemed to fade away.

That evening, after supper, they took their usual walk along the creek. Gordon was quiet, preoccupied, knowing that the time had come to talk to Eliza about the future—about leaving this valley. But what did he have to offer her as an alternative? Now that the bounty hunters knew the whereabouts of his cabin in the mountains he could never return to that place. So he didn't even have a roof to shelter his future wife from the elements. He was a man on the run, and he supposed that would always be the case. There was only one option, as far as he could tell, and it would mean forsaking the high country he had come to love.

He could go back to Ireland.

Not that he had any prospects there, to speak of, but he could find work, and save enough money eventually to buy a piece of worn-out land and become a potato farmer like his father had been. A bleak existence, but at least he would be out from under that murder charge. He was confident that no bounty hunter would bother him in Ireland. To leave the mountains would break his heart, but he resolved to do whatever was necessary—for Eliza's sake.

He was about to broach the subject when three riders loomed out of the gathering darkness, and they gave Gordon a scare because he was unarmed—the

Plains rifle was back in the Hancock cabin. But it was only Joseph, with two of the Flathead braves.

"You must come with Joseph at once, White Crow."

"Why? What's happened?"

"Jonathan Miller has been hurt."

"I'll go get the medicine kit," said Eliza.

"No," said Joseph. "You will both come now."

"We'd better do as he says," Gordon told her, and helped her up behind Joseph. He rode double with one of the other Flatheads as they followed the creek for several miles before turning due north—this was not the most direct route to the village, and Gordon knew it, but he didn't say anything. The stars were out and an early moon had risen by the time they reached their destination. The village looked abandoned. Everyone had taken refuge inside the skin lodges. *Something bad has happened,* mused Gordon, *or is about to.* They dismounted at Joseph's lodge, and Joseph took them inside while the other two braves waited outside. The skin lodge was empty.

"What's going on here, Joseph?" asked Gordon. "Where is your family?"

"They are safe."

"And Miller? Where's Miller? How badly is he hurt?"

Joseph went to the back of the skin lodge, and it was then that Gordon realized that there was someone lying beneath a buffalo robe. Lifting the robe, Joseph said, "He is here."

Eliza gasped in horror and turned away.

Miller was dead. His throat had been cut. His sightless eyes seemed to stare right through Gordon.

"Damn it, Joseph," rasped Gordon, putting an arm around Eliza. "Cover him up."

Joseph did as he was told. "The whirlwind has been set loose, White Crow."

"Why did you bring us here?"

"So that you would not die."

"My God," muttered Gordon, feeling sick to his stomach. He knew exactly what was happening now. Someone—perhaps the brother of the young widow— had murdered Jonathan Miller. That deed done, the decision had been made to drive the rest of the whites from the valley. Joseph had raced to the mission to save his friend. They had returned to the village by a roundabout route to avoid the war party that Joseph had known was coming along right behind him. Gordon figured that by now the Flathead warriors had arrived at the mission.

"I'm going back," he told Joseph.

"You must not."

"Do you honestly think you can stop me?"

"What is it?" asked Eliza. "What is happening?" She looked at Joseph, then up at Gordon—and then she, too, put the pieces of the puzzle together. "The mission," she gasped. "They're going to attack the mission." She broke free of Gordon's grasp and turned on Joseph, trembling, fists clenched. "How could you? Why didn't you warn my father?"

"Because it would have changed nothing."

"No, that's not why. You hate him, don't you? You hate him because of the way he treated you. That's why you abandoned us last winter. And it's why you didn't warn him tonight."

Joseph's features betrayed no emotion. "Your father would not have run away."

She looked at Gordon. "It's too late, isn't it?" she asked in a small voice, tears welling up in her eyes.

"Stay here," said Gordon.

"No. I'm coming with you."

He took her firmly by the shoulders. "You will stay here, Eliza," he said sternly. "I'll do everything that can be done. You'd just slow me down." He glanced at Joseph. "I'm taking your horse. You keep her here."

Joseph nodded. "No harm will come to her. You have Joseph's word."

Gordon was more than halfway to the mission when he saw riders up ahead, silhouetted against the night sky, and he veered Joseph's pony into a gully and hid there, unseen, as the dark shapes thundered past only a stone's throw away. It was the war party, returning to the village, their bloody task no doubt accomplished. Gordon knew then that it was too late to save the Hancocks. He rode the rest of the way to the mission with an aching emptiness inside him, fearful of what he would find when he arrived.

II.

By the time Joseph arrived with Eliza, early the next morning, Gordon had already buried Marcus and Letitia Hancock in graves side by side beneath the big wooden cross. He had worked through the night, and now he sat cross-legged on the ground beside the creek, numb with exhaustion and emotionally drained. Earlier, as the first streaks of dawn light probed the night sky, some of the Christian Indians had returned to their skin lodges. As far as Gordon could tell, none of them had been killed, though a few appeared to have sustained slight injuries. Apparently the war party had targeted only the Hancocks, sparing their own kind, but driving the converts away from the mission and tearing down some of their skin lodges. Now Hancock's scattered flock was straggling home to collect their few belongings. Some of them wept openly over the bodies of the minister and his wife. A few gathered their things and left, heading east for the Flathead village, while the rest lingered, uncertain what to do next, or where to go.

When Eliza arrived, Gordon forced himself to his feet. He watched her closely as she approached the gravesite. He wasn't sure what to expect from her, but she did not break down under the burden of her grief, only wept quietly as she knelt between the mounds of fresh dirt and prayed. Gordon glanced at Joseph, who sat his horse some distance away. The Indian had a pair of horses in tow, and Gordon recognized them as two of the ponies the Rocky Mountain Fur Company had provided the Hancocks; the Flathead killers had emptied the mission's stock pen. They had also taken a number of things from the cabin—Gordon's Plains rifle among them.

Gordon gave Eliza a few minutes alone and then went to her, helping her to her feet.

"I'm sorry," he said, wishing there was more he could say, her grief-stricken expression wrenching at his heart. "I'm truly sorry."

She swiped at the tears on her cheek.

"I guess I always knew this could happen," she said. "I think my father actually expected it to end this way."

"If you want I'll say a few words over them." He had no idea what he would say, but figured he ought to make the offer.

"No, I've already done that." She glanced at the cabin, and a violent shudder wracked her slender body. "Gordon, will you please take me away from here? Far, far away."

"I'll be right back."

He walked out to where Joseph was waiting. As Gordon neared, the Flathead tossed him the Hawken rifle.

"Killing them was bad enough," said Joseph. "But stealing . . ." He shook his head. "Joseph is ashamed of his people today."

Gordon took the reins to the two horses. Both were saddled, and he was relieved to see that his shot pouch hung from the pommel of one of the saddles. Joseph had no doubt gone to some trouble to retrieve the stolen horses and the gun, perhaps had even put himself at risk, confronting warriors whose blood was up from a killing spree. *I suppose I ought to thank him,* mused Gordon. But he found that hard to do.

"Believe this, White Crow. Joseph did not want this to happen."

"No, but it happened." Gordon couldn't help but wonder just how culpable Joseph really was. Had he hated Marcus Hancock, as Eliza suspected? Had he been forced to make a choice between Hancock and the Christian faith, and the old ways of his own people? Had he somehow redeemed himself in the eyes of his tribe by turning against the missionaries? "Well," said Gordon, climbing aboard one of the horses and giving Joseph a long look, "I know one thing. The man who sits on the fence is usually the first one to get cut. So long."

"Where will White Crow go now?"

Gordon racked the Hawken on his shoulder and kicked the horse under him into motion. "Where no one will ever find me, I hope," he replied.

He rode back to the wooden cross, and Eliza mounted the other horse. She had been in the cabin, emerging with only one thing—her father's Bible.

"Where would you like to go?" he asked her.

"With you," she replied.

They left the valley the way he had come into it, by way of the north fork of the Clearwater, across the Lolo Pass and down the east face of the Bitterroot Range. Then they turned south, because he wanted to take her as far away from the Blackfoot threat as possible. He could not fail to notice that the trees were beginning to turn. The nights were getting cooler. In less than two moons the first snows would fall. That meant he could not be on the move for long; soon he would have to begin work on yet another cabin, if he expected to get it finished and lay in a winter's supply of firewood and meat. Consequently he kept his eyes open for a likely spot.

He found just what he was looking for ten days' travel from the mission—a small, hidden valley with a pond fed by a mountainside creek tumbling down a rocky slope. There was plenty of timber and adequate graze for the horses. Best of all, the evidence was clear that the beaver had long since been trapped out of the pond. That meant it was unlikely they would be bothered by trappers; mountain men were generally too busy searching for new beaver country to waste time revisiting old stomping grounds where they knew they wouldn't find any "brown gold." No trappers meant in all likelihood there would be no Indian visitors, either; the valley was too small to sustain a band's encampment. There was enough game, though, for two people.

Best of all, the valley was but two days' hard ride from the canyon where Gordon had built his first cabin. They visited that site because he needed some of the things he had left behind in his haste to escape the bounty hunters. Mindful that the remains of Ben Talley were no doubt still in the cabin, Gordon left Eliza at the foot of the game trail and went up to the table by himself. There wasn't much left of Talley—coyotes had found the body. Ignoring the grisly remains, Gordon collected what was left of his salt, coffee, and flour. He also retrieved a pot, a blanket and, most importantly, his ax.

Returning to the small valley, he went to work with a vengeance. Eliza helped all she could. Every afternoon he went hunting, and in a week's time had bagged several deer and a black bear. He noted with some concern that he was down to about a dozen cartridges and as many percussion caps. That would have to last him until next spring, when he could afford to take the time to make a trip to the Rocky Mountain Fur Company's outpost on the Missouri River.

One day he was returning from a hunt along the shore of the pond when he heard splashing up ahead. Breaking through a thicket, he saw Eliza standing hip deep in the water, bathing. Hearing him, she whirled, covering her breasts with her arms, and he turned quickly away, flustered, mumbling an apology. He started to flee back into the trees, but she called out for him to wait, and he listened nervously as she came out of the pond. A moment later she touched his shoulder and he turned to face her, tentatively. She had slipped her dress on, but it clung very immodestly to her wet skin, and he looked away.

"Gordon," she said softly, "why haven't you made love to me?"

"What?"

"You heard me."

"Well I . . . I . . ." Gordon had never been so tongue-tied in his life.

"The nights are getting very cold," she said.

"Yeah, but . . . well, we're . . . we're not married, Eliza, and I . . ."

"I don't think we'll find very many ordained ministers in these parts, and I don't want to wait." She curled her wet blond hair behind her ear and tilted her head to one side. "Why don't we marry ourselves? I'm sure God won't mind, under the circumstances."

"Marry ourselves?"

"I'll say my vows to you, and you say yours to me."

Unsure how to respond, Gordon just nodded, and set aside his rifle.

She took his hands in hers. "I, Eliza Hancock," she said, barely above a whisper, "take you, Gordon Hawkes, to be my wedded husband, to have and to hold, to love and to cherish, from this day forward, in sickness and in health, till death do us part. Now you say it."

Gordon swallowed the lump in his throat. "I, Gordon Hawkes, take you, Eliza Hancock, to be my wife, to have and to hold, to love and . . . and . . ."

"To love and to cherish."

"To love and to cherish, in sickness . . ."

"You forgot the part about from this day forward."

"Sorry. To love and to cherish, from this day forward, in sickness and in health, till death do us part."

"Now kiss me," she said.

He did as he was told. Her passion surprised him. Her body felt like it was on fire. She sank to the ground and pulled him down on top of her and somehow they squirmed out of their clothes and made love there beside the pond, beneath the soaring mountains and the big sky.

III.

The cabin they built stood at the top of a long grassy slope angling steeply down to the north end of the pond, with the forested shoulders of a snow-clad peak behind it, and a good view of the length of the valley. About four miles to the south you could see, from the cabin door, the rocky saddle between two mountains by which they had entered the valley. There was another way in or out—a high and difficult pass to the west, but the first heavy snow would render it impassable. Then they would be boxed in. But Gordon didn't worry too much about that. He was too happy to worry about much of anything. He figured he had to be the happiest man in the whole world. Not to mention the luckiest. He had everything he wanted—he was living in the high country with a woman who owned his heart.

He watched in wonder as Eliza gradually mastered her grief. She was a strong person, and she accepted the loss of her parents and was able to move on much more quickly than he had expected. It was clear that her faith helped her cope with the tragedy. Her love for him also helped. Often he lay awake at night, holding her body against him, wrapped in bearskin and blanket against the chill, and savoring every precious moment of the experience.

They talked about everything, wanting to know all there was to know about each other's past, and then there were times when they would sit for hours around an evening cook fire, holding hands and saying nothing, the looks they gave one another speaking volumes. They made love every day—sometimes two or three times a day—delighting in the process of learning the most secret things about the other. There was something very tender and magical about their lovemaking that Gordon had not experienced with Mokamea, and because of that it was, somehow, far more gratifying. Gordon understood now that he had never truly loved the Absaroka maiden; his feelings for her did not compare to the way he felt about Eliza. He had desired the Indian beauty, but he realized it had been a completely physical attraction. He was attracted to Eliza in the same way and to an even greater degree, but there was more to his feelings for Eliza. In a few short weeks she became a part of him, and he felt as though he had known her all his life, and he couldn't imagine what life would be like without her. He knew he wouldn't be able to live without her, any more than he could survive without the air in his lungs and the blood in his veins. She was absolutely everything to him—friend, lover, heart, soul, world.

Best of all, his doubts about her adaptability to mountain existence were soon put to rest. She loved the life they were making every bit as much as he did. She proved to be far stronger physically than he had imagined she would be; she worked as hard as he did in finishing the cabin and building a pole corral for the horses and gathering fodder and firewood. She demonstrated an aptitude for cleaning and curing the skins of the game he killed. She also showed a remarkable skill in spearing fish, wading out into the pond's shallows with a long, sharpened stick as a makeshift lance.

As for the future, she told him that she would be quite content to stay in the high country with him. If it happened that they associated with friendly Indians, she would try to introduce them to the English language and the Christian faith. She felt compelled to continue her father's work, and Gordon respected her wishes. She did not share her father's all-consuming passion for the saving of heathen souls. If anything, it would be a pastime. "A person can have only one obsession," she told him, "and you are mine."

With the cabin completed, Gordon concentrated on hunting. To save on ammunition he fashioned yet another bow and several dozen arrows. But as the days grew colder and shorter, the game became harder to find. The signs were pointing to a long and especially harsh winter, and the creatures of the high country took note of the rapid changing of the seasons. He began to spend much of the day away from Eliza, ranging far afield, regretting the necessity but knowing he had to lay in more meat before the snows came. He set his goal at three more deer, and it took him a fortnight to make his quota. Each kill he skinned and butchered on the spot, leaving only the skeleton and the offal, carrying the meat home in the skin, slung over his shoulder like a sack.

He soon learned that a pack of wolves had moved into the valley; the presence of the predators was part of the reason for the scarcity of game. For quite a long time he never actually saw them—only their sign and, occasionally, an eerie, mournful howl that made his skin crawl. On the day he made his third kill he finally did lay eyes on them, gray shapes flitting through the trees, shadowing him as he made his way back to the cabin. Their presence unnerved his horse, and eventually Gordon had to dismount, tie the deer bundle to his saddle, and lead the horse, his Hawken rifle primed and ready and in hand. This slowed him down some, and his anxiety soared, because he had at least a mile to go and the day was fast coming to a close and he wanted to get home before dark.

Having had no prior experience with wolves, he didn't know what to expect from them. He had heard tall tales told by RMFC men around the campfire or barracks hearth; it was generally held that wolves were the smartest of God's creatures in the mountains and, next to a grizzly, the most dangerous. A pack was the perfect killing machine, all the members working in remarkable unison to bring down their prey. Gordon wondered if this pack—there were five, maybe six, wolves—would attack him. They wanted the deer meat, and he considered leaving it behind. But he decided he couldn't afford to. The first snow was on its way, and he and Eliza needed that meat, and there was no telling how long it would take him to track down another deer. No, this kill belonged to him, and by God he would not let a pack of wolves take it from him. Not without a fight.

He heard a noise behind him and whirled, holding on tightly to the reins of his spooked horse—and saw one of the wolves standing not thirty yards away, head down, fangs bared, growling deep in its throat. He thought about trying a one-handed shot, but the damn horse was pulling him off balance, and he doubted that he could hit his mark, even at this close range.

Suddenly the wolf turned and vanished like a ghost into the deepening gloom of the twilight that was gathering beneath the trees.

Dumbfounded, Gordon looked around for the rest of the pack—and saw no signs of them. They had simply disappeared. Were they really gone? Had they run off? If so, why?

Wild-eyed, the horse jerked its head back, trying to pull the reins out of Gordon's grasp, and Gordon, holding on for dear life, was jerked off his feet—just as the bullet blew past him, so close he imagined he could feel the wind of its passage. There was a loud *crack*! followed in the next instant by the thunderous boom of the rifle's report, echoing through the valley. The bullet hit a tree trunk, throwing splinters. Gordon let go of the horse, dropped the bundle of deer meat, and hurled himself to the ground, rolling onto his belly and spotting the horseman about fifty yards off through the trees. He couldn't identify the man—the light wasn't good enough for that—but the rider was dressed like a trapper. He was reloading his rifle, and Gordon took his shot. He hit the mark; the man made a grunting noise and rocked violently in the saddle. But he didn't fall. Instead, he kicked his horse into motion, galloping straight for Gordon.

Muttering a curse, Gordon rolled behind a tree and proceeded to reload the Plains rifle. He could do it in about twenty seconds flat—fish a new cartridge from his shot pouch, tear it with his teeth, pour the powder down the barrel, then the ball, then the paper, and tamp it down with the ramrod, then place a new percussion cap over the nipple. By this time, though, the horseman had closed the gap; Gordon came out from behind the tree on his knees, bringing the Hawken up and firing in one smooth motion, and his adversary fired a second later. His bullet struck the Hawken's barrel a glancing blow and went screaming off in a ricochet, and yet the impact nearly kicked the rifle out of Gordon's hands. Gordon's bullet hit the man high in the shoulder, and this time it knocked him out of the saddle. Gordon closed in, wielding the empty Plains rifle like a club. But the man was on his feet in a hurry, drawing a pistol from his belt, and in that instant Gordon recognized him. It was Johnny Ornsdorff, and he had two of Gordon's bullets in him; his hunting shirt was soaked with blood. But it was obviously going to take more than two bullets to kill him.

Swinging the Hawken with all his might, Gordon hit Ornsdorff's arm so hard both bone and rifle stock shattered. The pistol went off, and the bullet went wild. Staggered, and growling like a maddened grizzly, Ornsdorff whipped a knife from its belt sheath, but Gordon hit him again with what was left of the Hawken, this time aiming for a knee, and with a mighty roar of pain Ornsdorff went down like a felled tree. Gordon drove the shattered stock of his rifle into

Ornsdorff's throat, and jumped nimbly back out of range of the trapper's knife. Clutching at his ruined throat, Ornsdorff got to his hands and knees, making horrible gurgling sounds, blood pouring through his fingers. Gordon looked around for a weapon, wondering what it was going to take to put this man down for good. He grabbed a fallen tree limb, about four feet long and as thick as his arm. Closing in on Ornsdorff, he hit the man at the base of the skull just as he was rising. Ornsdorff went sprawling, and this time he didn't get up.

Winded, Gordon backed off, wondering if his adversary was really dead. Ornsdorff didn't move, and Gordon cautiously stepped closer, ready to strike again with the tree limb, if necessary. Ornsdorff didn't seem to be breathing, though; Gordon knelt and pried the knife out of the trapper's hand, then felt for a pulse. There was none.

His mind racing, Gordon searched the gathering darkness. If Ornsdorff was here, could Three Fingers Batterson and the two bounty hunters, McCree and Kennedy, be far away? He didn't waste time worrying over how they had found him. His first concern was for Eliza. Fear grabbed him like an invisible hand clutching at his throat—fear for Eliza. Casting the tree limb aside, he gathered up Ornsdorff's rifle. The latter was a J. Henry rifle, .52 caliber, converted from flintlock to percussion. Gordon went back to the corpse and retrieved Ornsdorff's shot pouch. Then he slowly approached the dead trapper's horse, which stood a little ways off, eyeing him warily. Gordon's own horse had made for the tall timber; in an unforgiving mood, Gordon half hoped the wolves would run it down. He focused all his attention on Ornsdorff's pony, knowing that if he could get into the saddle he would reach Eliza a lot quicker. He was almost within reach of the horse when it turned and moseyed away, stopping to look back. "Damn you," muttered Gordon. "Stand still." The horse whickered softly; this time it let him come up and take the dragging reins. Swinging into the saddle, Gordon offered silent thanks to God, wheeled the horse around, and whipped it into a gallop—reloading the Henry as he clung to the saddle with his knees.

When he reached the cabin, Gordon spotted a strange horse ground-hitched nearby—and in the same instant heard a scream from inside the cabin that made the blood in his veins turn to ice. Dismounting on the run, he burst inside. Three Fingers Batterson had Eliza bent backward over the table; she struggled ineffectually, pinned beneath him. As Gordon charged in, Batterson wheeled, swinging Eliza around in front of him as a shield. Gordon's fury turned white-hot as he saw that her dress had been torn. He stepped forward, aching to kill Batterson—but froze in his tracks as the trapper put the blade of a Bowie knife to Eliza's slender throat.

"One more step and I'll take her head right off," said Batterson with a growl. "Now you go on and drop that there rifle."

"Don't do it!" gasped Eliza.

"Shuddup!" roared Batterson, squeezing the breath out of her. "I'd sure hate to kill a purty little thing like you, but I'll do it." He leered at Gordon. "She's a bit on the thin side for my taste, but beggars can't be choosers. Ain't that so, Hawkes?"

"I killed your friends, Talley and Ornsdorff," said Gordon bleakly. "You're next."

"You're the one fixin' to die, boy. And after you're dead I'm gonna have my way with your gal here. I'll show her a real good time—'fore I kill her, too."

Gordon brought the rifle to his shoulder and fired in one quick motion, almost faster than the eye could follow. The bullet struck Batterson in the forehead, and seemed to hurl the trapper's body violently backward. The Bowie's blade grazed Eliza's throat, drawing blood, but the razor-sharp steel did not cut too deeply, and Gordon threw the rifle away and rushed to her side, sweeping her up in his arms, holding her trembling body close.

"It's over," he breathed. "You're fine, Eliza. I'm so sorry. God I love you. It's finished now. Everything is going to be all right. I promise."

"I'm afraid that's one promise you won't be able to keep," said McCree.

Gordon spun around to see the bounty hunter standing in the doorway, a pair of pistols in his hands.

"No sudden moves, Mr. Hawkes, or your woman might get hurt."

He was a tall, thin man, wearing buckskin leggins tucked into boots, a red vest beneath a fringed buckskin coat, and a battered beaver hat on his head. His gaunt features were framed by lank, shoulder-length black hair. His eyes were as cold and blue as a high mountain lake in winter time. Gordon had no doubt that McCree would carry through with the threat; he was a man fully capable of killing an innocent person without blinking an eye.

Gordon placed himself in front of Eliza. "I won't

give you any trouble if you give me your word that no harm will come to her."

"Gordon, no!" cried Eliza.

"Be quiet!" he said.

"I've got no reason to kill her, unless you force me to," replied the bounty hunter. "I've got no interest in her one way or the other, unlike Batterson."

"You used him for bait, didn't you? You stood back and let me kill him and Ornsdorff. That way you don't have to share the reward."

"I knew you were a smart one. Batterson didn't think very highly of you, but I knew better. Guess he knows better, too, now."

"What about your partner?" asked Gordon. "Kennedy?"

"Oh, he gave up not long after we left the mission. Just lit out one night when he was supposed to be on guard duty and the rest of us were asleep. He figured chasing you was a waste of time. I was beginning to think so, too—until we got word about what happened at the mission. News like that travels real fast. Heard tell of someone named White Crow, a white man who'd been living with the Absarokas. Knew right off that had to be you. So me and Batterson and Ornsdorff, we turned right around and made tracks back to the mission. Some of the Injuns told us you and the girl had lit out along the north fork of the Clearwater. Seemed logical to me that you'd head south once you got across the Bitterroots. Figured you'd look for a likely place to winter. Took some time, but we finally found you."

"So now what?" asked Gordon—though he was pretty sure he already knew the answer.

"Now I'm gonna have to kill you, Hawkes."

"No!" cried Eliza, and tried to position herself between Gordon and the bounty hunter, but Gordon pushed her back.

"For God's sake, Eliza. Stay alive. For my sake, just stay alive."

"Gordon," she whispered, forlorn tears streaming down her cheeks.

"Sorry, miss," said McCree. He didn't sound sorry at all. "But Hawkes here is too damn clever to take any chances with. It'll make my life a whole lot easier if I take him back dead. So why don't you step outside," he told Gordon. "No call to do it in front of her."

Gordon nodded. "Thanks for that."

McCree stepped to one side and motioned to the door with one of the pistols. "Let's get it done."

Gordon took one last look at Eliza. "I love you."

Overcome with emotion, she couldn't speak.

Gordon went outside, took three steps, and turned. McCree was in the doorway again, facing him, the pistols held rock steady and aimed at his chest.

"You might as well forget about Stewart," said Gordon. "You'll never find him."

"Don't be too sure. I found you, didn't I?" McCree raised the pistols slightly, smiling coldly. "You gonna run on me?"

"I wouldn't give you the satisfaction." Gordon forced himself to look the bounty hunter straight in the eye.

McCree nodded approvingly—and then his eyes flared open wide with shock, and an incoherent cry issued from his gaping mouth. His arms jerked upward, and the pistols discharged harmlessly at the darkening

sky, and then he pitched forward. Gordon saw the
Bowie knife buried to the hilt between the man's
shoulder blades; and looked up to see Eliza slumped
against the door frame, hands covering her face, mumbling, "God forgive me. God forgive me." He went to
her, and she threw her arms around his neck, holding
on so tight that he could scarcely breathe, but he didn't
mind, and as she kissed him he tasted the salt of her
tears.

IV.

The first snow fell a week later, and about two weeks
after that they had another visitor. Gordon was down at
the pond, fetching water in the pot, when he saw
movement out of the corner of his eye and whirled,
dragging one of McCree's pistols out of his belt. A
rider emerged from the tree line, and Gordon recognized the buckskin horse even before he identified the
man in the saddle.

It was Stewart.

Gordon just stood there in amazement and waited
for the Scotsman to ride up to him.

"What in heaven's name are you doing here?" asked
Gordon in disbelief. "I thought you'd be halfway to
England by this time."

"Me, too." Stewart dismounted and gave Gordon an
enthusiastic bear hug, clapping him soundly on the
back a few times and then holding him at arm's length
and shaking his head. "You've changed quite a bit
since the last time I saw you."

"You haven't changed at all. What are you doing
here?"

"It's a long story. I was, um, detained in Oregon by a young lady, so I missed the boat bound for home."

Gordon laughed. "That doesn't surprise me."

"Then I got word of the massacre at the mission. When I got there I found out about you and Eliza from a Flathead Indian named Joseph. I also heard all about the bounty hunters. I'm surprised you haven't heard from them."

"I did. They're buried over yonder."

"Indeed!" Stewart was surprised—and visibly impressed. "You've done well for yourself, lad."

"I had help."

"You mean Eliza?" Stewart glanced toward the cabin. "Is she well?"

"She is. But how did you find me?"

"It wasn't all that difficult. There is a band of Absaroka Indians in a winter camp one valley over. They know you're here. They know all about you. It's not Little Raven's band, but you've got quite a reputation among the Indians, you know. Believe me, they have no intention of bothering you."

Gordon shook his head. "I'm going to have to do a lot better job of finding a hiding place."

Stewart put an arm around his shoulder. "So come on. I want to say hello to Eliza. You know, I always thought that somehow the two of you would end up together. You were born to love her, Gordon, just as you were born to these mountains."

"Amen," said Gordon, with feeling, and bent his steps for home.

AFTERWORD

Many of the characters in this novel are actual historical figures. For instance, there was a Robert Campbell who led an overland expedition to the headwaters of the Missouri for the purpose of opening the Rocky Mountain Fur Company's first outpost. There was a Kenneth McKenzie, who acted as John Jacob Astor's chief lieutenant in the wild country, and who was charged by Astor with the task of putting the Rocky Mountain Fur Company out of business. Louis Vasquez, Charles Larpenteur, and Benjamin Harrison were real people.

So was Captain William Drummond Stewart. The thirty-seven-year-old Scotsman was the brother of Sir John Archibald Stewart. William had joined the Sixth Dragoon Guards at the age of seventeen and became a lieutenant in the King's Hussars. He fought at Waterloo. After the Napoleonic Wars he was mustered out and thereafter traveled the world as a hunter and sportsman. Stewart did visit the United States, and we know that he spent some time in New Orleans, where he learned that his bankers had refused to pay his bills.

Stewart, described by one observer as a man who stood about five feet nine inches tall, liked strong drink, had strong prejudices and equally strong appetites, left a few letters behind; a streak of Byronic romanticism can be detected in them.

Unable to pay his debts in New Orleans, Stewart went west, accompanied by a young companion, reportedly English. He would spent six years in the West, but ventured there initially in the company of Robert Campbell, leaving St. Louis on April 13, 1833. It is from the journal of Charles Larpenteur that we learn about Stewart's involvement in the caravan, as well as the presence of Benjamin Harrison, son of William Henry Harrison, and a gentleman-physician who apparently had a taste for strong whiskey and wild adventures.

Stewart met Marcus and Narcissa Whitman, Methodist missionaries, after whom the characters Marcus and Letitia Hancock have been modeled, although in fairness to Mrs. Whitman, it must be said that she was reputedly quite a beauty, so much so that Stewart fell in love with her, at least according to Nathaniel J. Wyeth, the canny Yankee businessman who went to Oregon hoping to make his fortune with a scheme to transport furs by sea.

The Whitmans established a mission among the Cayuse Indians in the Oregon Territory. The white man's diseases wiped out half of the Cayuse tribe, and in 1847 a violent altercation between Whitman and an Indian resulted in a massacre that left eleven men, including Whitman, dead, along with two children and the lovely Narcissa. The bodies of many of the whites were hacked to pieces with axes. Narcissa was buried at the mission, but her body was dug up by wolves.

Much of the background for this novel was derived from a classic work on Western Americana, Bernard DeVoto's *Across the Wide Missouri,* and the author strongly recommends that book for all those interested in learning more details about the Whitmans, the Rocky Mountain Fur Company, and Captain William Drummond Stewart.

Don't miss Gordon Hawkes'
next thrilling adventure in
MOUNTAIN MASSACRE,
coming summer 1999
from Signet books.

As he always did when he was about to leave his mountain sanctuary, Gordon Hawkes rose before the sun, slipping out of the cabin with no more sound than a ghost might have made, leaving his wife and young son undisturbed in their slumbers. He went to the corral where his horse, a dun-colored mountain mustang, still shaggy with its winter coat, whickered a soft recognition, while its two companions, the mules, eyed him warily. Saddling the mustang quickly, Hawkes secured to the hull his Plains rifle, cocooned in a fringed buckskin sheath, and looped his cartridge pouch and possibles bag over the horn. The long winter was over, the snow beginning to melt beneath the onslaught of the spring sun, yet the nights remained cold, and his breath clouded as he gave the cinch one last hard tug, fit a moccasined foot into stirrup, and hoisted himself into the saddle. With one final look at the darkened cabin, he turned into the evergreens that rimmed the sloping meadow.

Finding the familiar trail, he began to ascend the steep, wooded mountain shoulder. Now and then he could see the valley below as the trees thinned at rocky outcroppings. The soft gold of the morning sun touched the snowcapped peaks opposite, even as night shadows clung stubbornly to the lowlands. Hawkes knew that before long Eliza would be rising, stirring up the embers of last night's fire, adding kindling and a log or two. She would not be alarmed by his absence. She would know, based on past experience, what he was up to, for today they would leave the valley, leave it for the first time in many months, and though he seldom discussed his anxieties, she was well aware of his reluctance to venture forth into the world.

And why shouldn't he be reluctant? Gordon Hawkes had received more than his fair share of misery at the hands of his fellow man. At least that was his conviction. Born the son of a poor Irish potato farmer, he had watched his father die by inches from ship fever during the voyage to America. Tom Hawkes had dreamed grand dreams of a new beginning in the new land, but he'd found only a watery grave instead, hundreds of miles from the promised land that had so beguiled him.

His father's wretched death had been only the beginning for Hawkes. It had been a long and difficult journey from that sad day until more than a year later when he had first set eyes on the Shining Mountains, and many more months of betrayal and disillusionment and danger until he had finally found his refuge—Eliza Hancock, the frail, yellow-haired daughter of a Methodist missionary slain by Indians.

But Eliza was only part of his refuge. This valley, where they had lived in relative peace for eight years, was the rest of it. Here they had made Cameron, now seven years of age. Hawkes smiled as he imagined Cameron's excitement as he woke to the day he had longed for all those long winter months—the day he went with his father and mother to Fort Bridger. This was the outpost the famous mountain man and Indian fighter, Jim Bridger, "Old Gabe" as his friends called him, had built on Black's Fork of the Green River, in Shoshone country down by the Uinta range, and hard by the Oregon Trail. More and more emigrants were rolling west these days, and while, like most mountain men, Bridger didn't have much good to say about emigrants, he was wise enough to know that the fur trade was dying and there was a future in catering to the needs of the pioneers. His post, complete with black-smith forge, and stocked to the rafters with provisions, was meant to provide supplies and repairs to the emigrant families. It was also a favorite gathering place of that fast-vanishing breed, the mountain man.

Fort Bridger was a good ten-day journey south of this valley, but it was the nearest source for the few supplies Hawkes needed—powder and shot, some coffee and sugar and a little tobacco for his pipe. Eliza and Cameron looked forward to the annual visit for other reasons. Unlike Hawkes, they missed the society of others. Now and then someone would drop in on them, an acquaintance from the days when Hawkes had been associated with the Rocky Mountain Fur Company, or an occasional party of Absaroka Crow braves passing through and stopping to visit their white brother. For the most part, though, they lived in complete isolation. And that suited Hawkes.

But was it fair to Eliza, and especially to Cameron? Hawkes felt a little guilty as he rode ever higher up the mountain trail astride his surefooted dun. If Cameron wasn't up by now, he soon would be, itching to go, and impatient for his father's return. Cameron needed to be with other children, and there were always children at Fort Bridger. A few lived there year-round now, and there were always many more passing through, the off-spring of trappers or traders and their Indian wives, or emigrants bound for points west.

The only other opportunity for Cameron to associate with those of his own age was on the rare occasions that Hawkes called on the Absaroka Crows. In late autumn, as the gold and russet leaves of the hardwoods began to fall, an Absaroka band made its winter camp a few days' hard riding north of the valley, at the southern limits of Crow country, and every now and again Hawkes would go see them. If he did not, they would come looking for him sooner or later. They called him White Crow, and by now every band in the tribe knew who he was and what he had done. Hawkes had saved the lives of a chief's wife and son, and while he'd had a bit of trouble with the tribe later on, thanks to his refusal to participate in a raid on a defenseless Blackfoot village, he remained their brother, and would until the day he died. No Crow would raise a hand in anger against him. So when Hawkes visited, he brought Cameron and Eliza along, and Cameron played with the Indian boys. It was good experience for him, thought Hawkes, who assumed that his son would make these mountains his home when he was old enough to decide for himself the course his life would take. After all, a mountain man's life was the only one worth living.

At last Hawkes reached his destination, a high shelf of land at the timberline, where he could stand on a rocky, windswept ledge and view the length and breadth of his valley thousands of feet below. Or he could gaze beyond the nearest peaks to the east and see the majestic sweep of the mountains, jagged and blue and snowcapped and extending as far as his eye could see. Dismounting, Hawkes took the precaution of removing the sheathed Plains rifle from the saddle, ground-hitched the mustang, and went to stand at the brink of the ledge; ordinarily, the horse remained close by, but Hawkes wasn't one to make mistakes like leaving the rifle with the dun. A .41-caliber percussion pistol and Bowie knife adorned the wide leather belt at his waist, but Hawkes relied mainly on his long gun. Grizzlies and other bears roamed these high slopes. He'd been confronted by the great beasts on more than one occasion, and he had a healthy respect for them. Survival in the high country meant avoiding those greenhorn errors in judgment. As Old Gabe was fond of saying, Hell was chockful of greenhorns.

He stood there for a long while, a tall and slender man, a man of scars and sinew, his sandy hair and beard already flecked with gray, though he was only in his twenty-sixth year. The beard made him look older, and so did the creases on his weathered brow, and the piercing squint of his sun-faded eyes. From top to bottom he was garbed in buckskin, blackened in places from long use, from his moccasins to the "half-breeds" that covered the lower part of his leggins to his long-fringed hunting shirt. Over it all he wore a long buckskin coat lined with fur. Eliza had made it for him. She had become as handy as any Indian woman when it came to working with quill and hide. On his head was a broad-brimmed beaver hat with a low crown.

The wind whispered its seductive song to him as he gazed upon the world he had made his own, watching the night shadows retreat at last as the sunlight flooded the valley floor. He did not feel as though he had conquered this land in any fashion, but rather that he and the land had come to a mutual understanding. And unlike many of the people who populated his past, the land would not betray his trust so long as he did not betray the land. These mountains did not embrace everyone. The bleached bones and unmarked graves of those who had not measured up to its demands were many. He was one of the few who had measured up. He had earned the privilege to call these mountains his home. In return, he honored the mountains, while they sustained him.

More than that, they protected him. They were his refuge precisely because they resisted the encroachment of civilization, which was made up, in the vast majority, of people who lacked the traits required to survive in the high country. And it was, after all, civilization that Hawkes spurned. This wasn't just because of the murder charge that still, he assumed, hung over his head. Ten years ago he had been falsely accused of the murder of a Louisiana planter. He had killed several men who had thought to collect the bounty placed on his head. But even without the murder charge, even without the threat it posed, he would not have left the mountains, his sanctuary.

Even going so far afield as Fort Bridger was cause for concern. He didn't like the emigrants. Not because they were bad people, because most of them weren't, but because they brought civilization with them. It lurked like an unseen contagion in their wagons as well as in their dreams, ready to spread across this land and change it in ways Hawkes knew he would not like. They were coming with the idea that they could tame the land, and if for no other reason than that Hawkes would have set his heart against them. There was more, though, to his distrust of them—something intensely personal, something rooted in his past, in all the times that society had chewed him up and spit him out. He wanted nothing to do with society, even the primitive society of a remote frontier outpost like Old Gabe's place. But he had to go. Not just for powder and shot and some Ol' Virginny tobacco, but more importantly for Eliza and Cameron.

He had to go—and yet he lingered on the high ledge, soaking in the serenity and beauty of the majestic panorama before him, letting it calm his troubled soul and give him strength. He felt the warmth of the sun between his shoulder blades as it cleared the high reaches behind him. He breathed deep the clean crisp air redolent with the fragrance of the sturdy conifers. From somewhere far off came the rampant cry of an eagle. Each time he came here it was the same—the same sounds, the same smells, the same sights. But of course that was what he valued most, what brought him back, the unchanging nature of the mountains. He always knew what to expect. The same could not be said when it came to dealing with people.

But his thoughts continued to stray to Eliza and Cameron, and his guilt grew more burdensome. He was being selfish, indulging his fears, while they waited. Finally, reluctantly, he turned away from the ledge and went to the mustang, tied his rifle to the saddle, and mounted up.

Arriving at the cabin, Hawkes saw that the two mules had been made ready, one with an old Absaroka "squaw" saddle, the other with a sawbuck pack saddle laden with provisions necessary for the journey, lashed down under hides with a diamond-hitched rope. It was a very good job, he noted with approval. Both Eliza and Cameron were adept in mountain ways. Both could pack a mule, set a trap, skin a deer, shoot a rifle, read sign, and do all the myriad things a body had to know how to do in order to live in the high country.

Cameron busted out of the cabin as Hawkes rode in,

great expectations illuminating his innocent face. Laying eyes on his son—Eliza said Cameron was his father's spitting image—never failed to fill Hawkes with wonder and gratitude. Filled him, too, with a fierce determination to protect his son from the cruel disillusionment he himself had known in his younger years.

"Are we going now, Pa?" Cameron asked hopefully. "Are we?"

"You bet." Dismounting, Hawkes tousled the boy's sandy hair, and then Eliza emerged from the cabin, and smiled knowingly and forgivingly at him, and as always happened when he saw her, Hawkes wondered why he had been so blessed.

"Run inside and fetch your hat and coat, Cam," she said, and when their son had gone, she stepped closer to her husband and put her arms around him, laying her head against his chest. This, Hawkes thought, was his greatest refuge, here in the arms of the woman he loved, and who loved him without reservation. .

"We don't have to go," said Eliza, "if you'd rather not."

"No. We'll go."

"I'd just as soon not go, actually," she said, very earnest, and he held her at arm's length, searching her eyes and seeing that she was deeply troubled.

"What's wrong, Eliza?"

"It's nothing, really."

"Tell me straight out."

She shrugged, expressing the inconsequence of what she was about to confess. "I had a bad dream, that's all." Seeing that this was not enough to satisfy him, she added, "It was about you, Gordon."

"Well, I should hope so," he joked, but the feeble attempt at levity fell flat.

"You were being chased by bad men, and they shot you, and then there was this . . . this angel who came to you and . . . and she took you away. . . ." She shook her head fiercely, her fingers curling a stray tendril of pale yellow hair behind an ear. "Like I said, it was just a silly dream."

Cameron came bolting out of the cabin again. "I'm ready!" he declared. "Let's get a move on! I can't wait to get to the fort, can you, Ma?"

She smiled gently at his enthusiasm. "No, I can't wait either, Cam." She glanced at Hawkes, and he nodded, for they both knew not going would break their son's heart, and so they put aside their fears for Cameron's sake. Hawkes helped them aboard the saddle mule, and then led the way, astride the shaggy mountain mustang, leading the pack mule, and leaving the valley's protection behind.

SIGNET BOOKS

Jason Manning

The Texas Volunteers gallop into their third adventure!

☐ **THE MARAUDERS**   0-451-19145-5/$5.99

The battle for Texas independence is over, and the volunteers who fought for that freedom have settled down to live peacefully in their new land. But a border town revolt occurs when its corrupt sheriff is gunned down, and not even the Texas Rangers can restore order. The son of Black Jack John Henry McAllen joins a new volunteer group to stop the rebellion. But when he is captured by the enemy, his father decides to come out of retirement...and take justice into his own hands.

Don't miss these first two adventures:

☐   **THE BLACK JACKS**   0-451-19141-2/$5.99
☐   **TEXAS BOUND**   0-451-19142-0/$5.99

Prices slightly higher in Canada

Payable in U.S. funds only. No cash/COD accepted. Postage & handling: U.S./CAN. $2.75 for one book, $1.00 for each additional, not to exceed $6.75; Int'l $5.00 for one book, $1.00 each additional. We accept Visa, Amex, MC ($10.00 min.), checks ($15.00 fee for returned checks) and money orders. Call 800-788-6262 or 201-933-9292, fax 201-896-8569; refer to ad #SHFIC1

Penguin Putnam Inc.   Bill my: ☐Visa ☐MasterCard ☐Amex_____(expires)
P.O. Box 12289, Dept. B   Card#_____
Newark, NJ 07101-5289
Please allow 4-6 weeks for delivery.   Signature_____
Foreign and Canadian delivery 6-8 weeks.

Bill to:
Name_____
Address_____City_____
State/ZIP_____
Daytime Phone#_____

Ship to:
Name_____   Book Total $_____
Address_____   Applicable Sales Tax $_____
City_____   Postage & Handling $_____
State/ZIP_____   Total Amount Due $_____

This offer subject to change without notice.

SIGNET BOOKS

"A writer in the tradition of Louis L'Amour
and Zane Grey!"—*Huntsville Times*

RALPH COMPTON

☐THE AUTUMN OF THE GUN   0-451-19045-9/$5.99

☐THE BORDER EMPIRE   0-451-19209-5/$5.99

☐THE DAWN OF FURY   0-451-18631-1/$5.99

☐DEVIL'S CANYON: The Sundown Riders

         0-451-19519-1/$5.99

☐THE KILLING SEASON   0-451-18787-3/$5.99

☐SIX-GUNS AND DOUBLE EAGLES

         0-451-19331-8/$5.99

Prices slightly higher in Canada

Payable in U.S. funds only. No cash/COD accepted. Postage & handling: U.S./CAN. $2.75 for
one book, $1.00 for each additional, not to exceed $6.75; Int'l $5.00 for one book, $1.00 each
additional. We accept Visa, Amex, MC ($10.00 min.), checks ($15.00 fee for returned checks)
and money orders. Call 800-788-6262 or 201-933-9292, fax 201-896-8569; refer to ad # WES6

Penguin Putnam Inc.	**Bill my:** ☐Visa ☐MasterCard ☐Amex _____(expires)
P.O. Box 12289, Dept. B	Card#_____
Newark, NJ 07101-5289	
Please allow 4-6 weeks for delivery.	Signature_____
Foreign and Canadian delivery 6-8 weeks.	

Bill to:

Name_____

Address_____City_____

State/ZIP_____

Daytime Phone#_____

Ship to:

Name_____	Book Total $_____
Address_____	Applicable Sales Tax $_____
City_____	Postage & Handling $_____
State/ZIP_____	Total Amount Due $_____

This offer subject to change without notice.